BITTER
BLOOD

CYNTHIA
EDEN

CHAPTER ONE

The scent of blood hit her—sweet and tempting—and New Orleans Police Detective Mary Jane—*just Jane*—Hart clenched her teeth as she rushed toward the yawning mouth of a nearby alley. She also prayed that her new fangs wouldn't decide to burst out right then and there…because that would be bad, very, very bad.

The victim ran toward her and yelled, "He stabbed me! The crazy bastard *stabbed* me!"

The bleeding victim was young, probably in his early twenties, with bright blond hair and blue eyes. It was dark right then, well after midnight, and the alley was nearly black, but Jane could still see him perfectly.

At least there was one benefit to being a vampire. Excellent night vision.

But that guy is getting way too close to me. Her teeth were aching because the coppery scent of blood flooded her nostrils. "Stop!" Jane ordered as she lifted a hand. "I'm a cop!"

He staggered to a stop. "I need a freaking ambulance!"

Yes, he did. But if he kept coming at her, he was going to get bitten. She didn't like human blood. Actually, she couldn't keep it down at all, but her vamp instincts were still kicking in with a vengeance. When fresh blood came running right up to you, well, it was hard to resist a bite.

"Just stay there," Jane gritted out.

She looked over her shoulder. She'd been walking the street alone, trying to get her damn thoughts together. She wasn't even on the clock that night. But, no, of course, she would have run into a bloody victim. That was her luck, right?

And helping him is my job, whether I'm on the clock or not. I might be undead now, but I'm still a detective.

"Where is your attacker?" She inched deeper into the alley. Her gun was holstered at her side. With her new vamp strength, she didn't even need it anymore. Not really.

"B-back there…" His voice stuttered as he glanced over his shoulder. The blood had soaked through his coat.

Her eyes narrowed. The alley was only about six feet wide, but it was long, stretching between the old buildings. She didn't see anyone back there but…

I can hear him. The faintest rustle of footsteps. The perp was probably hiding, just out of sight. Waiting.

Jane determinedly marched toward her victim. "It's going to be all right." Going closer to him meant the smell of that tempting blood just got stronger. *Human blood makes you gag. Remember that. It may smell like candy, but you can't handle that crap.* Her gaze slid over him. The blood was all coming from his right shoulder. A stab wound? "The wound isn't that deep. You're going to be all right." A few stitches and he'd be good as new. Provided she got him out of that alley and away from the attacker who could spring again at any moment. "Just stay behind me." She slid past him and—

"*Bitch,*" the blond victim whispered. "I know what you are."

She whirled back to face him.

Too late, she saw him reaching into his coat. The guy didn't look so scared and hurt any longer. His face was twisted with hate and he was—oh, hell, he was yanking a wooden stake out of his coat!

I know what you are. Yes, yes, he did know.

And she heard the fast rush of footsteps coming from the back of that alley. The guy that she'd *thought* was the attacker—hell, he must be working with the blond male.

I'm their target. I'm the victim.

Or, at least, that was what they thought. Adrenaline fired her blood and when that stake came slashing toward her heart, Jane grabbed the guy's wrist in a tight grip, stopping him. "I don't think so," Jane whispered. Then she snapped his wrist. One fast jerk. He howled and immediately went down to his knees, clutching his broken wrist desperately.

Jane whirled to face the other threat. "You think you'll stake me, too?"

The guy coming at her was big, easily over six foot two, and built like a linebacker. He lifted his hand—

No stake. A gun.

"Blood loss, vamp," he snarled. "I know it can take you down."

He fired.

She dodged the bullet. Actually freaking dodged it. Jane was still not used to the increased speed she had—moving that way made her feel dizzy, but being dizzy was better than having bullets littering her chest. The guy cried out in fury when he missed her, then he started just firing wildly.

Left, right. Up. Down.

His partner screamed when a bullet hit *him.* But nothing had touched Jane, not yet.

And she was now close enough to grab the shooter.

She swiped the gun from his hand and threw it against the alley wall. Then she locked her hand around the shooter's neck and shoved *him* against that alley wall. He outweighed her by at least one hundred and fifty pounds. He dwarfed her smaller frame but…

He couldn't get out of her hold. She was stronger. Far stronger than he'd ever be. "Now who is the bitch?" Jane whispered and she flashed her fangs at him.

He screamed.

That was right. He should be afraid. He should—

Boom. Boom. Boom.

The bullets slammed into her back, one after the other. Her body jerked, like a puppet on a string, and she spun to see the blond guy on the ground—he'd pulled out a gun from his coat. *How many damn weapons did he have hidden in that thing?* The blond was still on the ground, the gun still clutched in his shaking hand, and he was preparing to fire at her again. *I should have broken both of his wrists.* Her mistake.

"*Jane!*" The roar of her name shook the alley. And she knew the two men who'd come here for her—humans who had made such a terrible mistake—were about to pay.

In the next moment, Aidan Locke was there. Tall, strong, too powerful. His blue eyes glowed with the rage of his beast even as razor sharp claws sprang from the tips of his fingers.

The blond with the gun fired at him, but the fool—he wasn't using silver bullets and the hits didn't slow Aidan down for even a moment. Aidan slashed out with his claws, cutting that guy's wrist, and blood flew into the alley.

More blood.

Jane's clothes were soaked with blood. She sagged to her knees. "Aidan…" His name came from her as a rasp.

The blond jumped to his feet and charged at Aidan. He ran right at him and—

Jane's eyes sagged closed. She fell forward, slamming into the cement.

Footsteps thudded toward her and a hard hand fisted her hair. "Not so tough now, are you?"

It was the linebacker-wanna-be. Spittle flew from his mouth as he wrenched her hair back even more. "You're not nearly as strong as I—"

Bam. This time, she was the one who'd fired. Good thing she still carried her service weapon. *And here I was…thinking I didn't need it any longer.* The blast went right into his chest, a perfect hit to the heart, and her attacker fell down beside her, gasping out his last breath.

Jane forced her eyelids to stay open a little longer. She was bleeding so much, and an insidious cold swept over her body. *Aidan*. She needed to get to Aidan…

"Baby, what the hell did they do to you?"

He was above her, no, bending *over* her. Aidan gently scooped her into his arms and held her so very carefully.

As if she were precious.

As if she weren't a monster.

Because to him, she wasn't.

"S-set-up," Jane managed to whisper. Humans lying in wait for her. Not a good thing. And that could mean… "Need to g-get out of here…could have…r-reinforcements." She was stuttering. That was bad. She never stuttered and she never felt this cold.

Aidan's handsome face was locked in lines of fury. "They'll find the dead when they come looking for their men."

So he'd killed the blond. Too bad. She would've liked to question him. She—

"Shit, baby, how much blood have you lost?"

Enough to make her weak. "Think the bullets…are still…in me…"

He cursed—wonderful, dark inventive curses that had a smile tugging at her lips even as he clutched her tighter and raced from that alley. She hurt, so much, but Jane wasn't scared. Not when Aidan was there. He'd take care of her. She knew it with certainty.

Death wasn't an option for her. He'd give her his blood — his wonderful, strong alpha werewolf blood, and she'd heal so quickly.

And once she was healed…

I'll find out just who the hell planned that set-up in the alley.

And payback would be such a bitch.

***

He waited until the werewolf left. The alpha had been in such a blind rage when he rushed away, looking neither to the left nor the right as he hurried to get help for the vampire.

Mary Jane Hart.

His prey of choice.

He stepped over the body of the first human. His gaze swept over him carefully. Claws to the jugular had taken out that fellow. His face was frozen in lines of terror and blood had sprayed into his blond hair. The fellow probably hadn't expected to die. He'd thought he was the predator.

Wrong. You were the bait. The test.

He kicked the blond with his shoe, wanting to make sure he was gone.

The man was.

So he looked at test subject number two. This fellow interested him the most because…*Jane killed him.* He'd had a small surveillance camera placed in the alley, the better to watch from a safe distance. Even when she'd been shot—four times in the back—Jane had still managed to kill this man before he'd had the opportunity to end *her*.

But, interestingly enough, she hadn't used her fangs to attack him. She'd fired at him, shot just like a human cop would have done when confronted with an assailant who wouldn't stop.

Blood permeated the alley, a temptation that no new vampire should be able to resist. Yet…

Jane Hart hadn't taken so much as a sip. She hadn't used her fangs even when biting would have saved her.

How very interesting.

He pulled out his phone and called his boss. "You'll want to get a clean-up crew here. Immediately." Before anyone stumbled into the alley and saw hell.

"Disappointing results? Did Jane fail?"

He smiled as he looked at the dead men. "No, it was a promising night. Very, very promising…" A near perfect start.

***

Jane's blood was on his hands.

Aidan fucking hated that.

He carried Jane up the stairs and into his office at Hell's Gate. The club was packed, filled with humans and werewolves, but no one even glanced twice at him as he held Jane. Why would they? The humans didn't see the blood, he had her pulled too close for that. And the werewolves knew better than to question him about Jane.

He went up the stairs and two of his pack members immediately took up a position on the ground floor, blocking the bottom of the staircase. They'd make sure he wasn't followed.

And he could focus on what mattered most — Jane.

"Aidan…" Her voice was so husky and weak. "I…I need blood." A hushed confession. Shamed.

Jane should never be ashamed. Not of anything.

He took her inside his office. Kicked the door shut. Then he hurried across the room and put her on his couch. She gave a little moan when her back made contact with the leather.

"Baby…" He brought his wrist to her mouth. "Take everything that you need."

Her lips closed over his wrist. He felt the quick lick of her tongue, the press of her teeth and then —

Pleasure. White hot. Seeming to race along his veins and go straight to his heart. Need, lust, a dark desire built inside of him. He clenched his teeth and locked down his muscles, refusing to move. Jane was hurt. Jane needed his blood — she didn't need him falling all over her like a sex-crazed madman.

She was shot. Bleeding out. Those bastards wanted to kill my Jane.

And he was sick of her being prey.

Her dark eyes met his. He could see the strength coming back to her and the link they shared—that deep, basic, primitive link that always seemed to bind them—grew even stronger. She licked his wrist once more, then eased back. "Aidan." Her lips curved faintly. A drop of his blood was on her bottom lip. "Aidan, you have to take the bullets out. I…I can't heal until they're out."

He knew that, dammit. Just as he knew the *last* thing he ever wanted to do was hurt her.

But Jane was rolling over, his blood having given her strength. She pressed her stomach to the couch and her blood-soaked back was inches from him.

"Don't worry," Jane said quickly. "I won't move, I promise." Her voice was stronger. "I won't make a sound…"

Because she didn't want him to hear how much he was hurting her.

"I can get a doctor," Aidan muttered. "Dr. Bob will be here in—"

"I need them out." She spoke quietly as she added, "They…they're close to my spine, Aidan, too close, and I-I can't feel my legs."

His heart stopped beating. He remembered when she'd been shot. The way she'd fallen. He'd thought her knees had just given way but—

Jane turned her head to look back at him. "Vamps heal." She nodded determinedly. "Once they're out, I'll heal."

Pain clawed at his insides. He wanted to bellow his fury. This shouldn't be happening. Darkness bled around his eyes. The rage was so strong and hot—his claws burst out, his canines lengthened, and the beast he kept chained deep inside tried to leap out of him.

No. Not now. Not yet.

His fingers were trembling when he reached for her. The hands of a beast with dark claws that could—and had—killed a man in mere seconds. He cut away her shirt and saw the wounds in her back, wounds that still bled, and, yes, they were far too close to Jane's spine.

"Let me get the doctor," he said again, his chest aching as he stared at her skin. Dr. Bob Heider was the main medical examiner in town, but the doctor was also on Aidan's payroll. When supernaturals needed patching up, Dr. Bob was called in for the job. Dr. Bob could come now and use far more care as he treated Jane. He wouldn't cut into her with claws—

"No need for Dr. Bob. We both know…it will just prolong the pain." Her eyes were closed. Her cheek was turned toward him. "Please, Aidan. Get them out."

He swallowed and his claws cut into her skin. She stiffened at the first cut but didn't make a sound, just as she promised. No moans of pain. No screams. Nothing.

But Aidan saw the tear that slid down her silken cheek and it felt as if she'd just gutted him.

One bullet. It came out easily — *a fucking wooden bullet.*

He'd known the men weren't firing silver bullets. As soon as they'd hit him, he'd known. But…

Wooden bullets meant they were in that alley for one purpose — to kill a vampire. To kill my Jane.

His claws reached a second bullet. He pulled it out. Stained with her blood. So small.

So dangerous.

The third bullet was next. He had to dig deeper to get it. Still, Jane didn't cry out. She was statue still beneath him. No anesthesia, no drugs at all. Just feeling the pain that *he* gave to her.

He wanted to kill those bastards in that alley all over again.

The fourth bullet was the hardest to get. Nausea swirled in him because he had to cut her so deeply to get it out. Her breath rasped out and another tear slid down her cheek. His fingers were shaking worse and he was afraid —

"I love you, Aidan," Jane whispered.

She trusted him with her life.

He got that bullet out. Flung it across the room. Then he was putting his wrist back to her mouth. "Drink, now." Because his blood was special. Sure, all werewolf blood was strong, downright delicious for a vamp, but…

An alpha werewolf's blood could heal like no other.

Jane's lips pressed to his pulse. Her little fangs slid into his skin. His eyes closed as he released a slow breath. Jane was alive. Jane was okay. Jane was safe…*again.* She drank from him and he bent his head, relief surging through him. His Jane. *His* fucking Jane.

Right then, he wanted to pull her close. To hold her against his heart and know that she was safe.

And after that…

He wanted to beat her sweet ass.

She'd told him that she was just going for a walk. A fucking walk. How had a walk turned into that blood bath?

Her tongue licked over his wrist. She pressed a soft kiss to his hand. "Thank you." The words were soft, husky. He knew sleep pulled at her. She'd heal while she slept.

His fingers slid over her cheek, wiping away the tears. "When you wake up, we're talking."

Her long lashes cast a shadow over her cheek.

"You're not doing this shit again," Aidan growled. "You can't risk yourself like this. I won't allow it." He was the alpha in the city. The one who controlled all the paranormals. And as of very, very recently…Jane was no longer human.

She was a paranormal, just like the others under his command.

Whether she liked it or not, she had to follow his orders.

And order number one for his beautiful Jane…

Don't get hurt. Because her pain gutted him.

A sharp knock sounded at his office door. He knew only one wolf would have the balls to see him right then, only one guy would have been able to get past the guards below — Aidan's first in command, Paris Cole.

Jane's breathing was deep, easy. Humans thought vampires didn't breathe — that they were cold. That their hearts didn't beat. But that was all bullshit. Hollywood hype. Vampires breathed. Their hearts beat. They *lived.*

Their deaths were fleeting. They came back, stronger, far more powerful than ever.

He turned and headed for the door. Jane's blood was still on his hands when he yanked that door open. Paris stood there, one brow raised and curiosity glinting in his golden eyes. The tall, African American wolf was dressed in a tux, and he looked as far from a beast as it was possible to get.

Then Paris inhaled and his gaze dropped to focus on the blood that coated Aidan's hands. "What happened?"

"An ambush." He stepped back so that his best friend could enter the office. At least, that was what it had looked like to him. *Jane went for a walk and wound up nearly dead.*

"Someone tried to take you on?" Paris demanded as he crossed the threshold.

"No." Aidan shook his head. "Someone tried to take out Jane."

Paris's gaze immediately cut toward the couch — and a heavily sleeping Jane. Her back was still bare and bloody. "Sonofabitch." His hands tightened into fists. "I'm assuming the fools are dead?"

"Good assumption." Aidan nodded. "And I'll be taking a team out to the alley because I want to personally search the scene. They had *wooden* bullets. If I hadn't gotten there when I did…" But he stopped because he wasn't going to finish that sentence.

He felt his friend's gaze on him. Once more, Paris inhaled and then he said, voice halting, "All of the blood isn't hers."

No.

"You were shot," Paris added.

He'd barely felt the pain. Now, he just shoved his claws into his gut and pulled out the two bullets. "Wood, not silver. They were for her, not me." He'd just been in the way so the blond bastard had fired at him.

But Jane? *Those two had wanted to kill her.*

Paris gave a low whistle. "Okay, the way I see it…we have a few very big problems." He paced toward the couch. Toward Jane. He put his hands on his hips as he stared down at her sleeping form. "Problem one…Jane's secret is out. Obviously, there are people who know exactly what your girlfriend is."

Vampire. Only Jane hadn't been a vamp, not until a few days before. Then her human life had ended and—well, shit, they were still adjusting to the change.

His pack was adjusting.

He was adjusting.

So the hell was she.

Normally, vamps and werewolves were natural enemies. When a werewolf scented a vampire, the primitive instinct to attack, to kill, took over. As an alpha werewolf, Aidan should have immediately killed Jane when she turned.

But he hadn't.

Because she's mine.

Jane wasn't like other vampires. Because of him, werewolf blood had flowed in her veins before her change. So when she'd transformed, she hadn't just woken as a vampire. She was something so much more.

And too many people were afraid of that *more*.

Some in New Orleans believed that Jane was too dangerous. That she was going to be the end of them all.

"Since Jane is so new to the vamp world," Paris continued, voice thoughtful, "humans shouldn't know what she is, not yet. Hell, I would only think *one* vamp in town knew what she was."

The vampire who'd helped to end Jane's human life. Vincent Connor. Only that bastard had made himself absent lately. Probably because he knew Aidan intended to kill him at the absolute first opportunity. *Payback is coming, asshole.*

Paris glanced back at him. "You think Vincent is spreading the word about her?"

Aidan's claws were still out. "I think it's past time for me to have a little one-on-one chat with the guy."

Paris exhaled slowly. "Problem two…The people who know Jane's secret? Well, the fact that she's covered in blood means they want her dead. They know what she is, and they want to end her."

Obviously. "Two humans were in the alley with her. Neither of them made it out alive." That meant there were two less people hunting Jane.

"So either they're the only two who were involved in this mess and the threat to her is already gone or…" Paris shook his head. "Or there's a boss somewhere, hiding in the shadows. Someone who set that attack in motion."

That was precisely what Aidan feared. "Stay with Jane." The order came out fast and hard. There were two people in the world that Aidan trusted completely. Paris…

And Jane.

"Uh, I stay—and what do you do?" Paris asked as his brow furrowed.

"I go back to the alley. I follow any scents left behind." Because no one else had a nose like an alpha. "And I hunt down any other fools who were in on the attack tonight." He knew the attack went beyond the two humans who'd died that night. More was at play, he could feel it. When it came to the paranormal world, there was always more at work than what met the eye. It was a rule to live by.

He hurried back to Jane. She slept deeply, a healing sleep. His hand lifted and his bloody fingers lightly smoothed over her cheek.

"Yeah," Paris's voice was grim. "That brings me to problem three."

Aidan pulled his hand away from Jane, but before he could move back, Paris had grabbed his wrist. Paris turned over Aidan's hand, staring at the faint bite marks on his inner wrist.

"Problem three." Paris slowly lifted his gaze to meet Aidan's. "Problem three is that you can't keep giving her your blood."

Aidan yanked his hand away from Paris. "What the hell did you think I was going to do? Let Jane bleed to death?" Hell, no. Not an option for him.

"I think…I think you have to be careful." Paris seemed to measure his words. "Every time that you give her your blood…she could become more powerful."

Aidan tensed. "You worried she'll grow too strong?"

"I worry that she isn't done changing." The faint lines near Paris's mouth tightened. "And that you aren't, either. You're giving her your blood, man. A werewolf wasn't meant to feed a vamp that way."

A werewolf wasn't meant to feed a vamp at all. They were supposed to be natural enemies.

"We don't know what the connection you have with her…" Paris said doggedly. "We don't know what it will do to you. Or her."

Because there'd never been another mated pair like him and Jane. When she'd transformed, she should have killed him.

He'd been duty bound to kill her but…

I didn't. Neither did she. "Watch her," he snapped out. "Make sure that she stays in this room until I get back." He turned on his heel and stalked to the bathroom. A new sink and countertop gleamed in the spacious bathroom. He washed his hands at that sink, watching his blood and Jane's blood disappear down the drain. Then, his hands free of blood — for the moment — he marched back into his office. "You *are* going to keep her here, right, Paris?" He threw out the question as he headed for the door.

"Oh, right," Paris drawled. "Because it's easy to keep a super vamp in place. I mean…the woman is just prophesized to be *the end.* No big deal. I've definitely got this covered."

Aidan glanced back at him and Aidan just *stared* at his best friend for a moment. Stared, glared, same thing.

Paris swallowed. And straightened. "Right, alpha." He gave a quick little smart-ass salute. "She won't leave the room."

Good. Because when Aidan got back, he and Jane were going to fucking clear the air. She didn't get to risk herself over and over. She didn't get to run into danger.

She was his.

And if something happened to her…

I will go insane.

Hell, maybe he already was insane. Plenty of his pack members suspected he was. After all, what sane werewolf would mate with a vampire?

I would. I'd do anything for Jane.

That was the problem.

But he was also the paranormal boss in the city, and it was time that Jane started paying attention to the rules in place. *His* rules.

CHAPTER TWO

The alley was clean. It had looked like a blood bath just an hour before but now the place was practically spotless.

Aidan's nostrils twitched.

Bleach. Someone had even used damn bleach at the scene. He stared down at the ground. A body should have been there, close to the trash bin. The blond bastard that he'd killed with his claws. But the guy was gone. So was his partner.

A low whistle came from behind him. Aidan didn't move at the sound. He waited as Garrison, one of his younger pack members, approached. Garrison's arm brushed against Aidan's as he studied the scene. "Somebody sure moved fast, alpha," Garrison mused.

Somebody sure as hell had.

And the bleach was overpowering — nearly wiping out all the other scents.

"At least we don't have to clean up the bodies, though," Garrison added, his voice sounding a bit brighter. "That's something, right?"

Aidan turned his head and focused on the redheaded wolf. Garrison was still young—Aidan reminded himself of that fact for about the hundredth time. *He's young. He'll learn. He's only an asshole some days.* "The bodies would have told me something." But now—

He stiffened. He'd just caught sight of a faint green light from the corner of his eye. A light that should *not* have been in that alley. His head tilted up, then to the left. *There.* Small, dark—a video camera. The faint green light was glowing from the bottom corner of the camera.

Someone is watching.

His eyes narrowed on that camera. Someone had been watching while Jane was attacked? While she lay on the ground, fighting for her life? And now…someone was *still* watching as he came to find answers.

"Uh, alpha…" Garrison began nervously.

Aidan leapt up into the air—far higher than any basketball player could ever dream. His claws drove into the camera and he wrenched it down.

No more green light. No more watching.

The wolves who'd come with him to that alley were dead silent.

A video camera…one that had recorded a vampire and a werewolf that night. "Trace it," Aidan ordered. When it came to tech, his pack knew their shit. "Find out where the feed was going. Find out who the hell put this camera up there. Find out…" His voice dropped to a growl. "Who was watching."

Who was watching while Jane nearly died.

***

The dream came again. Dream, nightmare, memory — to Jane, there was no difference.

She was tied down, secured on the top of an old table. In the basement of *her* house. When she turned her head, Jane could see her mom. Her mother was tossed on the floor, her limbs all twisted and a big pool of red underneath her body. Her dad…he was there, too. Another quick turn of her head showed Jane her dad's form. The only father she'd ever known, not by blood, but by love. He'd loved her so much, all the way until the very end.

His eyes were still open, but she didn't think he saw her, not anymore.

"*There, there…no need for tears, little one. It's all for you.*" That voice was back. The voice she hated. Mean and cold and cruel and she wouldn't look at him. She just *wouldn't.*

"We waited a long time for you. You'd better not disappoint."

She looked back at her dad. This was her house. Her mom's house. Her dad's house. They were supposed to be safe there. *Why aren't we safe?*

"You can scream if you want," that cold voice told her.

It was all the warning she got. Pain came then. So hot. Burning, branding. She screamed and screamed but it didn't stop. And she could smell something — something funny. Something —

It's me. I'm burning.

Her voice broke and her cries stopped.

"Good girl."

She didn't want to be good. Not if he liked that.

"I'll be back soon." He stroked back her hair, and his green eyes gleamed down at her. "We'll take a little break. Let you get a bit of strength back so that we can finish things up." His blond hair was swept away from his face. A face that seemed so normal.

It isn't. He's not normal. He's evil. Monster. Monster. Monster!

Vampire.

There were no tears on her cheeks. She'd stopped crying after...*Daddy.*

The green-eyed man — *monster* — shut the door on the way out. Her home. He had taken over as if he owned the place. *They had.* In the middle of the night, monsters had come for her.

Her mom had told her that monsters weren't real. That she should never be afraid of them.

Her mom had been wrong.

She heard faint squeaks. The softest of rustles. Her eyes had closed. When had they closed? She should look around and see what was happening.

But she was afraid and she didn't think she wanted to see anything else.

Her right side kept hurting. Throbbing. She could still smell that terrible scent in the air. *I think that's me.*

"Mary Jane…" A soft voice called. Her brother Drew's voice. "Mary Jane…are you okay?"

Don't be here. Don't. Run away.

"Y-you didn't tell them I was here."

Now she did cry. One long tear slid down her cheek.

"I'm gonna…I'm gonna get you out."

She shook her head and kept her eyes closed. But she felt him pulling on the ropes that held her ankles down. There was a faint sawing motion. It sounded so loud to her ears. She was afraid *he* would hear. "Stop." The barest of whispers.

But the rope gave way. Her legs were free and her feet *hurt* because it felt like needles were shoved into them. She bit her lower lip as hard as she could, trying to hold back her cries. Now wasn't the time to scream. She knew that.

Her eyes opened.

Her dad's sightless eyes stared back at her.

No, look away. Look away!

Then the rope was gone from her wrists. Sawed away. He'd cut her wrists with the knife he had, but she didn't care about that small pain. Then he was pulling her, pushing her toward the window. Such a small window. They were in the basement. And that window was up high.

"I'll go through first," he said. He shimmied up and vanished.

I don't want to leave mom and dad. But…they were already gone. They'd left her. They weren't suffering anymore. No one could ever make them suffer again.

"Mary Jane!" Drew reached down for her. His hand was small, barely bigger than hers. Dirty. Bloody. "Come with me, Mary Jane!"

Had he been hiding during everything? Hiding and waiting? He'd seen everything, too, just as she had. She looked up into his eyes — eyes that were the exact shade of her own. He'd been crying. He never cried.

Her gaze darted back to his hand just as she heard the basement door opening — the faintest of clicks from the top of the stairs. The monster was coming for her again.

She grabbed for the dirty little hand, and he pulled her up, yanking with all of his strength. Her body slid through the narrow opening of the window. Her shoulders. Her chest. Her stomach. Her—

The monster grabbed her feet.

"No!" she screamed. And then she held that dirty little hand even tighter. "Drew, help me!"

***

The nightmare-slash-dream-slash-walk-into-hell faded. Jane cracked open one eye. She wasn't in the old basement any longer. Her face was shoved into a familiar leather couch—Aidan's couch. She moved just a bit and saw the floor of his office and—

Legs. Legs in fancy black pants.

"Rise and shine, Jane," an amused voice murmured. A voice that did *not* belong to Aidan.

Her head lifted and she stared at Paris. He smiled at her.

And she realized she was naked from the waist up. Good thing she'd only lifted her head. Jane took stock of her body, checking for aches and pains, but she actually felt good. No, better than good. *Strong. Powerful.*

She flexed her back but didn't feel the pull from her wounds.

"Already healed," Paris told her, rather helpfully. "It was quite amazing to watch, really. Your skin just starting closing about an hour ago. Like it was stitching itself up."

"You've been watching me?"

"Um."

That wasn't an answer.

So she tried a different question. "Where's Aidan?"

"Where else?" He waved one hand in a rather bored gesture. "Out looking for the men who attacked you. Come on, Jane. You know how he gets. Anyone hurts you and he flips the hell out." Some of the amusement slipped from his golden eyes. "A very dangerous thing for an alpha of his power."

"The men who attacked me are dead." She distinctly remembered sending one to hell. "So there was no need—"

"Aidan thinks more is at play. More involved in the game than just two humans deciding they were going to kill you. After all, they were packing wooden bullets." He walked to Aidan's desk and lifted one blood-stained bullet. The bloody bullets had been lined up in a neat little row on top of the desk. "Wooden bullets mean they were after special prey. They knew what you were, and they were ready to see you die."

She swallowed. Twice. "How—how did—" Jane broke off. Okay, no, she would not keep talking to him without a shirt on. "Turn around."

He quirked one brow but did as she asked. Paris was the charmer, the lady killer. So, yes, he'd probably seen hundreds of women without their tops, but he wasn't seeing *her* that way.

She sat up and quickly grabbed for a nearby jacket—one that smelled of Aidan. She pulled it on and rose to her feet. Her steps weren't even shaky as she paced away from the couch. Definite improvement considering that when she'd arrived in Aidan's office, just breathing had been hard.

Jane headed for the bathroom. She'd wash off the blood that still marked her body, get the extra clothes that Aidan kept for her in the bathroom closet, and then she could square off with Paris.

"You shouldn't keep taking his blood."

Jane's steps faltered. "Um, I was dying."

"That's a habit you have. A rather nasty one." He turned to face her. "Do you just expect him to appear these days? Kind of like Lois Lane and Superman? You think you can tackle anything because your safety net will always be there to save the day? To save *you*?"

He was angry and that wasn't like Paris. Normally, he was the mellow one. And… "I'm not Lois Lane. He's not Superman." And she wasn't waiting around for *anyone* to save her.

"Right. Not Superman." Paris nodded. "Aidan's an alpha werewolf and you're a vampire. The two of you should stay as far away from each other as possible."

Even with the coat, a chill skated over her body. "Do we have a problem, Paris?" Because she hadn't thought so but...

Jane was still new to the vamp life, but she realized there were plenty of werewolves out there who didn't like what she was—didn't like *her*.

I just didn't suspect Paris was one of them.

Testing now, she eased out a quick breath and said, "When you're near me, do you want to attack?" Because that was the werewolf way. Get close to a vamp and primitive instincts take over and—

"You made yourself different."

She didn't know what he meant.

"Aidan's blood," Paris gritted out. "You had too much of it before your transformation, so when you became a vampire—that blood of his changed with you. You're not just a vamp, Jane. You're more—hell, I don't even know *what* you really are."

That was...insulting?

Scary?

Both, Jane decided. Definitely both.

"He changed you," Paris said, a muscle jerking along his hard jaw. "And I'm worried that you're changing him."

"I-I need to get the blood off me." No, what she needed was to get away from Paris for a few moments because Jane didn't know what to say to him. She turned away. "Excuse me a moment, would you?"

"Stop taking his blood."

Her hand grabbed the bathroom's door frame. "You know I can only take werewolf blood." She'd tried to drink human blood—both bagged and from a live source. She'd vomited it right back up. Jane licked her lips. "You're right. Aidan's blood did change me—it altered something inside of me so that I crave werewolf blood." *Not human blood.* "If I didn't get it…" Her hold tightened on the door frame. "I would die."

Silence.

Then, after a tense moment, Paris asked, "Will any werewolf's blood work? Or is it just Aidan's that you crave?"

Would it? Jane didn't know. It wasn't as if other werewolves had been offering up their blood for her to try. She hurried into the bathroom, shut the door and made certain not to look at herself in the mirror.

The whole mirror-avoidance routine wasn't because of the old legend about vamps not having a reflection. She still had one.

She didn't look because she was afraid she'd see a monster staring back at her.

With a quick flick of her wrist, Jane turned the water on in the shower. Aidan had one lush bathroom—and the shower was certainly big enough for two.

But she didn't linger to enjoy the hot water. She showered briskly, watching the blood turn the water red before it disappeared down the drain. Paris's words had gotten beneath her skin. *Changing Aidan.*

Was it even possible for a vamp to change a werewolf? She had no clue. But Jane knew someone who might be able to answer that question…

Too bad that *someone* was the vampire who'd broken her neck a few days before. *Vincent Connor.* He was a powerful born vampire who she really didn't want to see, not ever again.

Unfortunately, he was the only man who might have the answers that she needed.

She dried off and opened the nearby closet. Aidan kept her clothes in there—his, too, of course. He had to keep extra clothes on hand because when he shifted into the form of a wolf, well, his shirts and pants had a tendency to shred.

And when your lover was a werewolf who had incredible strength…*my clothes tend to shred when he takes them off me.*

So…extra clothes.

She pulled on fresh jeans and a loose shirt and after sliding her shoes on, Jane hurried back to face Paris. He was standing in front of Aidan's desk, a wooden bullet still cradled in his fingers.

"I don't want to hurt Aidan." The words came from her, stark and desperate and so very true.

His head lifted. "I know." He'd rolled up the sleeves of his white dress shirt. "That's why you and I are about to have a little experiment."

"Experiment?" Jane didn't like the sound of that. She shook her head. "No, I have to go. I need to get out there and do damage control on those bodies—"

"Aidan will make them vanish. We both know he's good at cleaning up paranormal messes." He'd rolled the sleeves of his shirt all the way to his elbows. "Your genetic tests showed that your blood cells looked like Aidan's. That you were a vamp with wolf power flowing through you. Aidan thought that you could only drink from werewolves because you needed the blood of your own kind to survive."

"And I have been surviving on his blood." Just his—only Aidan's. The idea of biting someone else wasn't exactly appealing. Actually, that idea made her nauseous. Having a blood diet was bad enough. Letting her teeth sink into someone else?

No, thank you.

Though technically, she *had* bitten one other werewolf, but the guy had met a fast and brutal death shortly after that bite. So…

Paris cleared his throat. "Well, let's see what happens when you take my blood." He stepped toward her. "Because I can't have you endangering my alpha. I can't let you change him anymore."

Her gaze darted down to his wrist. When she concentrated hard enough, she could hear the racing thud of his pulse. Paris was nervous. So was she. "I don't want your blood." It was true. She didn't. She *hated* drinking blood, but at least when it came from Aidan, she could tolerate it.

"Jane…" His face was hard. "There is more at play here than you realize. You want to protect Aidan, don't you?"

Always.

"Then try my blood. Because I would damn well rather you change me than him." He offered his wrist to her.

Jane's hand flew up and her fingers curled around his hand. Her fangs weren't even out. Take his blood? Every part of her rebelled against the idea. *He isn't Aidan. He isn't.*

And…she only wanted Aidan.

"No." Jane shook her head. "I can't."

"Jane." The faint lines near his mouth seemed to deepen. "I have to see what you're doing to him. I need to feel the changes myself so that I can help him, too. He's my best friend. I can't have him walking through fire alone."

Wait…in that little scenario…was she the fire?

Before she could tell him that she was *not* damn fire, the office door opened. Jane and Paris turned together, with her still holding his hand.

Aidan stood there. His bright blue stare swept over them and lingered on their hands. He blinked, once, twice, and the tension in the room seemed to ratchet up.

"Someone want to tell me…" Aidan said, voice low, too low. "What the hell is going on?"

"Nothing." Jane dropped Paris's hand. "Nothing is—"

"I want Jane to bite me." Paris straightened his shoulders. "That's what's happening."

Jeez. Just once…*once*…couldn't Paris have lied to Aidan? Would that have broken the bro code too much?

Very slowly, Aidan shut the door behind him. "Want to tell me why?" His eyes glowed with the power of his beast. "Why you want *my* Jane to put her teeth in you?"

Paris jerked up his chin. "Because it's too dangerous for her to keep taking from you! You're changing, Aidan! You can't give her any more blood—we both know it. You—"

In a flash, Aidan was across the room. He'd grabbed Paris by the front of his shirt. "Jane drinks from me. Only me." His voice was so…deadly. She shouldn't have found that scary growl to be sexy. She was probably messed up on the inside. *Because I do think it's sexy.*

"Aidan, let him go." Jane sprang forward and shoved between the two men. "I'd already said I wasn't drinking *before* you got here. He's just worried about you. That's all. Because he's your friend." As if Aidan needed that reminder.

Aidan stared at Paris. "She drinks from me." A cold order.

Paris gave a grim nod. "But at what cost? Do you even realize what's happening to you?"

"I am in full control." That was the alpha talking. She could hear the authority in Aidan's voice.

"I sure as hell hope so." Paris backed away. "For everyone's sake." Then he headed for the door.

When it closed behind him with a soft click, Jane's shoulders slumped. "That was awkward."

Aidan didn't speak.

"I-I wasn't going to drink from him." Just so they were clear. "He's worried about you. About what might happen and—"

Aidan grabbed Jane and pulled her close. Her hand flew against his chest as he lifted her up, holding her easily, and his mouth crashed down on hers.

The kiss was hard. Rough. Deep.

Hot.

So very Aidan.

And she loved it. Her mouth met his eagerly, her tongue tasting him, her body already yearning because when they kissed — they ignited. Imploded.

The chemistry between them had always been off the charts. But lately, since her change…

She wanted him even more.

For a vampire, physical lust and blood lust combined. Desire went soul-deep. Her hunger wasn't sated with quick sex. She needed more. Longer. Hotter.

Aidan.

"You healed?" He bit the words off against her mouth.

"Yes…"

He whirled her around. Sat her on the edge of his desk and shoved her legs apart. Jane's hands flew back, slamming onto the surface of his desk, narrowly avoiding a collision with his laptop as she fought to find her balance.

"Need to be…in you…" And his voice was that rough growl again. The one that made goosebumps rise on her skin. That made her nipples pebble.

That made her wet.

"I want that, too," Jane whispered as her hands curled against the desk. *Aidan, in her. Sinking deep.* Her nails scraped over the wooden surface and Aidan's fingers — he was yanking at the button of her jeans, pulling down the zipper, then pretty much jerking the jeans and her shoes right off her.

Her underwear vanished with the jeans. A very good thing. The cool air hit her skin and Jane let out a quick gasp when Aidan's hands came back. Big, strong hands. They pushed her thighs farther apart and then his fingers were stroking *into* her. Pushing into her sex even as his thumb worked her clit.

That was her Aidan, all right. Zero to implosion in way less than sixty seconds.

"Aidan—" Jane began, desire sharpening her voice. The room was sound-proofed, so she knew no one outside would hear them. When you had a bar that was normally packed with werewolves and their enhanced hearing, you *had* to take precautions—hence the soundproofing. She knew she could yell, could scream with her climax, and no one but Aidan would hear her.

Only Aidan.

"Can't wait," he gritted.

She nodded. Did she *look* like she wanted him to wait?

"Too scared…" His eyes were definitely glowing. "Too…*pissed*."

Uh, oh. "Aidan?"

He'd jerked open his own jeans. His cock— big, long, fully erect—pushed at the entrance to her sex. Their eyes met, then he drove deep.

So deep that she lost her breath.

So deep that her whole body shuddered.

So deep…Jane thought that for a moment, they were one.

The bond is always there with him.

Her nails scraped over his desk, then she was grabbing his shoulders. Holding on tight. She could handle all of him now that she was a vampire. No worries about him hurting the delicate human. She could have him all, and all— *all* was exactly what she wanted.

He withdrew, then slammed into her. Again and again. Her fangs burned in her mouth, the bloodlust aroused by her physical desire for him. But Jane kept her lips clamped shut. This wasn't some life-or-death emergency, she wasn't going to bite him again—especially not with Paris's warnings fresh in her mind.

His hand was between their bodies. His thumb still stroking her clit and her orgasm built, her whole body quaking. It was so close. She was—

Aidan put his mouth at the curve of her shoulder, right there, at the bottom of her neck. She felt the press of his teeth and then he…he…*bit* her.

Pleasure lashed through her and she squeezed her eyes shut. Her legs were locked tightly around his hips and her body arched against him, rocking hard again and again as the climax erupted. She couldn't get enough air to scream, couldn't do anything but take and take that pleasure as he thrust into her once more…

And then he was the one erupting. She felt the hot splash of his release inside of her, and then Aidan was pulling his mouth from her and roaring out her name.

She rather liked that roar.

Her heartbeat thundered in her ears. Her body quivered. Her sex pulsed. And slowly, very slowly, her lashes lifted as she stared at him and —

There was blood on his mouth. A little drop of blood that had dripped from the corner of his lips.

Her blood.

Only…

Since when do werewolves drink blood?

Her thundering heartbeat seemed to stutter as she stared into his eyes. Eyes that were still glowing too bright with the power of his beast.

Aidan licked the drop of blood away. "You taste fucking delicious," he whispered.

A shiver slid over her body. A shiver that had nothing to do with pleasure and everything to do with fear. Paris's words whispered through her mind once more…

I'm worried that you're changing him.

She…was.

CHAPTER THREE

Jane was afraid of him.

Aidan paced in front of his desk. Jane was in the bathroom. He could hear the blast of the shower. He'd wanted to go in there with her, but…

Jane is afraid.

Did she think he didn't know? He'd smelled her fear. Fear had a distinct scent—coppery, bitter. Jane had stared at him, even while he was still balls deep in her body, and she'd been afraid. Her hands had flown between their bodies and she'd pushed him away, muttering about needing to freshen up.

What. The. Fuck?

He stopped pacing and glared at the bathroom door. Had he been too rough with her? Yeah, okay, going straight into the office and immediately fucking her didn't exactly shout romance, but he'd been at the damn edge. Jane had nearly died. Again. That shit had to stop. She was too important to him. She needed to realize it.

He spun from the door and marched to his desk. He stared down and then…

Then his fingers traced the deep gouges that she'd left across the top of his desk. Claw marks. Her hands had scraped over the desk right before she'd grabbed onto him. When her claws had curled into his shoulders, he'd loved the burn of pain.

Even as he knew just what it meant.

I did this — I did this to Jane.

Paris had warned him, over and over, that Jane was different. No average vamp. Because of Aidan, she wasn't. Because of Aidan, hell, he wasn't even sure *what* Jane truly was. A hybrid? Half-vampire, half-werewolf? Something else?

Something…worse?

The shower had turned off. His shoulders stiffened as he listened to the soft rustles of movement from inside the bathroom. A few moments later, the door creaked open. He caught Jane's scent drifting in the air — soft, sweet, feminine.

Not the bitterness of fear, not any longer.

The breath he'd been holding slipped away. "Jane, I—"

"I've done something to you." Her voice was stilted. Sad.

Not Jane.

He spun to face her. She was pale—okay, yeah, most vamps were a little pale, but this was different.

"I'm sorry," Jane said, and her fingers rose to press against her neck. "I never meant to hurt you."

Hurt *him?* In a flash, he was right in front of her. "You scared the hell out of me, baby." He pulled her into his arms and held her close. "When I came into that alley and saw you—shit, don't do that crap to me again, got it? My heart can only take so much."

She was tense in his arms.

He didn't want that. Aidan squeezed her tighter. "Okay, so I flipped out a bit. That happens when the woman I love is attacked. It happens when—"

"You bit me."

His body tensed.

"When we were having sex, you bit me, Aidan."

Handle with fucking care. "You…didn't like that?"

Her hands curled over his shoulders and she pushed back so that she was staring up at his face. "I thought I was supposed to be the vamp in this relationship. Paris said—"

Shit, shit, shit! Paris needed to stop saying things.

"Paris said I was changing you. That can't happen, Aidan. I can't hurt you. Not you. You can't become—"

He made himself speak carefully as he explained, "Werewolves mark their mates. They bite them."

She stepped back. Her hands slid from him.

"They bite them…" Aidan continued, and he was the one to reach out and touch her. His fingers trailed over her collarbone then slid to the soft curve where her shoulder and neck met. "Right here." The sweet spot. Not *the* sweetest spot, though. That area was lower on her lovely body. "I bit because you're mine, Jane."

Her lips parted. "You…you drank my blood."

Tread carefully. "Did I?" He shook his head. "Paris doesn't know what he's talking about. The guy's a worrier. Always has been. You aren't hurting me. You aren't doing anything to make me weaker." That was the absolute truth. "Together, we will always be stronger."

Her gaze searched his. He saw the exact moment when she decided to believe him. A relieved breath slipped from her and her eyes gleamed. "Always."

He knew the storm had passed, for the moment. "Glad that's settled," Aidan muttered. His hand slid up the delicate column of her throat and he leaned toward her, pressing a quick kiss to her lips. Jane leaned into him, kissing him back so sweetly and then when he pulled back, she smiled at him.

His beautiful Jane.

Mine.

Hell, yes, he'd marked her. No other werewolf had better get close to her, and if Paris thought she'd drink from *him…*

Think again, buddy. Think the hell again.

"Are you going to tell me what you found in that alley?" Jane murmured. A furrow appeared between her brows. "I guess the clean-up is all handled now and—"

Right. Time to get back to business. Though the pleasure part of their relationship had certainly been fun. "Someone beat me to that particular job."

The furrow deepened. "Come again?"

Oh, baby, I plan to. At the first available opportunity. He cleared his throat. "The bodies were gone. The alley reeked of bleach. No work for me there."

She blinked. "But…who did it? Why?"

Might as well tell her all now. The better for her to be ready for the threat that *would* come again. "I found a video camera out there. Someone was watching you, baby. Those humans in the alley? They might have thought they were there to take you out, but I suspect they were really just bait. Someone wanted to watch you. Maybe see how strong you were."

"*What?*" Then she gave a bitter laugh. "Well, if that's the case, then that someone saw me nearly get taken out. If you hadn't been there, I—"

"Even at death's door, you killed your attacker," he said flatly. "That's what the watcher saw. He knows how you fight now. Knows that you don't stop, even when you barely have a breath in your body."

Sadness darkened her expression. "Two men died tonight."

Yeah, he wouldn't exactly be grieving over them. "Why'd you go into the alley?" His hand was still curved around her neck. He could feel her pulse jerking beneath his touch.

"Because I smelled the blood." Her gaze turned distant. "Someone was hurt. The blond man was yelling, saying he needed help." She shrugged. "I might be a vamp, but I'm still a cop, too. So I went to help him."

"And got ambushed."

"Yes."

His voice roughened as he said, "The next time you hear someone calling out for help, you're not even going to hesitate, are you?"

"Aidan…"

"You were warned before, Jane. Being a hero will just get you killed." That particular warning had come from a very powerful voodoo queen, a queen who had foreseen Jane's fate.

Sometimes, you couldn't change fate, no matter how hard you tried.

Jane's lashes lowered. "I already died once."

His hand slid from her neck.

"And I can't just watch while an innocent suffers." Her hand was at her side, pressing against the scar that marked her. No, not a scar. A burn.

A burn left by a sadistic vampire long ago.

"That's not who I am," Jane said.

No, it wasn't.

She gave him a tight smile. "I have to go now. I need to…to check in at the station." Her chin notched up. "I'm supposed to see my brother today."

Aidan's body iced. "That's a bad idea. Very, very bad." He'd prefer for her to never get anywhere near Drew Hart again. The guy was a ticking time bomb—one who had already exploded once and Aidan knew for certain, Drew would again.

"After he got out of intensive care at the hospital, Drew was transferred to a maximum security psych ward. I can't just leave him there."

Why not? As far as Aidan was concerned, the dick was getting off too lightly. Jane's brother Drew had shot her—he'd been the one to set in motion the horrible chain of events that resulted in Jane's transformation into a vampire.

No, I'm the one who did that. I'm the one who brought her brother to this town. Because Aidan had mistakenly thought he was doing something to make Jane happy. He hadn't realized her precious Drew was a nutjob.

He tried to kill me, but Jane got caught in the cross-fire. He took her out.

And I will destroy him.

"Drew hasn't spoken to anyone, not since he woke up in the hospital. I need to see him."

"The guy opened fire at a college campus. He needs to stay locked away."

Jane swallowed. "Once upon a time, he saved me." She turned away from Aidan and took two steps. "He —"

"Bullshit." Aidan grabbed her wrist. "Once upon a time, a sadistic vampire bastard broke into your house. He killed your mother and step-father. The vamp tied you up and tortured you and your *brother* left you to that hell."

Tears gleamed in her beautiful eyes. "Drew hid to protect himself. When it was safe, he came back for me. He got me out of there. He —"

Time for hard truths. "He wants supernaturals dead. You're a supernatural now. What do you think that means?"

She looked down at her hand, then back up at him. "It means I have to see him. Drew is my responsibility."

Fuck. There she went. Being all noble again. He had to break that habit before it killed her—a second time.

"I'll do some digging and see what I can possibly uncover about those jerks in the alley." She pulled her hand free. "I'll check some mug shots. Guys like that—maybe they've got a criminal record. I get a name to match a face, and it will be the perfect lead to take me to whoever was pulling the strings in that alley."

That wasn't exactly a face-off that he wanted. "Don't charge into battle without me." He had leads that he'd be following up on as well.

She stared at him, and her face softened. "You won't change, will you?"

He made himself smile. "Baby, I can already shift into the form of a wolf. What more change do you want from me?"

She smiled back at him. Such a beautiful sight. Then Jane was walking away. His gaze dropped to her ass and the sweet sway of her hips.

Another beautiful sight.

Jane unlocked the office door and left him. He turned back to his desk. He touched those claw marks once more.

And he swore that he could still taste Jane's blood on his tongue. He could taste it — and he wanted more.

His hand fisted over those marks. *What am I becoming?*

***

Paris paused outside of the Voodoo Shop. He was going behind his alpha's back, and that didn't sit right with him. As a rule, he never kept secrets from Aidan. Aidan was his best freaking friend. Aidan was family but…

Aidan is also in danger. And the guy can't see the danger because it's wrapped up in a sexy Mary Jane bow. His hand lifted and he started to pound on the shop's door, but the door swung inward before he could make contact and Paris found himself standing face to face with the infamous voodoo queen.

Annette Benoit.

Drop-dead gorgeous and far too deadly Annette Benoit. The woman he'd secretly been fantasizing about for far too long.

"Well, well," Annette gave him a slow smile, one that didn't quite reach her dark eyes. "If it isn't the handsome Paris. Coming to pay me *another* visit?" She moved back, motioning with her hand for him to enter. "If you're not careful, I'll start to think you like me."

He crossed the threshold and his body brushed against hers. "I do."

Annette's face—absolute damn poetry to him—softened with surprise.

"But I'm here on business." Because he wasn't sure either of them were ready to cross *that* particular line yet. He'd known Annette's last lover, known the guy well—and had come to hate the bastard. Would Annette really be open to trusting another werewolf? The last thing he wanted was to get shot down by her.

Better to have his fantasies.

She hurried past him, all smooth, chocolate cream skin and sweet-smelling woman. She wore a long, flowing dress, one that did little to hide her perfect curves, and hoop ear-rings adorned her delicate ears. No other jewelry, not for Annette. She didn't exactly need other adornment.

The woman is perfect as she is.

She led him into the back room and pointed toward her table. Shards of broken, black glass were carefully positioned on that table. "Why don't you have a seat?"

He kept standing. "How can you even see anything, with your scrying mirror shattered that way?"

She eased into her chair and stared down at the chunks of glass. "All of the power in that mirror…it came from *me*." She looked up at him, her light brown gaze glinting with determination. "I'm still strong, Paris. So if you are looking for weakness—"

He had to laugh. "Annette, you're as far from weak as a woman can get."

She smiled at him. A real, breath-taking smile.

I am in such trouble with her.

Paris cleared his throat. "I came about Aidan."

Her fingers tapped on the table. "Of course, you did. It's not as if you came by to ask me out on a date."

Ah…hell, no, he wasn't going to touch that one. *Not yet.* But…what kind of date would impress a voodoo queen?

"What's happening to the fearless alpha?" Annette asked.

His fingers curled over the back of the nearby chair, but he still didn't sit. "He's changing."

Her smile vanished.

"He keeps giving Jane his blood. She was attacked earlier tonight and he let her drink from him again. The bond between them just gets stronger."

"Jane isn't evil." She looked down at her broken chunks of glass. "You and I both know that."

"It's not Jane I'm worried about." And it pained him to say this. "Alpha werewolves aren't like the rest of the pack. They're stronger, deadlier, and…more vicious." Because sometimes, you had to be vicious when you were the boss of all the paranormals in town. "So what will happen to him if he keeps changing? What will happen to his beast? It's sure as all hell not going to be some *peaceful* change. His blood is mutating, we both know that." Because they'd taken some of Aidan's blood and some of Jane's blood…and they'd given it to the doctor on the pack's payroll, Dr. Bob Heider, so he could run some tests. "He's already starting to show vamp traits, and that shouldn't be possible."

She picked up a chunk of glass and shivered. "You think Aidan is the one we need to fear."

"I think Aidan is already powerful enough. I think vampires—Jane being the damn exception—live to kill and destroy. What the fuck happens to an alpha werewolf when he suddenly has all of those dark desires?" *I don't want Aidan losing the humanity he has.* "I tried to get Jane to drink from me instead. I thought maybe that would be safer."

Her hand fisted around the glass. "Let me guess, Aidan didn't like that plan."

He raked his hand over his face. "Serious understatement."

Her gaze met his.

"So what am I supposed to do now? How do I help him?"

She put down the chunk of glass and slowly rose to her feet. Her steps were silent as she rounded the table and came to his side. Then her hand lifted and touched his arm. Paris swore that touch singed him. "You be his friend. You stay close to him. And if you see him crossing a line…" Her breath whispered out. "Stop him."

"That's easier said than done." Like stopping an alpha was child's play.

"I'll see what else I can learn. I'll scry. I'll check my books. We *will* fix this. Aidan is a good man. And Jane isn't going to let him go into the darkness." For an instant, he could actually feel the swirl of magic around them. He stared into Annette's eyes and saw her gaze go distant, as if she were watching something he couldn't see. "She'd follow him into the darkness," Annette murmured. "Long before she ever surrendered him."

That didn't make him feel better. It made him worry even more.

***

Annette watched Paris as he drove away. His shoulders had slumped as he left the Voodoo Shop, as if he carried a terrible burden.

He did.

Paris was right to be afraid. All of the wolves should be afraid. A change was coming, she could practically feel it in the air. She went back inside, making sure to shut and lock the door behind her. She wasn't in the mood for tourists that day. Didn't feel like making love potions or telling of what fates might come.

She almost wanted to hide because the danger she felt...it was that consuming.

Annette headed into the back of the shop — into the room that was her haven. Her steps quickened and —

"I was starting to think the wolf would never leave."

She stilled.

The man who'd been waiting for her — the *vampire* who'd arrived to visit her just moments before Paris appeared on her doorstep — lifted one brow. "What? You knew I was waiting." Vincent Connor smiled at her.

Yes, she'd known he was hiding out of sight, but Paris hadn't so much as scented the vamp, a bad thing. Werewolves were supposed to have the best noses in the world. "You really do have some powerful magic." Or rather, she suspected he had one very powerful witch working for him.

Vincent laughed. "It's just a little trick to disguise my scent. And if I didn't move, I knew the wolf wouldn't hear me. It's not like Paris is an alpha."

No, but Paris was still plenty strong and dangerous. There was a reason he was the alpha's assassin.

Vincent lifted both of his hands and put them in front of his body. A gesture that she knew was supposed to show he was no threat.

Too bad she always believed vamps were threats.

"Despite what the alpha believes, I am really not here to hurt anyone. I don't know how many times I have to say it but…not all vamps are monsters. We aren't all driven mad by bloodlust. Born vampires—vamps like me, vamps like Jane—we stay in control. We were meant to be this way. It's only the ones who are transformed that go mad. And really, how can you blame them? They are becoming something that nature never intended. Humans weren't meant to be vampires. They can't handle that kind of power."

She scooped up a few chunks of broken glass. "What about werewolves?"

His hands fell. "I heard what Paris said."

I know you did.

"And I've maintained, all along, that Jane and Aidan never should have been involved. Vamps and werewolves aren't meant to be together. I'm afraid that when Jane tries to leave him, Aidan won't be quite…sane about it."

Now she was the one to laugh, a shocked laugh of disbelief. "You actually think Jane will leave Aidan? She loves him."

"Love isn't always enough. Especially where monsters are concerned." He paced closer to her and his index finger tapped against her fist, the fist that she'd made over the chunks of glass. "So that's what became of your magic mirror."

Her eyes turned to slits. The guy was *mocking* her?

"Too bad. I think we could have all used your foresight about now." He exhaled. "How are we supposed to stop the threats, if we never see them coming?"

Such a very good question.

His hand slipped away from hers. "The alpha wants me to stay away from Jane."

She dropped the glass onto the table. "Do you blame him?"

"I'm not Jane's enemy, no matter what he thinks. Everything I've done, it's been because I wanted to help her achieve her destiny."

Now he was getting all sanctimonious on her.

"Soon enough, Jane will see reason. And when she does…" He handed her a slip of paper. "Make sure she gives me a call. I will *always* be there to help Jane."

Right. Fabulous. "I think you'd better focus more on getting out of the city. Aidan isn't a man you want as an enemy, but you sure have pissed him off."

His lips thinned. "I don't run from wolves."

Maybe you should.

"Goodbye...for now, voodoo queen." He gave her a little bow and then sauntered away.

She put his card on her table, right next to her broken chunks of glass. She stared into the glass and, for just an instant, she saw fire.

Fire...

And a vamp rising.

***

"You sure you can handle this?"

Jane glanced over at her police captain. Vivian Harris stood with her in the too bright hallway of the Hathway Psychiatric Facility. Vivian's badge was pinned to her belt, but the captain didn't have her weapon with her—both Jane and Vivian had been ordered to surrender their weapons at check-in.

It didn't exactly work out well to have loaded firearms around mental patients.

A guard stood just a few feet away, watching the exchange between Jane and Vivian.

"I can talk to the prisoner," Vivian assured her. "You don't have to do this." Vivian's suit didn't sport so much as a single wrinkle and her hair was pulled back in a twist, emphasizing the elegant lines of her cheeks and jaw. Her coffee skin gleamed, even under the horrible lights, and her gaze was steady as it focused on Jane.

Sympathy. Jane could see the emotion in her captain's eyes. Vivian pitied her. Just when Jane had thought things couldn't get worse. *I want Vivian's respect, not her pity.*

Jane's shoulders straightened. "Drew hasn't talked to anyone else. He's not going to speak, not unless he's talking to me." She had to go into that little room and see her brother. She'd been dreading this meeting…dreading it from the moment she realized that death wasn't going to keep her in its tight grip. Drew would know that she should have died after that shooting spree that *he'd* initiated. And when she walked into that room…

What will happen then?

"Just make sure the security camera in his room is turned off," Jane whispered. "We don't exactly want anyone getting a record of this little chat."

Vivian knew the score. After all, she was a werewolf, one of the many wolves in positions of power in New Orleans.

"Don't worry," Vivian assured her as she inclined her head toward the silent, watchful guard. "That's already been handled."

The guard nodded back toward her.

Another werewolf? And to think Jane hadn't even been aware of the werewolves, not until a few months ago. How quickly things had changed.

"Your brother has been restrained," Vivian told her. "So you don't have to worry—"

Jane's sad smile stopped her words. "I don't have to worry that—what? He'll try to kill me? Been there, done that." But she still hesitated to put her hand on the door knob and open the damn door. *Coward. I am a coward at my core.* Jane licked her lips and risked a quick glance at Vivian once more. "Are we good?" She blurted out those words in a really, terribly awkward way.

Vivian's dark brows shot up. "Good?"

Jane waved her hand between them. "Yeah. Me. You. Me being all…" Jane pointed at her mouth. *Vampire-like.* Only there was no "like" to it. She was a vampire. And as a werewolf, how did that make Vivian feel? Did it—

"You don't come at my throat, you don't start draining any humans, and yes, we're good," Vivian said briskly.

But Jane still had to push. "You don't…feel the urge to attack me?" It was that way for other vampires. Aidan *should* have killed her as soon as she'd transformed. Paris should have gone for her throat but…

They hadn't.

Because I had so much of Aidan's blood in me. Werewolf and vampire all combined.

"I don't," Vivian said simply. Her head cocked. "You want to tell me why that's so?"

I'm a crazy vamp-slash-werewolf. That's why. Jane knew her smile was weak as she said, "I'd better go and talk to my brother." Before any *non*-werewolf guards started their shifts and wondered why the video surveillance in Drew Hart's room wasn't working.

Squaring her shoulders, Jane took a deep breath. Then she reached for the handle on his door and she stepped inside.

The walls were yellow. Cheery. Sunlight spilled through the blinds and through the bars that were on the lone window.

A sharp gasp came from the right and Jane's head turned—and her eyes clashed with a gaze that was just as dark as her own. Her older brother, Drew, was in bed. *Strapped* down to the bed. His dark hair was a stark contrast to the white pillow case. His body strained on the bed as he twisted and heaved against the restraints. "*Mary Jane.*" His gaze widened as he seemed to drink her in. "Thank God…*Mary Jane.*"

She shut the door behind her and then Jane pressed her back to it. Not a wooden door—metal. Reinforced. She stared at her brother as her heart twisted in her chest.

"You're okay." His voice was rasping. "So glad you're okay."

She was far from okay.

"I had to kill the werewolf, you understand that, right?" His hands had fisted. "He was evil. Dangerous."

"Aidan isn't evil." She couldn't move. Her brother's face was lined, pale, showing the strain from his recent hospital stay. But she'd read the reports on him — he was healing fast. Almost too fast.

At her words, Drew's dark brows shot up. "Isn't...*isn't evil. Isn't?*" Drew heaved against the restraints once more. His handsome face reddened. "I shot him! Are you saying he's still alive? He should've died! He should've —"

"You shot *me*." She kept her voice flat with an effort. Her brother had apparently been dead silent for days but the minute he saw her...

I knew he'd talk.

"You jumped in front of him," Drew muttered. "I never meant to hit you. I was so scared. So worried...but you're here. You're alive."

And she couldn't help it. Jane shook her head.

He stopped struggling against his restraints. "Mary Jane?"

"You have to let go of all that rage you carry inside," she told him, her chest still burning. "It's destroying you. I saw it…for years. Like a festering wound. Just getting worse and worse, never better. I stayed away from you because I saw what you'd become. I thought I was making it all worse. Making you remember…"

Vampires. Death.

Hell.

She took a step away from the wall. Then another. She walked slowly until she reached the edge of his bed, then she stared down at Drew. His hair was mussed, sweat beaded his brow, and his eyes….

"You killed me, Drew. *You* did that."

"No!" He screamed the denial. "I was just trying to stop the werewolf! He's a monster! He thought you *loved* him!" Drew gave a hard, negative shake of his head. "You don't belong with someone like that. Some*thing* like that!"

"I do love him."

Drew shook his head.

"And I love you." That part hurt so much. "Even with what you did, I still love you." That was why it hurt so much to look at him. When Jane gazed at her brother, she remembered the boy who'd pulled her from hell one dark night. A dirty hand, reaching out to help her.

Her side seemed to burn. Her side—her scar. The twisting mark that she'd been given when she was just eleven years old. A twisted, sadistic vampire named Thane Durant had broken into her home. He'd killed her mother and step-father, then he'd tied Jane to the table in the basement. He'd pulled out a soldering pen and burned the Greek letter Omega into her skin as she screamed.

Omega. *The end. Is that what I am?*

"You aren't dead, Mary Jane." Drew wasn't screaming any longer. He was whispering. "I see you. You're right here. You're breathing. You're talking. You're—"

Jane leaned down close to him and in his ear, she whispered, "I'm a vampire."

His whole body jerked as he tried to pull away—from her. Her gaze slid to his forearm and the tattoo there, a tattoo of the Greek letter Omega. A tattoo to match her burn. Only he'd chosen to get that tattoo. He'd said he'd done it to remind him of her.

The pain in her heart just got worse.

"If you get free," Jane asked him, "what will you do?"

He wasn't looking at her. Just staring at the far wall.

"Will you come after me again? Go after Aidan?"

Again, no answer. Drew just kept staring at that wall as if it held all the secrets in the universe.

Her laughter was sad. "The silent treatment, huh? Aren't you tired of that bit?" Then, driven too far, Jane just broke. She caught his chin in her hand and wrenched his face toward her. She stared at him, their faces inches apart. "I am not your enemy."

His jaw hardened. "Get me the fuck out of here."

"What will you do," Jane asked again, "if you get free?" Because she could still feel the fire of his bullet going into her chest.

"I won't stop," he rasped. "Not until I destroy the monsters."

She jerked back from him, as if she'd been burned. *Again.* Jane marched into the bathroom, her gaze searching frantically around. And then—then she looked into the mirror. She hadn't wanted to look in the mirror at Aidan's place…*because I knew I wouldn't like what I had to see.* But, sometimes, you had to face the monsters. Her eyes narrowed as she stared at herself. Jane drew back her hand and drove her fist right into the mirror. It shattered.

She grabbed a big chunk of that mirror and marched back to Drew.

The door to his room flew open. Vivian stood there, her body ready to attack. "Jane, what happened?"

Jane just shook her head, and she shoved that broken mirror before Drew's face. "Take a good long look in there," she ordered him. "And you'll see a monster staring back at you." *Because I'm not the only monster in the family.*

His gaze locked on his reflection.

"Aidan never did anything to you. He never would have gone after you. And me...well, I just wanted to love you. You are the only family I have left." The mirror was shaking in her hand.

Vivian crept closer to the bed. "Jane..."

"You destroyed your own life, Drew." She was just sad now. "What comes next, well, it will be on you." She moved away from the bed, taking the mirror with her as she and Vivian headed for the door.

"Mary Jane..." Drew called.

She stopped. Looked back.

Drew smiled at her. "You won't leave me here."

What else was she supposed to do with him? Let him out so he could go and attack again? Go after Aidan? Hurt innocent people who got in his way?

"I didn't leave you," Drew reminded her softly. "When the vampire had you in our basement. When he was burning your skin and you were crying, I didn't leave you. I got you out of there. I saved your life."

She swallowed.

"You won't leave me," Drew said, utterly confident.

Jane turned away from him once more. Her eyes squeezed shut. "Goodbye." And she walked out, as fast as her shaking legs could carry her.

He bellowed her name. She didn't look back.

He *screamed* for her.

Jane kept walking. From the corner of her eye, she saw Vivian jerk her head toward the guard and then point to Drew's room. The guard quickly ran inside.

But those screams followed Jane.

"Aidan can make him forget," Vivian said, voice brisk. "He can make sure that your brother forgets everything that happened in New Orleans. You know an alpha werewolf can control a human— Aidan can control Drew. He can make it so that your brother—"

The screaming had stopped.

Jane looked at Vivian. "So that Drew forgets me?" Because he'd have to forget her—otherwise, she'd just be another monster that he had to hunt.

I didn't leave you. Jane exhaled on a ragged breath. "Keep a guard with him until I can get Aidan back here." Because only an alpha werewolf had the power to control a human's mind that completely. Other werewolves could influence humans, could charm them, sway them, but an alpha…

Mind-freaking-control. An alpha was a whole other level of power.

"I'll make sure my man stays here," Vivian assured her.

Jane nodded. She looked down at her hand and realized she was still holding the chunk of broken mirror. Her reflection stared back at her.

Hello, monster.

Jane shoved that piece of glass into the nearest garbage can. Then she reached for her phone as she rushed down the long corridor. Unfortunately, there was no signal in that place.

No signal, but she could have sworn she heard the echo of her brother's screams.

CHAPTER FOUR

Drew Hart glared at the guard who stood just inside of his room — *more like my prison*. The guy was tall, thin, but with an intense gaze that wouldn't freaking leave Drew's face.

Is he one of them? One of the monsters? For years, Drew had thought that he only had to worry about vampires, but then a werewolf had appeared, literally on his doorstep. A beast who'd worked for Aidan Locke — the bastard who *thought* he was going to keep Jane at his side.

"Get the restraints off me," Drew demanded.

The guy just smirked at him. "Relax, buddy. You aren't going anywhere. Captain Harris sent me in to keep an eye on you."

Captain Harris…Yes, he knew her. She'd tried to interview him a few times but he'd given her nothing. Then she'd come running into his room a few minutes ago, her badge gleaming like she was some kind of big deal. She wasn't. "I've got to *piss*," Drew threw back at him. *I am not your buddy.* "I'm about to piss all over this bed. So get the restraints *off*." He heaved once more. "Where are the nurses? The doctors? They should be coming around. They *always* come around at this time." That had been the drill since he arrived in the looney bin. He'd gotten patched up at the hospital, then been sent to this hell.

"There was a change of plans for today."

That wasn't good. Just what did Mary Jane have in mind? She'd really left him — deserted him. What would happen next?

"The alpha will be coming soon," the guard added, his eyes gleaming.

Oh, hell, no. He'd met Aidan Locke once, tried to kill him on the same day. Drew did *not* want to tangle with that fellow again. "I'm going to piss myself."

The guard nodded. "Yep, that's the reaction most folks have to Aidan."

What? He jerked again as he fought his restraints. "Just let me go to the damn bathroom! You can tie me down again as soon as I'm done. There's no window in the bathroom — no way out for me at all." Then, hating it, he added, "Please." Begging. So humiliating.

But the guard actually seemed to soften at the last word. "You're right. Nowhere for you to go. Not like you'd get past me." He sighed as he headed for the bed. "And I really don't want to smell your piss on the sheets." A few moments later, the straps were gone and Drew was lurching his way to the bathroom.

"Thank you," he managed, voice nearly strangled. Then he shut the door on the guy. No lock, of course not. But…

Drew smiled.

The guard shouted, "I don't hear you pissing!"

Drew flipped on the water. Then he bent down and picked up one of the broken mirror shards. The guard should have bothered to look in the bathroom. Hadn't he heard the breaking glass? Captain Harris had sure run in fast enough.

Drew hid the shard behind his back as he left the bathroom.

"You left the water on, man," the guard grumbled. "Conserve the damn earth, you know? Take care of it or…" The guard marched toward the bathroom, obviously intending to turn off the water himself. "Or it won't take care of you," the guard finished. His body brushed against Drew's.

Drew attacked. He yanked up that shard of mirror and drove it into the man's stomach. Once in his stomach.

Then one long slice across the guard's throat. *The better to stop any screams.*

"I take care of myself," Drew muttered. "Always." Then he reached for the keys on the guard's belt.

It was time for him to get the hell out of there, before Mary Jane came back with her alpha lover.

He couldn't trust her, not anymore.

She'd changed. Now...

You're one of them, Mary Jane.

And that broke his heart.

***

Aidan kicked open the door of the apartment that sat on the edge of the French Quarter. The place was on the second floor of one of the historic homes that dotted the area. The place had been updated, so that while the outside of the building spoke of its age, the interior was hipster trendy. He and two of his pack members rushed inside, even though he already knew...

The apartment is empty. He hadn't been able to pick up any sounds from the apartment as he'd climbed up the stairs, so he knew his prey wasn't waiting for him.

But this *was* the place that the video camera in that damn god-forsaken alley had been transmitting to—a laptop was still up, still sitting on a desk and a cup of coffee was even perched beside it. Aidan's pack techs had traced the signal right to this location, and Aidan had closed in for the hunt.

Garrison strode forward and touched the mug. "Still warm," he murmured. His red head tilted as he stared at the open laptop. "And the computer is still on. Looks as if someone was trying to delete files."

Files…video footage? "We'll take it to our techs." They could retrieve the files, he had no doubt about that.

Paris began to prowl around the apartment. Aidan had picked Garrison and Paris to accompany him on this hunt…mostly because it was particularly personal and he trusted those two the most. Garrison might be reckless, but Aidan knew pack always came first for the guy.

"Fancy place," Paris murmured. "The guy who was here has money."

The guy liked lots of leather and big screen TVs and tech. Plenty of tech. The laptop wasn't the only computer in the place. There were plenty of monitors and desktops. And…cameras.

Aidan had pulled strings and gotten the name of the guy who supposedly had been renting the apartment. John Smith. A bullshit name? Oh, he was fucking sure it was. And the fact that the guy had been paying in cash…*You were trying to cover your tracks.*

But when a werewolf was hunting, it was impossible to cover those tracks completely.

"There's no scent here," Paris announced, a frown pulling his lips down. "Humans always leave scents."

"I don't think we're dealing with an average human," Aidan said. If only it were that easy. "The guy knew what Jane was. He sent out his bait to lure her in, and he just watched while she was ambushed." Which fucking pissed him off. The guy had been watching while Jane had fought for her life. He nodded toward Garrison. "Search the place. Every inch of it, got me?" Because maybe the watcher had been smart enough to cover his scent, but he might have been dumb enough to leave some other clue behind. A clue that cops—human cops—might overlook.

But a clue that werewolves wouldn't miss.

"Yes, sir." Garrison sprang to attention. The guy almost saluted. Jeez. Aidan barely contained an eye roll as Garrison hurried toward the hallway.

"He's...improving," Paris allowed.

Aidan just raised his brows. Garrison had been trouble from the start but...Aidan understood the guy. No, he felt *responsible* for him. Garrison's parents had been killed by a vampire—by the same bastard who had murdered Jane's mother and her step-father. Aidan had arrived too late to help Garrison's

family, but he had been able to carry the guy —
just a kid back then — out of that blood bath.

And I've been watching out for him ever since.
Yeah, Garrison could be a pain in the ass but…

He's pack. Pack is family. Pack is life.

"About earlier…" Paris began, his voice a bit
stilted.

Someone save me. Aidan's brows shot up.
"You aren't about to pull some sentimental BS are
you?"

Paris rolled one shoulder. "Just going to say
that you're a dick most days, but I'd still hate to
see anything bad happen to you."

"Jane *isn't* anything bad." Now he was
getting angry. He was — his phone rang, stopping
him before he could say more. Aidan pulled the
phone from his pocket and saw Jane's face on the
screen.

"Speak of the devil," Paris murmured.

Aidan's eyes turned to slits. *Don't keep
pushing, Paris.*

Paris coughed. "I'll just…" He pointed down
the hallway. "I'll go and help Garrison. You
know, search for clues. We'll Scooby Doo the shit
out of this place."

Aidan growled as his friend retreated. Then
he turned his back and put the phone to his ear.
"Jane? What's wrong?"

A pause, then she said, "You always assume
something is wrong."

Mostly because with them, something *was* generally wrong. It wasn't like she usually called and asked him to pick up milk from the store. Instead she called when people were dying or chaos was erupting. Standard shit for them.

"I need you to make him forget," she said, voice soft. "Can you come to the Hathway Psychiatric Facility? I—I hate asking, you *know* I hate asking, but I'm afraid he'll just attack again if you don't use your power on him to make him forget and—"

"I can't."

"Wh-what? Aidan, please, okay? *Please.* This is me, begging you for—"

"You never have to beg me for anything." He could hear the others in the hallway. They'd just opened a door. It gave a long squeak.

"Then do this for me. Just—"

He wished that he could help her. "My power doesn't work on him."

Silence. "What? Aidan, no, that's not—"

"I thought it did, the first time I met him. I thought I got him to tell me his secrets, but he was holding back on me." Aidan had been over that scene, again and again, in his mind. "That's how he was able to attack. He fooled me, Jane." It wasn't something he was proud of admitting. It was something that enraged him. "So making him forget isn't an option. If you think Drew won't stop coming after us, then the guy needs to

stay locked up or he needs to be taken out."
There were only two options, and Aidan knew
which option he favored.

Kill the bastard.

The problem was that the bastard in question
was Jane's brother.

A brother who fired fucking silver bullets at me.
Aidan still didn't know where the guy had gotten
those bullets. Drew had acted shocked to learn
Aidan was a werewolf. *But if he already had silver
bullets, where had the fucking shock come from?*

"I can't kill my own brother," she whispered.

Why not, baby? He killed you. But Aidan didn't
say those brutally true words.

Another door squeaked open, the sound
coming from the back of the hallway. Garrison
and Paris were continuing their search. They
were—

Snick.

A bitter, acidic scent hit Aidan's nose. He
whirled, every primal instinct he possessed
screaming at him. "No!" Aidan bellowed as he
dropped the phone and rushed down the
hallway. "Get out! *Get*—"

Paris turned toward him. His face showed his
shock—and his fear. He must have caught the
scent in the air, too. Maybe he'd heard that faint
snick sound. Paris was starting to run back
toward Aidan.

Garrison still stood frozen in the doorway. His head jerked at Aidan's roar. He looked at Aidan, utterly terrified, his wide gaze holding the same wild fear that it had possessed when he was a child. When Aidan found him covered in blood, cowering in that death-filled house that had been Garrison's home.

"*Aidan?*" Garrison mouthed his name.

Then the flames erupted. They shot out of the room behind Garrison and the force of that blast lifted him up, throwing the younger wolf toward Aidan.

And then the fire seemed to swallow them all.

***

The sunlight poured down on Jane as she stood just outside of the Hathway Psychiatric Facility. That light was too bright. Too hot. "Aidan?" Jane whispered.

But there was nothing. No response. No whisper of breath. Not even any beeping to signal they'd been disconnected.

"Aidan?" She'd heard him yelling for someone to get out. There had been fear in his voice. Aidan wasn't normally afraid. He wasn't...

The bright sky was suddenly dark. Her head tilted as she stared up at a big, black puff of smoke that was rising in the air, rising near the French Quarter.

Jane slowly lowered the phone as she stared at that smoke. *Aidan.* No, no, it didn't have to be him. The smoke did *not* have to be related to Aidan. It didn't have to be, but—

Her chest hurt. She felt as if someone were trying to carve out her heart. Trying to *take* her heart right from her.

She started running down the stone steps that led to the street.

"Jane?" It was Vivian's worried voice, calling out after her. "Jane, we need to—"

Jane didn't stop. She ran for her car. She dialed Aidan again on her phone, but he didn't answer. The phone just kept ringing.

Be okay. Be alive. Be —

A strong hand grabbed Jane's shoulder and spun her around.

"What's happening?" Vivian demanded as her hold tightened on Jane.

Jane tried to think—tried to shove back the fear that wanted to swallow her so she could focus. *Captain Harris.* Vivian had connections she could use. "I'm afraid something happened to Aidan…"

*I'm afraid…*The very stark truth that cut straight to her soul.

I'm afraid.

***

Fire engulfed the historic building at the edge of the French Quarter. The windows had exploded and glass littered the street. Jane ran toward the two-story building, leaving her car haphazardly parked near the curb, and fighting her way past the firefighters and cops who'd just arrived. Broken glass crunched beneath her boots and her frantic gaze stayed on that blaze.

Aidan might not be inside. He might not. He might —

"Get the hell off me!" A dark, dangerous bellow. A *familiar* bellow that stopped Jane in her tracks. "I have to get back in there — my best friend is in that building!"

Her gaze whipped toward that voice. Paris. He was there, currently being held back by five police officers. His clothes were half-burned. Singe covered him, and she could see blisters on his face and arms.

"Let him go!" Vivian bellowed as she rushed to Jane's side.

If Paris is here…

The flames crackled.

The cops looked at Vivian, recognized her, and followed her orders. They let Paris go and he surged to his feet, running toward the flames.

But Jane jumped in his path. She shoved her hands against his chest. "Stop! Not another step until you tell me exactly what is happening!"

The firefighters were spraying water at the building, trying desperately to control the blaze. It had already spread to the next building.

"Freaking six alarm fire," one of the uniformed firefighters snapped as he shot past them, his mask in place. "That's what's happening. The whole building is about to collapse, and we got reports that people are still trapped inside."

People? Jane stared at Paris. At his burns. "Aidan?" Saying his name hurt.

Paris flinched. "Aidan tossed me out a second story window," he confessed. She realized his right arm was twisted at an…unnatural angle and he was dragging his left leg. "The flames started—a bomb of some sort—seconds after we opened that back bedroom door in the second floor apartment."

"Aidan's still inside?" Jane whispered back to him.

His grim nod chilled her.

Jane turned and ran for the building.

She'd barely taken five steps when Paris tackled her right to the ground. "You *can't* go in!"

She rolled beneath him and tossed the guy off her. Even weakened during the day, she was still powerful. *Vampire strength, got to love —*

He grabbed her arms and jerked her toward him. "Know the fastest way to kill a vamp?" His voice was a deadly rumble. Behind him, Vivian was barking orders to the cops — and even to the firefighters. "It's fire. You go into those flames, and you don't come out."

"*He* hasn't come out!" Did Paris think that Jane was just going to stay out there while Aidan died?

"And if I let you burn, Aidan will take my head," Paris said the words with utter certainty. "Stay here, Jane. I'll go back in for him. Shit, I already would have been inside, but I blacked out when my head hit the concrete."

She could see blood trickling down the side of his head.

"Stay here," he said, voice low. "I'll get him."

Jane nodded. She didn't want to fight Paris. She also didn't want to waste time.

He let her go. He ran toward the building, shoving firefighters out of his way. Jane sucked in a deep breath and the smoke burned her lungs. She watched as a firefighter tried to stop Paris from rushing inside.

Not going to work. Paris was too determined. After a brief battle, Paris heaved the fellow to the side, then ran right into the flames.

Now it's my turn. Jane eased out a slow breath. If Paris thought she was just going to stand outside like some good little vampire, he needed to think again. Jane grabbed the smallest firefighter she saw—one who was only a few inches taller than she was. "Give me that uniform," Jane snarled. The uniform had to be better protection than her faded leather jacket. Firefighters wore turnout gear—she knew that stuff was supposed to be waterproof, heatproof and as damn sturdy as possible. If anything was going to save her vamp skin from the flames, that uniform would do the trick.

"My uniform?" The firefighter—a woman—stared at her in confusion. "Lady, you're crazy. You need to step behind the safe zone and let me do my job."

Jane's fangs burst out. She couldn't help it. She was scared and her adrenaline surge had her blood nearly boiling. "Give. Me. The. Uniform."

The female firefighter backed up. "What in the hell?"

"Give her the uniform," Vivian advised as she closed in. "You really don't want to fight on this…"

Screw fighting. If she had to do it, Jane would knock that woman out and take the gear. The scene was chaos. No one was paying any attention and—

"The place is about to collapse!" Two other firefighters ran out of the building. "Everyone needs to get clear, *now!*"

Jane yanked the coat off the other woman and snatched her mask. She'd take what she could get and she would haul ass.

Hold on, Aidan. I'm coming. It was her turn to save him.

Vivian yanked the gloves off the stunned female firefighter. "Take those, too, Jane, and *hurry*."

***

Jane Hart was going into the fire.

A suicide mission, of course. Vampires burned ever so quickly. But…

He lifted the binoculars to his eyes and watched her. She was going inside. Donning a firefighter's coat and mask, as if those items would help her. The trap he'd left burned particularly hot. He'd intended for the whole place to be destroyed.

He'd also aimed to take out any pesky wolves who'd come snooping. He wasn't interested in wolves. They were just beasts. Dogs that were in the way.

Vampires interested him.

Jane interested him. After all, she was his assignment. She had been, for quite some time. Longer than she could possibly realize.

The end. Oh, the stories that were spreading about her. Was she truly the one the vampires sought? He wasn't so sure, not yet.

Especially since she was doing dumbass shit like running into a fire.

"Should have let him burn," he muttered. "Fire hurts like a bitch when it bites you."

What would Jane look like when she came out of the fire? No longer so beautiful. No longer so perfect.

If she even came out…

Love. People were always spouting about how they'd risk everything for love. In Jane's case, it seemed that she truly might just do that.

Risk her life.

For a monster.

Pity. He hadn't realized she was insane. Maybe the vampire transformation had done that to her? Pushed her over an edge? And now Jane couldn't control herself.

She had a death wish.

Wish granted, Jane. Wish fucking granted.

CHAPTER FIVE

She nearly tripped over Paris. The guy was on the stairs, slumped down, choking on the smoke and flames.

Jane grabbed him and shook the werewolf, hard. *You were supposed to help with the rescue. Not become someone else I had to haul out of here!* "Paris!"

His eyes were closed.

And his head was bleeding — again. Or maybe it had never stopped bleeding.

She tightened her grip on him and hauled the guy *up* the stairs. There wasn't any time to go back outside. She could already hear the groans and creaks above her. The last thing she wanted was to waste time getting Paris out and *then* trying to run back into the building — that could be time that Aidan didn't have.

So she made it to the top of the stairs. There was only one door up there, one apartment from the look of things. The door to that apartment swung open. Had the firefighters bashed it in before they had to retreat? Maybe. Probably.

Smoke rises and I can barely see anything.

Jane went into that apartment and dragged Paris with her. *Where are you, Aidan? Where?*

Paris had said they were near the back bedroom when everything went to hell, right? So she kept walking straight ahead. The flames were on the walls, rolling above her and—

Paris was screaming. She looked back and saw that flames were on his legs. Oh, hell. She swatted her hands at them, trying to put the flames out. Then she focused on Paris, staring at him through the thin frame of the mask she wore.

His grim expression said what she was thinking.

We're both going to die in here.

No, they weren't. Because she'd just spotted an open window. Well, open in the sense that the glass had been blown out of it by the fire. Flames were everywhere. She was pretty much afraid to breathe, worried the heat would singe her lungs and she'd be DRT. A phrase she'd heard firefighters toss around before.

Dead right there.

She inched closer to that window. Flames started to eat at Paris's legs once again. *I'm sorry.* She squeezed her eyes shut and then threw him toward the window. He'd survived one fall…surely he'd survive another? *Please survive another.*

Paris never made a sound as his body hurtled to the street below.

Now she just had to get Aidan and get him out of there. Once Aidan was clear of the building, he'd be able to give Paris his blood and heal any injuries that the other werewolf had just sustained. That wonderful magical werewolf alpha blood was a cure-all.

I just have to find Aidan and get him out.

She turned back toward what she *thought* had been the hallway. She shuffled forward and saw flames up ahead, thick, greedy flames on the floor of that hallway and —

The flames are Aidan.

For an instant, the world stopped. It just stopped. Because he was burning, right in front of her.

"*No!*" Jane screamed the cry and heat singed her lungs. She ran forward, and her gloved fingers reached Aidan. He was burning so much — was he even alive? How *could* he be? The flames were eating at him, covering his back and his arms and —

Aidan.

She grabbed him with one hand and threw him toward the wall — but the wall gave way and Aidan flew right *through* it. He hurtled down to the street below.

At least he's out of the building. His wounds would be terrible, but he'd heal. He had to heal.

She stood there, her shoulders heaving, tears on her cheeks as she stared down at Aidan on the street below. He'd slammed into a parked car, denting the roof. Vivian and a few police officers swarmed near him and a firefighter sprayed at the flames still burning Aidan's body.

He can heal from that. Aidan can heal from anything. She wouldn't think of any other option. Jane stepped toward the gaping hole she'd just inadvertently created, intending to leap down to him. Screw any humans who might watching — they could just toss her actions up to a trick caused by all the smoke and flames.

The ceiling groaned above her.

She inched toward the edge of the building. It looked like such a big drop from up there. *But I'm a vamp. I can handle this fall…right?* Why was she even hesitating? Aidan and Paris had both not been given any option on the fall. She closed her eyes, wished for a safe landing and —

And something grabbed her foot. No, not *something.* Someone. Jane looked down and saw Garrison staring up at her. His face was ash streaked and blistered, but —

He's not covered in flames. Aidan was shielding him from the fire. That's why Aidan was still inside the apartment. That's why he was crouched in that hallway, he was leaning over Garrison, shielding Garrison with his own body. Shielding Garrison, as Aidan had burned.

The alpha protected his pack.

Garrison's lips parted. *"H-help — "*

The ceiling groaned again. Jane bent, grabbed his arm and she jumped out of that gaping hole in the wall. She leapt into the air, still holding Garrison tightly, and for a moment, she could hear the whistle of the wind around her. The people below her were screaming, she could see their open mouths, but she didn't *hear* those screams. Just the wind. Her body was light, weightless. She was soaring.

She was flying.

She was —

Falling.

Shit.

Garrison slipped from her hold. She tried to grab him, tried to grab —

She hit the concrete. The wind stopped whistling. Everything just stopped.

***

When Jane slammed into the concrete, the watcher's breath left him in a quick rush. He'd been standing in the crowd, blending perfectly because he'd followed Jane's lead and taken a firefighter's uniform. It had been easy enough to slip up behind one of the firefighters…and to slit his throat. The poor bastard was currently dead —

and naked—in a nearby dumpster. It was so easy to hide dark deeds in chaos.

Jane had just come hurtling from that building, dragging some smoking redhead with her—literally, the dumbass had smoke rising from his clothes—and they were both on the ground.

When she hit the pavement, no one moved at first. He watched, waiting for Jane to leap up and race to her werewolf lover.

Only she didn't move.

People began to inch toward her.

"Stay back!" A woman yelled. Then he saw the flash of a badge. "I'm police captain Vivian Harris, and I'm ordering everyone to stand the hell back so I can assess the scene and help these people!"

First of all…they weren't *people*. And second…they sure seemed pretty far from the whole "help" stage to him.

He backed away from Jane and turned his attention to Aidan.

Aidan Locke. Werewolf alpha. He'd met the wolf before, and he sure hadn't been impressed then. Aidan was covered in burns, but he was obviously still alive. His breath hissed out, and his eyelids were flickering.

"J-Jane…"

How unsurprising. Even hurt, his first thought was of her.

I'll make sure she's your last thought, too. After all, that was part of his job. To stop their bond. To shatter the link between them.

Soon enough, they'd tear each other apart. But right then, he had another assignment. He slipped away from the crowd and moved toward the ambulance on the right. Three ambulances were at the scene but he focused on *this* one. The one that housed Paris Cole.

Aidan's best friend.

Aidan's pack mate.

One EMT was in the back of the ambulance with Paris. A brace was around Paris's neck and Paris…he looked like hell. But then, that was expected considering the bomb that he'd left for the wolves up in that apartment. *John Smith.* Not his real name, of course. He couldn't use his real name now. It would have tipped off Jane and Aidan too much.

"How is he?" he asked, trying to sound concerned. And he was a bit concerned. If Paris was already dead, this little experiment wouldn't work. He'd have to find another guinea pig. Guinea wolf?

The blonde EMT jerked at his voice and glanced up at him. "I don't even know how he's still alive," she said, voice breathless. "But I'm praying he can make it to the hospital. Did you see him? He came from the second story!"

"They all did," he said quietly. "The building was collapsing. I don't think they had a choice. It was jump or die."

Her eyes widened.

"I have training," he said, still trying to sound like he cared. "Let me help you. There isn't anything else I can do back there." He jerked his thumb toward the fire. Then, without waiting for her response, he climbed into the back of the ambulance.

His gaze focused on Paris's neck. The brace was there, so…did that mean his neck was broken? *The guy is still breathing. So that means this shit should work.* His hand reached into his pocket.

"I've got this," the blonde said quickly. "My partner will be here soon and—"

He drove a needle into her neck. She immediately slumped over. The drug was fast, it knocked out its prey immediately, but unconsciousness only lasted for mere moments. He had to work fast, especially if her partner really was coming back.

He reached inside his borrowed uniform and took out another vial. One that was filled with a thick, red fluid. Blood.

Very special blood. He opened Paris's mouth and emptied that blood inside. "You were supposed to die today," he whispered. "But maybe this is even better." Paris swallowed automatically, a reflex that made things so much easier. When he was sure that Paris had gotten the blood down, he shoved the empty vial into a pocket. Then he leaned over Paris once more. "I don't think your neck is broken…" And Paris was starting to get color in his cheeks already. That just wouldn't do.

After all, he did need a good test subject.

"Here, let me help you with that." Fitting, considering the way Mary Jane Hart had been transformed. Smiling, he put his hands on either side of Paris's neck and he yanked, twisting as hard to the right as he could.

Paris jerked, then shuddered…and lay very, very still.

"That's so much better." He hurried from the ambulance. He jumped down just in time to see…

Jane. Being zipped up into a body bag.

Ah, Jane…I know you won't stay dead.

So did his boss.

***

Jane opened her eyes and sucked in a deep breath. Darkness surrounded her, complete and total. Her body ached and her fangs throbbed in her mouth. She strained, trying to see through the dark, trying to find light, but there was nothing.

Where is Aidan? What happened to me?

Her hands lifted and she discovered that something was over her. Some kind of — of fabric?

Hard, rough. She kicked out with her legs and found that they were trapped, too. It was as if she were sealed up in something. Locked up.

Bagged.

Oh, my God, no. Understanding hit her with a brutal punch. *A body bag.*

Revulsion built in her chest and she clawed at the bag above her head. Clawed until it ripped beneath her fingers and cool air spilled down to her. Air and light and—

"Easy, Jane."

She stilled.

A hand—with slightly plump fingers and super soft skin—touched her wrist. "You're okay," that reassuring voice told her. "A whole lot of humans just saw your swan dive out of the burning building, so Vivian and I had to do the best damage control we could." He pulled her up, easing her out of the bag.

She stared at Dr. Bob Heider, chief medical examiner. The medical examiner's eyes were worried behind the tortoiseshell frames of his glasses. The lines on his face were deeper and he smelled of smoke.

Wait, maybe that's me. I'm the smoky one.

"Had to tag you and bag you," he murmured, wincing a bit. "After all, everyone on the scene thought you were a corpse."

"I'm not." The words came out sounding funny because her fangs were fully extended. She was so freaking *thirsty.*

She was also sitting in the remains of her own body bag. Jane knew this horror scene would play through her head too many nights to come. *Just what I needed. A new nightmare.*

"Well, if we're going to get technical," Dr. Bob began, voice taking on that weird musing tone of his.

Her eyes narrowed on him. "Aidan." He'd better not be in a body bag, too—

"He still had a pulse on scene." Dr. Bob's lips turned down. "Vivian saw to it that he and Garrison were taken out to the werewolf compound for treatment. She's with them, don't worry. She'll make sure they are taken care of."

"*You* should be with them. You're the doctor who knows the score about them." Long before she'd stumbled into the werewolf world, Dr. Bob Heider had been on Aidan's payroll. Dr. Bob was the ME who always handled the paranormal cases. Or rather, he was the doc who made sure the paranormal victims never found their way into civilian hands. "You could help Aidan! You could—" But Jane stopped. She'd just realized that her hand looked funny. Dr. Bob still gripped her wrist with his soft fingers but her...her nails were wrong. Too long. Too sharp. A dark black.

They weren't nails at all. They were claws.

Claws like a werewolf would have. She'd *clawed* her way out of that bag.

"I saw them at the scene," he told her and his fingers slid away from her wrist. "Once I glimpsed that new manicure job of yours, I figured you'd need me when you woke up." He paused. "After all, the alpha can heal from anything, right? But you…I didn't know about you."

Tears stung her eyes. She couldn't look away from those claws. "How do I make them go away?"

"I don't know."

"How do I—" But then her head snapped up. She stared at him, her mind slowly processing all that he'd said in the moments after she'd woken. "Aidan…and Garrison." *Aidan was alive. Alive!* Dr. Bob had said they'd been taken to the werewolf compound—she knew that safe haven was hidden deep in the swamp. But they hadn't been the only werewolves in the fire. "What about…Paris?"

Dr. Bob looked away from her.

No, he wasn't looking away. He was looking *at* the other black body bag on the nearby exam table.

"No." Jane shook her head. "That's not happening."

"His…his neck broke, Jane. When he came flying from the building—"

"When I threw him from the building." Her body started shuddering. Jerking.

Dr. Bob swallowed. "He didn't make it. If we'd been able to give him Aidan's blood sooner, it might have made a difference, but…by the time I reached him in the ambulance, he was dead. The EMT was working frantically on him, I tried to help her, but…there was nothing to be done."

Jane shoved at the bag that still imprisoned her legs. She jumped from the slab—slab, table, whatever the hell it was—and staggered toward Paris. Her claws ripped into his bag, pushing it out of her way. His face was so still. Burned, blistered. His eyes were closed, his heavy lashes casting shadows on his cheeks.

Paris had always been so handsome. The ladies' man. Charming.

And…

Now he's dead. Because of me. "I tricked him into going back inside." Her words tumbled out. "Acted like he was the one going to rescue Aidan when I knew I'd be going into the flames, too."

"Jane…" Dr. Bob began.

"I did this."

Oh, God. She'd killed Paris. She'd killed Aidan's best friend. She'd done *this*.

Dr. Bob curled his hand around her shoulder and—

Paris's eyes flew open. He sucked in a sharp breath.

What?

His lips curled back from his teeth and she saw his growing…fangs.

"Fuck me," Dr. Bob swore as his hold tightened on Jane's shoulder. "You did this."

***

He hurt.

Aidan eased open one eye. He saw the familiar dark wood furniture of his bedroom. Saw the huddled figure of Police Captain Vivian Harris as she stared down at him from the right side of his bed.

"Jane…" Her name slipped from him. Jane needed to know about what had happened. She'd been on the phone with him. She'd been asking him to control her brother…

Then hell had exploded all around him.

It did more than explode…for a while there, I swear I was being dragged right down to hell. For a moment, he'd lost everything.

"The burns have faded," Vivian told him, her voice brisk. "I didn't think that even you could come back from damage that bad."

He opened his other eye. Sat up. Groaned as he felt the weakness in his body. Weakness and…

Hunger.

"You risked your life for Garrison." Now her voice was more angry than brisk. "If Jane hadn't gone into the fire after you, hell, you and the pup would both be dead—"

He grabbed her wrist. "Jane." His hand was trembling. He was trembling. He was so damn weak.

And he swore he could still feel the flames, melting away his skin. Destroying him. Killing him. Then…

Hunger…

Aidan swallowed. He ran his tongue over the edge of his teeth. His canines were sharp. Too sharp. "Jane…wasn't in the fire." Jane had been on the phone with him. She'd wanted him to help her brother.

The only help is death.

"Yes, she was there." Vivian met his stare directly. She'd always done that—never flinched away. She was one of the few werewolves who'd never feared him and who'd always had his back. "The woman ran into the fire and threw you out of that building. She knocked a wall down to do it, but…"

No. No. His hold tightened on her wrist. "Where is she now?" He needed to see her. Needed to make sure she never went into another fucking fire again.

Jane saved me? And he couldn't remember. He could only recall fire. Flames eating at his flesh. Garrison begging him to run.

But Aidan hadn't been able to leave the other wolf. He'd known Garrison would never survive the flames. He'd tried to protect him but—

Chill bumps rose on his skin. *The fire was too strong. Too strong even for me.*

"Jane's with Dr. Heider."

He freed Vivian and rolled to the edge of the bed. Aidan stood up.

And promptly fell on his ass.

"Aidan." She sighed his name as she bent to help him up. "I just watched your body completely regenerate over the course of *hours.* You should have been dead. You—damn, alpha, you looked like you'd literally walked through hell. Your skin was *melting.*"

Okay, that wasn't the best image to carry around, but he knew she spoke the truth. He'd felt it melting. He'd felt hell. Hell had wanted to hold tight to him but…

I came back.

"I get that you want to rush off to find Jane, but you aren't one hundred percent, not yet. So…" She shoved him back on the bed. "Keep your ass here until you finish recovering. Jane is tough. She saved you, right? She can handle a few more hours on her own."

It didn't make sense to him. If Jane had gotten him out, why wasn't she with him? Jane wouldn't just leave him.

Vivian's gaze darted away from him. "Sleep longer. We'll talk more later." She turned and headed for the door, her steps quick. "I'll let the others know that you're nearly back to fighting form." Her hand reached for the door knob.

"Was Jane hurt?" A vampire should never have gone into the fire. She'd risked death...

For me.

They seriously needed to get the hell out of town. Away from blood and fires and danger. Maybe they should go on a cruise or some shit. Do what normal people did for a change. Cruises left from New Orleans nearly every day. They could go drink some rum in Grand Cayman.

"Jane was hurt...a little," Vivian allowed. She hadn't looked back at him.

A lot. "She's alive."

Her shoulders squared.

"Look at me."

She turned. "She is alive but..."

He hated *buts.*

"But it was best for us to remove her from the scene in a body bag. People—humans—had just watched her fly out of a second story window and crash head-first into concrete. I wasn't sure if you were going to make it or not, so I couldn't count on you hunting down all of the witnesses and making them forget about Jane. So...we zipped her up."

He grabbed for the bed covers. "Body...bag?"

"The humans at the scene bought the act. She was knocked out, barely seemed to breathe, and Dr. Heider was the one who pronounced her dead." She paused. "Undead," Vivian muttered.

His eyes narrowed.

"We got her out of there. She'll wake up with him. He's got a new lab that he's using and he took her there."

Right. Because his last lab had been destroyed—Aidan remembered that destruction all too well.

"He'll check her out and then I'm sure Jane will be rushing back to your side." Vivian gave a hard nod. "So rest, alpha. Your mate is safe."

For the moment. "The place was wired to explode. The minute Garrison opened that back bedroom, he triggered a bomb. I heard the snick of the detonator. I only had *seconds* to get Paris out—" He gave a rough laugh. "He's going to be pissed at me for throwing him through the window."

"No." She turned away. Yanked open the door. "I'm sure he won't be pissed at all." Moments later, the door closed behind her with a soft click. He heard the pad of her footsteps as they faded away.

And…

Aidan heard her crying.

Strange. Vivian never cried. She never showed any weakness at all.

She was lying to me.

He slipped from the bed and pushed to his feet once more. Dizziness swept through him. Dizziness and a dark, twisting hunger.

A hunger for…

Blood.

He staggered toward his bathroom. His hands gripped the granite countertop and he stared at his reflection. His skin was a light pink, but there were no deep blisters. No blood. He could remember the horrible agony of his flesh burning. The smell had made him wretch. He'd been trying to think of a way to get Garrison out of there, but the fire had been out of control.

He'd been about to collapse, in so much agony, hurting beyond measure. Desperate and…

Hungry.

He leaned toward the mirror and saw that his canines had lengthened. Sharpened. Sure, that happened sometimes — his teeth got sharper when he shifted into the form of a wolf.

Only he wasn't shifting right then.

She's changing you. Paris's voice whispered through his mind.

There was a soft knock on his bedroom door. He inhaled and recognized his visitor's scent. "Come in!" Aidan called, his hands still gripping the countertop.

The door opened. Footsteps shuffled inside.

"Vivian said…she said you were okay."

Aidan shoved away from the sink. He stalked back into his bedroom. Garrison was there, pale, blistered, and…

Garrison ran his hand through his shaggy red hair. The tips of his hair seemed a bit singed. Maybe more than a bit. "I don't remember much…The flames were everywhere. You — you were yelling at me to stay down…"

Aidan froze a few feet from him.

"I thought we were both dead," Garrison whispered.

Aidan turned his back on the other man. He didn't want Garrison to see his fangs. *Vampire fangs.* "Not yet," he said.

But Aidan didn't know if those words were true. Had he just healed from the fire?

Or had he fucking died?

And he'd come back…as something else?

"I need Jane," Aidan rasped. She was the one who could help him. The one who could let him know just what in the hell was happening.

His anchor, in the fucking storm of his life.

He. Needed. Her.

"Vivian…she gave me your blood when we got here." Garrison swallowed and offered a weak smile. "Good thing we keep some of that powerful alpha blood on ice, isn't it?"

Aidan just stared at him. It was standard procedure to keep his blood stored on the premises so that any injured wolves would have access to it. An alpha werewolf's blood had amazing healing properties.

If I hadn't been an alpha, I'd be dead now.

Garrison's weak smile faded. "You saved my life again."

"Forget it." Aidan brushed past him and started grabbing clothes from his closet. *Jane should be here.* The fear he felt, the terrible tightness in his chest, wouldn't ease until he had her close again.

"I remember...when you saved me before."

Aidan glanced over at the guy. Garrison was staring at the floor.

"My parents were bleeding in front of me. No, they were *already* dead, and their blood soaked our wooden floor. I thought I would die then, too." His shoulders hunched forward.

"You didn't die," Aidan said.

Garrison gave a rough nod. "Because of you. Then...and now." His hands fisted at his sides. "I owe you more than I can ever repay, alpha."

"I don't want payback." He grabbed for his clothes.

"One day, you might." Garrison's voice was soft. "And when you do, I'll be there."

Aidan started jerking on his shirt. He didn't handle emotional shit well—not with anyone but Jane. Garrison, hell, he'd always felt protective of the guy, even though the younger wolf was a pain in the ass most days.

Isn't that why I burned for him?

Garrison's steps were shuffling toward the bedroom door. "I'm so sorry," Garrison whispered. "About Paris. He was…one of the good ones."

Aidan stilled.

The bedroom door began to crack open.

In a flash, Aidan was at that door, slamming it shut again. He'd moved even faster than he normally did and his fangs—*they're out again.*

Garrison blinked at him in confusion.

"You talk about Paris in the *past* tense."

Garrison's Adam's apple bobbed.

"Why?" Aidan growled. *Vivian was lying to me. I could sense it…*

"Y-you should speak to V-Vivian…" Garrison had paled.

"I'm speaking to you. Why are you sorry about Paris?"

Garrison licked his lips.

Aidan grabbed the guy's shoulders and jerked him up so that they were nose to nose. "Why are you sorry?"

"B-because I saw him being zipped into the body bag! He didn't make it…he…he died before his ambulance ever had a chance to leave the scene."

CHAPTER SIX

Paris lunged up, his fangs snapping toward Jane's throat.

Behind her, Dr. Bob let out a very high pitched scream. She heard his footsteps scurrying away.

Way to help out, Dr. Bob.

Right before Paris could plunge his new teeth into her, Jane drove her fist right into his face — the face that had *not* repaired itself since the fire. Paris's head slammed back onto the exam table with a clang, but he was only down a second before he came lunging up again.

This time, Jane threw him against the nearest wall. He growled at the impact, shook his head, and stared at her with the feral intensity of a beast.

Or of a starving vampire.

"See," Dr. Bob hissed from his hiding spot a few feet away — a spot that put him *under* his desk. "Vampires wake up *wrong*. Filled with bloodlust. All they want to do is attack and feed.

They don't care who they have to kill in order to get their fill of blood!"

Jane made sure to keep her body between Paris and the hiding ME. "Knowing that he was going to wake up as a vamp would really have helped us out here," she threw at him. "Aren't you supposed to be the one who checks the dead bodies for things like this?"

"I didn't know! I didn't realize you'd bitten him!"

"I didn't!"

"Well, somebody did," Dr. Bob yelled right back.

Paris lunged toward her, teeth snapping.

Those snapping teeth caught her shoulder. "Ow!" Jane screamed. She elbowed him, and then, for good measure, she head-butted him. "Paris, I'm not on your menu!"

"He has to be put down!" Dr. Bob called. "Stop playing with him. Just end this!"

Playing? *Playing*! "It's Paris," she snarled. "I'm not ending anything." But she could sure use some help. "Get me something to knock him out with! Don't you have some kind of drugs here?" Sure, the main ME building had burned the night *she'd* woken up as a vampire and they were in "temporary" quarters—another building that was a block away from the original medical examiner's office. But the place looked pretty well stocked to her.

So give me something to knock out Paris!

Paris charged at her again. She dodged his attack, barely. "I don't want to hurt you," Jane said. She felt guilty enough for breaking the guy's neck. After all, that broken neck must have come courtesy of her second-story toss. "You're Aidan's best friend —"

His fangs snapped at her.

"But you are not making a meal of me!" She kicked him in the stomach, then grabbed the exam table he'd been on. Her vamp strength was in full effect as she lifted that table up into the air. "Stay away from me, Paris!"

He wasn't speaking. His eyes were wild. Saliva dripped from his teeth. He wasn't the Paris she'd known. He was —

Attacking.

She tightened her hold on the table, preparing to swing it at him like a bat.

And —

Bam. Bam. Bam.

The bullets blasted into Paris, one after the other. They sank into his chest and he blinked, seemingly confused as blood began to ooze from his new wounds. Then he staggered, falling to his knees.

"About time you helped out," Jane snapped to Dr. Bob as she swung her gaze toward the shooter. Only...Dr. Bob wasn't the one who'd fired.

Someone else had slipped into the temporary lab during the chaos. A woman with smooth chocolate skin, long, dark hair, and a light brown gaze that was locked on Paris as he bled out on the floor. Tears glimmered in that gaze even as magic seemed to pulse in the air around the woman.

Annette Benoit. Voodoo queen extraordinaire.

Jane lowered the table. Paris's eyes had rolled back into his head and he'd slumped against the floor. "You have…really good timing," Jane said.

"I saw the fire in my mirror."

Goosebumps rose on Jane's arms. Yes, okay, she was a vampire. She knew all about the paranormal, but the fact that Annette could look into a black scrying mirror and see things — past, present, future — that still unnerved her.

"When I scried tonight, I saw him die," Annette said. She inched closer to Paris. A tear slid down her cheek. "I just came to tell him goodbye. I-I didn't know he'd rise."

Jane took the gun from Annette's hand and checked the weapon. *Silver bullets.* Silver, not wood.

"A woman needs protection." Annette barely glanced her way. "I always carry that gun with me…well, I do ever since my last werewolf lover tried to kill me." The words were said as an aside. Her focus was on Paris. There was so much pain on her face.

"He's not dead," Dr. Bob announced.

Jane saw him finally crawl out from beneath his desk. She glared at the doctor. "We know he's not dead. He's undead, that's the problem. A problem *you* weren't helping with."

"What? What was I supposed to do?" He pointed to his chest. "Human." He pointed at her. "Super vamp. I knew you could handle a few bites from him." Dr. Bob brushed off his white lab coat. "But he's not finished yet, so we need to take his head and end—"

"*No!*" Jane yelled.

"*No!*" Annette whispered.

Dr. Bob blinked. "But...he's a vampire."

"So am I," Jane reminded him, like he needed the reminder. "And you didn't take my head."

Dr. Bob rubbed his face and looked vaguely guilty. "If you'd come to drain me dry, despite our friendship, I sure would have tried." His hand fell. "Have you forgotten, Jane? They don't all rise like you. They come back as mindless beasts, driven to attack. To kill. To drain anyone close to them. You were different because you were—"

"A born vampire." Annette cut into his words.

Dr. Bob nodded. "Paris isn't a born vamp. He was a werewolf. He shouldn't even *be* a vamp."

No, he shouldn't be. "Get his blood," Jane ordered the doc. "Start running your tests. See what it looks like. If it's…like a normal vamp's or if it's something more."

But Dr. Bob didn't move. He stared at her, at Annette, and sympathy flashed on his face. "Do you know what job Paris had just weeks before?"

Jane shook her head.

"He and Aidan would eliminate the vampires that rose in my lab. They'd end them. Take their heads, stake their hearts. A bloody, terrible job that they did because they knew they were giving those poor turned bastards peace. I've seen vampires rise, again and again. They're mindless. They're *monsters*. They just want blood and they'd drain the young, the old, *anyone* who came close to them." He gave a sad shrug of his shoulders. "When Paris opened his eyes, when he came at you, Jane, he had that same wild look in his gaze. We have the chance to end this all, right now. *We* can give him peace."

She looked back at Paris. His blood dripped onto the floor, pooling beneath him. "Peace can wait a bit." *Because I am not ready to give up on him. I can't.* She turned her head to look at Annette. "You got some magic you can do to hold the guy in check until we find out more?"

Annette's hand went to the bag at her side. She reached her fingers in and pulled out a small doll. "I'm pretty good at controlling the dead." No emotion was in her voice.

Okay, the lady was just scary when she said stuff like that. "He's *un*dead," Jane clarified.

"I'll be able to control him." Annette began to sprinkle what looked like dirt around Paris's body. "For a time."

Well, that was something.

"He's not going to…stay here, is he?" Dr. Bob asked nervously. He looked around his makeshift office. "I mean, yeah, it's the middle of the night now, that's why no one came running when shots were fired. But people *will* be here tomorrow. I can't have some vamp sprawled out in my exam room—"

"I'll move him by dawn," Jane promised. She'd find a place to contain him. There had to be a place nearby…Vivian would know of a place.

Aidan would know.

Oh, God. I have to tell Aidan. But…

"Do the blood tests." Jane nodded briskly. "He shouldn't have changed. Find out what the hell happened."

"I will," Dr. Bob promised. "But you need to talk to someone who understands vamps one hell of a lot more than we do."

Yes, she did. The problem was that vamps weren't exactly cooperative. Not friendly at all. Not…

"You know who to contact," Annette said. She bent and dipped her little doll—not a doll really, more a figure that seemed to be made from sticks—into Paris's blood. "The vamp who brought you over." She looked up at Jane, her lips twisting. "Vincent Connor. The vamp that Aidan hates most is the one you need now." Annette's eyes had taken on a hazy, distant look. One that was creepy. She usually looked that way when she was peering into her black mirror.

Jane cleared her throat. Her shoulder throbbed where Paris had taken a chunk out of her. "Vincent Connor cut out of town. The guy said he'd guide me, then he split." Talk about deserting her in her time of need. "Not like he's going to help me—"

Annette rose. Her fingers brushed over Paris's hair. "Who told you he left?"

"Uh, Aidan and—"

"Every paranormal in the city knows that Aidan told him to stay the hell away from you…or else Vincent was going to lose his head."

Jane's lips parted.

"Well, I guess every paranormal but *you* knew," Annette added.

Great.

Annette inclined her head as she continued, "Vincent has been giving you some…space. But he hasn't left town. He's still here. He's been waiting on you."

Waiting on you. Goosebumps rose on Jane's arms. "How do you know that?"

Annette's fingers slid down Paris's ravaged face. "He told me."

"You *know* where he is?"

"I know how to reach him."

"Then do it. Get him here." They needed his help. Aidan could be pissed. He'd get over it if Vincent could help Paris.

"I'll call him," Annette said softly.

"Yeah, yeah, you do that." Jane started to pace. Then she looked down at herself…her clothes were singed. Bloody and…

I look like the walking freaking undead.

But wasn't that exactly what she was? What Paris had somehow turned into?

"Run the blood tests," Jane ordered Dr. Bob once more. "And let's see what Vincent has to say."

***

An hour later, Jane was pacing in the corridor just outside of Dr. Bob's lab. This building was definitely not as nice as the place they'd been in before. But, since his previous lab and the building that housed it had been destroyed, she knew the city hadn't exactly been plush with other options. So Dr. Bob had gotten bounced to the little building on the corner, a building that smelled of mildew and fresh paint. Smaller, tighter, but it was still a place for the dead to go.

Only some aren't staying dead.

What had happened with Paris? She hadn't bit him. She definitely hadn't given him her blood. So how in the hell had he become a vamp?

Jane shook her head and kept pacing. Vincent needed to hurry his ass up and get there. She'd borrowed the scrubs that Dr. Bob's assistant had left in her locker and taken a quick shower to wash the blood away from her body. They'd secured Paris to an exam table, strapping him down as tightly as possible. He hadn't stirred, not yet.

But she was afraid that he would, soon.

Where in the hell is the vampire? She hadn't seen Vincent Connor in days. And she'd been glad. The guy scared her. Mostly because…

He broke my neck.

And…

He's like me. Vincent was born, not made into a vampire. And he's old. Like Viking-freaking old. With age…came power? If the two of them had to tangle, Jane was very much afraid that Vincent would kick her ass. And she knew that Aidan pretty much hated the bastard so she'd hoped to keep those two away from each other.

The last thing she wanted was for Aidan to fight the vampire.

She heard the click of a door opening. Jane spun around. Footsteps were approaching her as someone stalked down that long, lonely hallway. Her nostrils flared, her body tensed and—

Aidan's familiar scent seemed to wrap around her.

Tears burned Jane's eyes and she stopped guarding that lab room door. She ran down the hallway—and straight into Aidan's arms. Her body slammed into his, but he didn't so much as stagger. His arms—warm and strong—wrapped around her, holding her tightly as he lifted her up against him.

His mouth met hers. No gentle, tentative kiss. Desperate, wild, frantic.

Aidan.

Alive. Safe.

Aidan.

Her arms were locked so fiercely around him. She never wanted to let him go. Never wanted to feel the terrible wrenching terror that came from knowing...

I can lose him.

To flames. To fire.

To...

She pulled back.

To the pain I'm about to cause him.

Her feet slowly slipped back to touch floor. Jane stared up at Aidan. So handsome. There were no marks on his face. Not even a single blister. He'd healed completely.

Amazingly.

"I'm so glad you're okay," she whispered.

His bright stare seemed to pierce right to her soul. "Never do it again."

"What?"

He leaned down and kissed her once more. A hot, open-mouthed kiss. "Never run into a fire for me again. I'm not worth it."

"You are to me," she immediately said. "Aidan, you're—"

"I'm not worth your life."

She wasn't going to argue with him. She also wasn't about to make him a promise she wouldn't keep. So Jane just asked, "What if I'd been in that building?"

His face hardened. "You *were* because of me."

"Aidan—"

"I was the bait this time, Jane. Don't you see that? The bomb was set, the place was rigged. He knew I'd be the one to track him. He set all of that for me. And you came rushing in to save me."

He. Who the hell was this he? "I'd do it again." And she wouldn't apologize. Wouldn't pretend that she'd ever rethink the situation. "Just as I know you'd do it for me." The tie between them cut both ways.

A muscle jerked in his jaw. "I love you so fucking much, Jane."

Her heart melted a bit. It was still new for her, to hear him say those words. And, sure, okay, they didn't come out all romantic and gentle from Aidan. Aidan *wasn't* romantic and gentle. But she knew he meant exactly what he'd just said—Aidan loved her.

Fangs and all.

"I love you, and you *can't* risk yourself," he muttered. "Not again. We were lucky this time."

No, they hadn't been. "Aidan…" Jane began. Oh, God, she had to tell him.

Paris was one of his oldest friends. More like a brother than a friend.

She knew Aidan was about to freak the hell out.

She heard Dr. Bob's door open behind her. The hinges squeaked.

"I'm so sorry," Jane said.

Aidan swallowed. "I know…about Paris."

Wait, what? Shock rolled through her.

"I need to see him."

"Aidan, I never meant for this to happen." Never in a million years. "I was trying to get him out of the fire. I was…" *I chose you. Oh, dammit. I chose you instead of helping him. I had the chance to take Paris out, but I was afraid you'd be dead before I got back upstairs. I did this. It is all on me.* "It's my fault," Jane said, voice sharpening. "And I want to fix it."

"You can't fix the dead."

A throat cleared behind them. "He's not dead yet," Annette announced.

Jane looked back at the other woman.

"Not fully, anyway," Annette said. She put her hands on her hips, glaring at Aidan. "And you won't be taking his head. You'll have to go through me in order to do that, alpha."

Aidan took a step forward. "Taking his head…" Confusion flashed on his face.

"He came back," Jane whispered. "Paris is…he's a vampire."

And Aidan lunged for that lab room.

Annette pushed her hands onto his chest, stopping him before he could blaze past her. Though Jane knew that if he'd wanted, he could have easily gotten around the other woman.

"You will not take his head," Annette said again. "He's stood by you time and time again, and I don't care *what* your wolf says when you enter that room and see him…you will not kill Paris."

Aidan…nodded. Then he glanced back at Jane. "If the instincts kick in…"

The werewolf's instincts to attack and destroy a vampire.

"Knock my ass out," Aidan said.

Jane released the breath she'd been holding. Then she hurried to Aidan's side. Her fingers curled around his.

Annette slipped out of the way.

Aidan opened the door, and they entered the cold lab together.

Paris was strapped down on the table. Dr. Bob was perched over a microscope and—

Aidan strode toward his friend. Paris seemed to be out cold, a good thing. Jane darted a quick glance at Aidan's face and she saw the torment there.

Enough pain to steal her breath.

Aidan lifted his hand. He touched Paris's shoulder.

Paris didn't move.

"He's under deep," Annette said from behind them. "I made sure of it…after he bit Jane, I didn't want to risk another attack."

Aidan looked up at Jane. "He…bit you?"

"He wasn't himself." No, far from it.

"That's because he's a vampire now," Dr. Bob huffed, rising from his stool. "I can see it in his blood. He's changed. The man you knew before is gone."

Vampire.

"How?" That was the part that Jane just didn't understand. "How could this happen?" It *shouldn't* have happened. "I don't—"

Aidan cut through her words, growling, "I…I can't stay this close to him."

"Aidan?"

His claws were out. He turned toward her and she saw the shadow of his beast on his face. "The wolf wants…to attack."

Jane shook her head. No, she'd been praying it would be different. She'd—

Aidan pushed past her and ran back into the hallway. She hurried after him and when she got into that hall, she saw Aidan on all fours. His hands had slapped against the floor and he was transforming. His muscles were swelling, thickening. His bones starting to pop and snap.

It was a werewolf alpha's primal reaction to a vampire. *Kill or be killed.* Only Aidan hadn't responded that way to *her,* so she'd hoped that he wouldn't attack Paris, either.

"Paris is your best friend," Jane whispered, lost.

Aidan turned back to look at her. His jaw had elongated. "That's why…" His voice was barely human. "He still…has…his head."

Tears pricked at her eyes. Someone had done this. Someone had *changed* Paris. Somehow, at the chaos of that fire scene, a vampire had gotten close to Paris. That was the only explanation she could think of.

And, thanks to Annette, Jane knew exactly which vampire was still in town.

She crept closer to Aidan. "There might be a way to fix this."

He laughed. Stuck in mid-shift, that laugh was a very scary sound. "Only fix…is death."

Then the fire of the change swept over him. Brutal, agonizing. The man he'd been vanished.

Fur burst along his skin. Razor-sharp teeth filled his mouth. His hands became the powerful paws and claws of a beast.

The change was fast, sweeping over him so quickly. One minute, he'd been a man. The next, a wolf and—

Footsteps. Coming toward them. She looked down the hallway and saw that Vincent Connor had finally decided to grace them with his presence.

Tall, with a powerful build. Dark hair, gleaming eyes.

Fangs bared.

Yes, that was Vincent, all right.

The wolf growled when he saw the man there—not a man, really, but a vampire.

Vincent froze as he stared at the beast. Jane raced forward and grabbed Aidan's fur, trying to hold him back before he attacked Vincent. "You can't kill him," Jane fired at Aidan. "We need him!"

"Guessing this isn't the best time, hmmm?" Vincent murmured as he offered her a tight smile. "Perhaps we should chat later."

"No!" Jane yelled.

The wolf growled.

"He wants to rip me apart, my dear," Vincent said. "And if he comes at me, I *will* fight back."

Dammit. Why couldn't Vincent have arrived a few moments *before* Aidan? Jane bent low to

Aidan's ear. "Don't do this, okay? I know you want to attack. I know…I just…we need him." For the moment. "He knows more about vampires than anyone else. He might be able to help Paris."

Doubtful but…maybe.

Jane looked up at Vincent. She made sure to keep a steady grip on Aidan. "There was a fire tonight," she said.

"Um, that would be why you smell like ash." Vincent shook his head. "I get that you're still new to the whole vamp game, but here's a tip…don't run into a burning building. That's a surefire way to end yourself."

"*Aidan* was inside."

Vincent rolled his eyes. "Like I care about—"

The wolf jerked from Jane's hold and lunged toward Vincent. The wolf took the vampire down, hard, and he put his front paws on Vincent's chest to pin him against the floor. The wolf's jaws were bared, hovering inches from Vincent's throat and the thin, gold chain that circled his neck.

But Aidan wasn't biting. Wasn't ripping Vincent's head off…yet.

"Aidan," Jane spoke quickly, sharply. "Aidan, I know you're in there. You have to stay in *control.*"

And Vincent laughed. "Of course, he's in there. He's fully aware of everything that he's doing." There was a pause. "Just as I am fully aware of what I'm doing. Do you feel the gun pressed to your underbelly, wolf? It's got silver bullets in it. Get even a breath closer to my throat, and I will fire."

"Stop it!" Jane jumped toward them. "I called you here because I wanted your help, Vincent. Not because I wanted you to hurt Aidan!" She sucked in a breath. "Aidan, back away."

His instincts would demand that he attack, but he'd held on to his control before. Aidan was supposed to be the strongest wolf in town. He was...

Backing away. But snarling. Obviously, the guy wasn't a happy camper.

Neither was she.

Aidan backed toward her. His big body bumped her legs.

Vincent stayed on the floor, his gun gripped in his hand. "That was...tense."

"Paris died tonight," Jane said. Vincent had been keeping tabs on her long before she'd become a vamp—she had no doubt that he knew all about Aidan's long friendship with the other wolf. "Only he...he came back as a vampire."

"No." Vincent shot to his feet. He tucked the gun in his waistband and adjusted the gold chain that looped around his neck and disappeared beneath his shirt. "Sorry, love, but that doesn't happen. Not with werewolves. They don't—"

"They do." She pointed toward the lab door. "Go take a look for yourself if you don't believe me. He *transformed.*"

Vincent frowned at her. She frowned back. Vincent wasn't exactly on her friend list. More of a *Watch-Very-Closely* list. "He transformed," Jane said again, "and I was wondering…were you the one who did this to him?"

The wolf snarled.

Vincent shook his head. "No! Of course not! Look, I told you, it can't be done."

In a flash, Jane was before him. "It is done." And she was terrified. Terrified because…*I don't want to end Paris.* "Now you helped me when I became a vampire, and I need you to help Paris now. I need you to *fix* him."

"Fix him?" Vincent laughed. "There is no fixing—"

Jane pointed to her shoulder. "He attacked me. He was wild. Manic."

The wolf growled behind her.

"We have to stop Paris. He can't be…he can't be like the others." The other vampires she'd encountered. The terrible ones who killed their own families. "Please."

Vincent's gaze sharpened on her. "If I help him…what will you give me?"

"This isn't a game!"

"No, no, it's not." Vincent's lips thinned. "There will be a price you have to pay."

Wasn't there always? Jane looked back at Aidan. Even as a beast, he carried pain in his eyes. "Just help him," Jane whispered. "And I'll pay whatever you want."

CHAPTER SEVEN

The old building near the cemetery used to be a BDSM club. That was why there were so many chains and ropes hanging from the walls and the ceiling, part of the leftover decor.

It had also been Jane's prison, once. For a time that Aidan didn't like remembering. When she'd first transformed into a vampire, Vincent had held Jane in that place. He'd been trying to make sure she didn't attack anyone.

Or so the vamp said.

I still think the bastard was just keeping my Jane from me.

"He's secure," Vincent said, as he tested the chains that now bound Paris's wrists and ankles. Not the old chains that had come with the building—those were just for show, but with new, gleaming manacles. Paris was still out cold, courtesy of Annette and her spells. He was on a mattress they'd brought in for him, chained hand and foot.

And it fucking infuriated Aidan. A hard rumble slipped from him. Werewolves weren't meant to be chained up.

Vincent's stare cut his way. "You doing all right, wolf?" His eyes swept over Aidan. "Or are you about to go all beast again?"

Aidan was back in the form of a man, and his control was holding, for the moment. He'd only lost it and shifted into a beast back at the ME's office because he'd been so shocked.

Paris would never want to be a vampire. He wouldn't want to live this way.

"Don't worry about me," Aidan gritted out the words. *Worry about yourself because I still owe you a reckoning.* He and Vincent would never be fucking friends. Enemies by blood.

Enemies until death.

I'll never forgive him for what he did to Jane. The vamp needs to get his ass out of my town. Aidan flexed his fingers. "The way I see it..." He took a step closer to Vincent. Jane and Annette tensed, and he could feel their stares on him. "Only a vampire could transform Paris. I know of two vampires in this town. Jane and...you. Since Jane didn't do this, well..." *Well, I think you're the tricky bastard who did.* Maybe Vincent had been the guy setting up all of the little tests for Jane.

Why? Because he wanted to see just what another born vampire could do?

Or maybe because he was just a crazy fuck who needed to be put out of his misery?

"It wasn't me," Vincent said, voice flat. "I haven't been near your pack in days. Not near them, not near Jane. I was—" But he broke off, looking away.

"You were what?" Jane called.

Vincent glanced over at her. "I was waiting for you to come to me."

Aidan wanted to rip out his heart. "Not happening."

"I can help her, in ways you will *never* understand. I can—"

"Forget me," Jane ordered him flatly. "Help Paris."

As if on cue, Paris let out a low groan.

"I can put him under again," Annette said. "I can—"

Vincent locked his fingers around Paris's jaw. "Do you want to live?"

Aidan stepped forward. The bastard needed to damn well be more careful with his friend—

"Yes...." A broken hiss that came from Paris.

Vincent looked back at Aidan. "He wants a fighting chance, so that means none of us will take his head, agreed?"

Why did everyone keep fucking looking at him when they said that?

Vincent turned back to Paris. "It's not going to be easy. It's—"

Paris lunged toward his throat. His teeth scraped over Vincent's neck and he—

Drank. Guzzled.

Vincent just let him. Didn't even fight and then…

Paris vomited blood. All over Vincent. Vincent slowly rose. He turned to Jane. Glared. "Now where have I seen that shit before?"

"Hun…gry…" Paris gasped out the words.

"Yes, well, we all get that," Vincent muttered as he swiped at the mess on him. "I guess we shouldn't have started at the top of the food chain."

"Bagged blood?" Annette whispered. She was standing near the wall, watching Paris with wide, haunted eyes. "Will he be able to take that?"

"We're about to find out." Vincent whirled away and marched from the room.

And Aidan found himself stepping closer to his friend.

Jane caught his arm. "Aidan, *don't*."

"I'm not killing him," Aidan said. His control was back and holding for the moment. He needed to talk with Paris. To try and understand just how this had happened. His claws were out, but the fury of the shift didn't fire Aidan's blood. He paced closer to Paris, but stopped about five feet away. "Paris."

Paris didn't look at him. He let out another low, desperate moan.

"Who did this to you?" Aidan demanded. "Who changed you?" *How?* Aidan hadn't even thought it was possible for a werewolf to change into a vamp. He'd never heard of a transformation like that one.

Mostly because…vamps weren't given the chance to bite werewolves. When a werewolf encountered a vamp…*our normal MO is to end them.*

His gaze slid to Jane and Aidan swallowed. *Normal doesn't count with her.* Right then, Aidan couldn't think of the changes that were occurring within his own body. He had to put Paris first. He'd deal with his own shit later.

I just changed into a wolf, so that means…no matter what else is happening, I'm still an alpha. My beast still has power. And he'd use that power to help his friend.

Paris's lashes lifted. He stared at Aidan, and there was *zero* recognition in his gaze. Just…hunger.

"Who. Did. This?" Rage fisted around Aidan's heart.

Paris lunged toward him, snapping his teeth, but the chains held him back, stopping Paris before he could get anywhere near Aidan's throat.

Jane's hand curled around Aidan's.

Paris's stare turned toward her, and the bloodlust—it seemed to burn even brighter in his eyes. He began to salivate as he stared at her. "Need…"

The one word was far from human. More like the beast that Paris couldn't be any longer.

"Step back, Jane," Aidan said softly.

"I want to help." Guilt and grief were heavy in her voice and obvious on her face. "I did this, Aidan. I didn't bite him, but I'm the one who didn't take more care with Paris. I was stuck on us all being these super monsters…like we could take on anything and survive. I thought even if he got hurt, your blood would heal him."

My fucking blood.

"I'm so sorry," Jane whispered.

Aidan glanced at her. She was staring at Paris, and tears glinted in her eyes. "I wish I could go back. I know you didn't want this. I am sorry!"

"Save the sorries," Annette ordered, voice flat. "We have to fix him. We get him stable, then we figure out how the hell this happened."

Jane swallowed.

Vincent hurried back into the room. He had a blood bag in his hand. Aidan stared at the bag and—

Are my canines lengthening? Shit, they were. Not normal, not at all damn normal.

Vincent ripped open the top of the bag. He caught the back of Paris's head with one hand and pushed the blood bag toward Paris's mouth. "Let's see how you like this one…"

Paris started to guzzle the blood. A faint smile curved Vincent's lips and—

Paris yanked his head away, retching up the blood.

"Fuck," Vincent snapped.

Annette's footsteps shuffled closer.

Paris let out a loud, desperate scream, one that made Aidan's muscles clench. There was so much pain and fury in that sound. And Paris…

His eyes were on Jane. Devouring her.

"Maybe…maybe he needs werewolf blood," Jane whispered. "The same way I did. I mean, he was a werewolf before, so maybe he has to have the same type of blood that I do."

Aidan turned his head and stared down at Jane. There were tear tracks drying on her cheeks.

"Jane couldn't keep down the other blood, either," Vincent said softly. "Not bagged human blood. Not blood straight from a human victim. The only time she was sane was when she had *your* blood." He stared at Aidan, his mouth tight. "Because you had already changed her."

I'd given Jane werewolf blood. Paris already was a werewolf before this change. Yeah, shit, okay, it made sense that his friend would need werewolf blood, too. Locking his teeth, Aidan stepped closer to Paris.

He lifted his wrist, offering it to Paris. "You still in there, buddy?" Aidan asked. He needed Paris to talk to him. Needed to know that his friend was still with him.

But Paris just growled. And he was jerking his head, trying to see around Aidan to look at Jane.

"He...He had some of my blood." Jane's voice was halting. "At Dr. Bob's lab...I told you that Paris bit me. He kept that blood down."

But it sure hadn't *calmed* him down from the look of things.

"I can give him more," Jane said quickly. "Just to tide him over."

But Aidan shook his head, and even though he hated to say it, he had to voice his fear. "What if your blood makes him...worse, Jane?"

She sucked in a sharp painful breath.

Shit. "Your blood is changing me." Why deny it? He figured they all needed to get past the denial stage. "We have no idea what it could do to him."

Vincent gave a grim nod. "Can't believe I'm saying this but...I agree with the alpha."

Paris snarled. Spittle flew from his mouth.

"He shouldn't even be a vamp," Vincent added "We don't want to fuck things up any more than they already are."

"So I'm fucked up now?" Jane's voice had gone completely flat.

No, to him, she was completely perfect but…

I don't want her giving up her blood. Aidan pushed his forearm against Paris's mouth. He felt those fangs slide deep into him, sinking hard and then—

Paris stilled. His lashes had closed when he bit Aidan. For a moment, they stayed closed as if he were savoring his meal, but then his lashes slowly lifted. The wildness seemed to fade from his golden gaze, the insanity cleared for a mere instant in time.

And Aidan was staring into his friend's eyes again.

Paris tore his mouth from Aidan. Blood dripped from his lips. "K-kill…me…" Paris rasped out the words.

Aidan shook his head. "No, you don't want—"

But Paris nodded, even as the sanity began to seep from his gaze. "Kill *me*…" Then, in a quick rush, he whispered, "Before I kill you."

And Paris lunged toward him, snapping the chain that bound his right wrist. Aidan grabbed his friend and slammed Paris back, ramming Paris's head into the heavy stone of the wall.

Thunk.

Paris dropped to the floor.

"You killed him!" Annette cried.

But Aidan shook his head. "He'll rise again in a few hours." Because if you wanted to kill a vamp, there were only a few tricks that really worked.

A stake to the heart.

A beheading.

Fire.

Annette scrambled to Paris's side, her fingers flying over him.

Aidan's hands clenched into fists.

"Well, that bought us a bit of time." Vincent inclined his head toward Aidan. "Why don't we finish this outside?"

Aidan would like to finish *him* outside. Ending the vamp's life had never been more tempting but…

We need him, for the moment. Jane had been right. So Aidan turned on his heel and walked away. He forced himself not to look back. If he did, he'd just see Paris's prone body. He'd hear his friend, begging him…

Kill me.

It was the job an alpha was supposed to perform — stopping blood-lust crazed vamps from hurting others. But…to kill Paris?

That's a job I never hoped to have.

***

Jane watched as Aidan walked away. His steps were rough, angry, and his hands were still clenched into tight fists.

"And *that's* the guy you think you want to spend eternity with?" Vincent mumbled under his breath. "Right, good luck with all of that."

Jane's gaze flew over to lock with his. "We need to secure Paris."

"I think the massive brain trauma that your boyfriend just gave him is security enough for the moment but…" Vincent turned away, headed for a closet, and came back with a new manacle and chain. In moments, he'd replaced the one that Paris had so effortlessly ripped from the wall. "That will hold him."

Maybe.

Annette was sitting on the floor near Paris, her legs tucked neatly under her. Her hand was lightly stroking his cheek, such a tender touch.

A lump rose in Jane's throat. She could see it now — the connection between Paris and Annette. "How long have you loved him?"

Annette's hand stilled. "Don't be ridiculous," she said, her voice emotionless. "I hardly know the man at all." Then she reached into her bag and pulled out — was that dirt? Sure looked like it. And Annette was sprinkling the dirt around Paris's body.

"What are you doing, witch?" Vincent demanded.

Annette's head turned, a bit snakelike, and her eyes locked on him. "I'm no witch."

He blinked. "I-I didn't mean any disrespect."

Annette rose to her feet. "I'm a voodoo queen, just like my mother, like my grandmother, like my great-grandmother. Power flows through my blood and through *me*. I get that you use a witch to work spells for you, and that's just grand for you. But I am Annette Benoit, and *no one* uses me."

He held up his hands. "My apologies," he said very formally. "I won't make that mistake again."

"You'd better not." Her gaze cut to Jane. "What I'm *doing*…I'm protecting all of us. And Paris. The dirt from the dead will keep Paris enclosed within the circle I create. He won't be able to get out and attack us. So we should have a chance to figure out what's going on—how we can *help* him."

"Dirt from the dead?" Jane repeated carefully.

"Dirt taken from a cemetery under the light of a full moon." Annette rolled one shoulder in a delicate shrug. "You'd be surprised what things hold incredible power in this world."

Jane thought she was looking at someone who held incredible power right then.

"I'll stay with him," Annette said, giving a quick nod. "Go talk to Aidan. Go…try to stop some of the chaos that's taking over this town."

Vincent had turned on his heel and stalked away. But Jane didn't move to follow him.

Because, to her, Paris turning into a vamp seemed like the biggest chaos right then. She should stay and—

Annette's lips curled down in a sad smile. "Your world is going to rip apart, Jane. I hope you're still standing when it's all over."

Great. More murky warnings from Annette. Must be Tuesday…or Wednesday…or Thursday. Or *any day.* "It would help me so much," Jane told her quietly, "if you just *said* what I needed to avoid. You know, before I became a vampire, it would have been awesome if you just *said,* 'Jane, don't go to Tulane! Your ass will get messed up there!'"

Annette blinked at her. "It doesn't work that way."

"If you *know* something bad will happen, you should tell me! What good is having an all-seeing friend if she won't tell me exactly *what* she sees?" Jane threw her hands into the air and turned away.

She'd only taken a few steps when Annette's soft voice stopped her. "Are we really friends now?"

Jane glanced back at her. "Yes, I think we are."

Annette licked her lips. "I can't see things…as well as I used to. The future, I mean. My mirror shattered and…" Once more, she shoved her hand into her bag. This time, she pulled out a few chunks of black, broken glass. "This is all I have left. So when I look, I see bits and pieces."

"You can still share those bits with me."

Annette nodded, but she still hesitated. "You owe me, Jane. Do you remember that? Once, you promised that you would pay me back a favor. You'd give me something I wanted, no questions asked."

She didn't exactly remember the no questions asked part but…

"Help me save Paris," Annette pleaded.

Tears stung Jane's eyes again. "I did this to him. I was just trying to get him out of the fire — I never meant — "

Annette's dark gaze held hers as Jane's words tumbled to a halt. "Help me."

"I will," Jane promised. "But not as some favor I owe. But because Paris is my family, too. I want him back. I want to fix this."

But inside she worried, she feared…

There are some things that can't be fixed.

***

As Jane's footsteps faded away, Annette knelt beside Paris once more. She brushed back his hair, and her fingers drifted over his cheek.

Paris Cole had been fighting darkness for most of his life. It didn't seem right that the

darkness should now try to cl
right at all.

How did a werewolf bec

Jane changed the rules, for ...
had known that truth, she just hadn't wa...
face it. Now, there was no choice, not for any of
them.

Carefully, she spread out the chunks of her
precious black mirror. She would have to forge a
new mirror soon, but building a mirror like that
would drain her power, and with all the danger
coming to their town, she couldn't afford to be
weak, not even for a moment.

So the new mirror had to wait.

Her fingers fluttered over the chunks of glass.
When she'd touched Paris's cheek, a drop of his
blood had gotten onto her finger. Now, she
smeared that blood on a chunk of the glass. She
wanted to look into that mirror, and see Paris
fighting the darkness. She wanted to see him
surviving. Having his control back.

She stared into the glass and her heart
chilled.

She could see Paris, an image shimmering in
her mind's eye. He was strong. He was whole. He
was...

*Sinking his teeth into Aidan. Drinking from the
alpha, gorging on his blood.*

Annette threw the chunks of glass against the
wall. A sob broke from her. "I won't let this be

end. I *won't.*" Then she began to chant, low and fast.

Who said magic couldn't change the world? Magic could change anything, even fate.

Provided, of course, that the magic used was very, very dark.

As dark as a werewolf's tortured soul.

***

"He must have been given vampire blood. No other explanation for it." Vincent paced along the sidewalk. Dawn had come, but the sun barely peeked in the sky. Darkness still hung heavily in the city.

Jane glanced at Vincent — suave, polished Vincent who barely had so much as a hair out of place, despite their hellish night. Then her gaze slid to Aidan. *Her* Aidan. His hair was thick and wild, his eyes blazing, and the t-shirt he wore stretched over the powerful muscles of his chest and shoulders.

It was a good thing Aidan kept spare clothes in his car. Because after that shift at the lab, he'd been stark naked.

"I never gave him vamp blood," Aidan spat. "So try another explanation."

"Maybe you didn't…" Now Vincent focused on Jane. "But maybe *she* did."

What? Jane held up her hands. "Slow down there, asshole. I did *not*. I didn't so much as even nip the guy when he asked me to, all right? I know how werewolves feel about vamps. It's not like I'd ever want to give him this fate."

Her fate.

"I've *never* known of a werewolf to become a vampire," Vincent said as he began to rub the back of his neck. "And I've been around a long time. It's just…not done."

"Uh, obviously, it's done." Jane pointed to the building behind them. "Got an undead buddy in there who is proof of that fact."

Vincent's mouth clamped shut.

Aidan crossed his arms over his chest and studied the vamp. "You're telling me that you've *never* heard of this before? I thought your ass was alive when the Vikings were here—"

"I *was* a Viking," Vincent began hotly, "so don't tell me—"

"Because I'm not buying," Aidan continued, cutting right over his words. "That this has never happened before. Someone knows what is going on. Someone can fix this!"

"I'll put a call in to my witch." Before Aidan could respond, Vincent threw up his hand. "And, yes, she's a real witch, with more power than anyone I know." He hesitated. "Aside from Annette Benoit."

Jane inched closer to him. "Will your witch be able to help?"

"Possibly. Maybe. I don't know."

So he wasn't exactly building them up on hope.

"I'll get Lena out here as soon as I can, okay? She was a bit angry at me the last time I saw her, but I can convince her to help us out."

That was something.

"In the meantime, we keep Paris here," Vincent added doggedly. "We keep trying to feed him blood — your blood, alpha. He didn't spit it back up, so that means he can survive on it. We give him enough, and maybe we'll reach the guy's humanity once more. If his control can hold, then he'll have a fighting chance." But he shook his head grimly. "Either you were born to change, or you weren't. Humans weren't meant to grow fangs, and werewolves — hell, they definitely weren't meant to live on a blood diet."

"The rules have changed," Aidan said.

Jane's head turned toward him. He was staring at her, and his eyes seemed to shine with the power of his beast. A shiver slid over her.

"You changed the rules," Aidan said, almost as an accusation.

Another shiver. "I never meant to," Jane said. She'd never wanted to be a vampire. That choice — it hadn't been one that she'd ever wanted. She squared her shoulders and marched closer to him. "We're going to find a way to help Paris."

He stared back at her. "We *are*," Jane said. "Stronger when we're together, remember? We can do this."

Vincent gave a bark of rough laughter, drawing her stare. "Stronger together? You two are *lethal* together, when are you going to realize that? A werewolf with a vampire—it's an abomination to nature. *That's* why your friend is in there suffering. Because the two of you wouldn't fucking stay apart. How many others will you destroy before you finally get a clue?" He shook his head and turned away from them.

Aidan strode away from Jane and grabbed Vincent's shoulder. "You and I aren't done."

A muscle jerked in Vincent's jaw. "Still mad because I made sure she came back as a vampire, huh? You know, instead of being all enraged, maybe you should try being grateful. After all, I'm the one who made it so that Jane is around, permanently. No death for her—provided, of course, she doesn't get herself burned to ash because she's saving your sorry hide."

Aidan's eyes took on a beastly glow.

"Aidan," Jane said quickly. "Don't." She knew he wanted to rip Vincent apart but… "We need him, remember? Let the guy go and get his witch. For Paris."

Aidan held Vincent's gaze for a moment longer. She honestly thought there was a fifty-fifty shot that Aidan would ignore her and just cut off the vamp's head right then and there. Jane tensed…

But then Aidan was reaching for her. His fingers tangled with hers and held tight.

Vincent's gaze dropped to their hands. "And there it is." His lips twisted in a mocking smile. "She'll be the death of you one day, alpha."

And then…the vamp vanished. Oh, Jane knew he hadn't just disappeared into thin air. He used magic to make it seem as if he'd faded into nothing. Magic provided by the mysterious Lena.

"Can't wait to meet his witch," Jane murmured. "I want her to take away whatever spell lets him do that shit."

Aidan pulled her closer.

She glanced up and fury blazed at her from the depths of his blue eyes, and, hell, it was a fury that he was more than entitled to feel. Jane lifted her chin. "I'm going to make this right, I swear, I am—"

In a flash, he'd shoved her against the brick walls of that old club. His hands locked hers above her head. And his grip was…strong. Very, very strong. So strong that even with her vamp enhancements, Jane wasn't sure she could break away from him.

"You went into the fire," Aidan snarled.

Were they back to that? "Aidan…"

He kissed her. Angry, rough, but, jeez, it was still Aidan and when Aidan kissed her, her body reacted with an instant fever. She got turned on, she got hot, she got…

I want him.

His mouth lifted from hers. "I can't do it without you."

Jane blinked up at him.

"I can feel myself changing. Every damn minute, my sanity…my hold on my humanity…Jane, it's slipping away."

Fear had her heart racing faster. "What?"

"You and Paris…you two are my anchors. You keep me in check. But now he's in there…" And he stepped away from her. He freed her hands and started to pace. "Shit, he's in there, chained up, and the bastard wants me to kill him!"

Her heart drummed even faster. "He's half-mad from the change. He doesn't know — "

Aidan scrubbed his hands over his eyes. "He knows. When he told me to kill him, he was Paris, not some blood-lust insane vamp. He wanted me to end him." His hand fell. "And I didn't."

She wanted to reach out to him. Wanted to pull him close. To take away his pain. But Jane didn't know how.

Especially since I think I'm the one who caused his pain. "Aidan…"

He drove his hand into the brick wall. The bricks cracked, chunks went flying, and Jane saw the deep indention that had been left by his blow.

"I…I'm the fucking leader." His fist stayed embedded in the wall. His head tilted forward as his shoulders slumped. "I know what I should do. As a werewolf alpha, I *know*."

His pain was gutting her. She reached out for him, but when Jane touched his arm, Aidan flinched, then he whirled toward her.

And she saw his face.

His…fangs.

They were out. Sharp. Wicked, wicked sharp. The fangs of a vampire, not a wolf.

"Aidan?"

"But I'm not just a werewolf any longer." And even his voice had changed. Deeper. Darker. "I won't give up what's mine. Not my friend."

She was frozen to the spot.

He wasn't. He reached for her. Pulled Jane close. She could feel the hot stir of his breath on her neck.

"And not you. Not ever fucking *you*." His fangs sank into her. No marking from a werewolf, but a vampire's bite. The pain was a white-hot flash, and then…pleasure. Seeming to burn through her veins. She gasped and held on to him, shuddering. Her breasts tightened, her nipples ached, and Jane found herself pushing closer to him, needing to touch him, wanting more of him. Wanting everything. Wanting—

He wrenched his mouth from her neck. "Jane?"

Her breath sawed out of her lungs. She peered up at him from beneath her lashes.

"Your…your neck…" He stumbled back and rammed into the brick wall. "I bit you." His face reflected his horror.

Her hand lifted to her neck, and Jane felt the blood drops there. "It's okay, Aidan." She tried to make her voice soothing.

But he shook his head, once, hard. "No, no, it's not. I *drank* your blood."

"Aidan…"

His hands were at his sides and she could see the claws curling from his fingertips. His eyes were glowing, such a bright, intense blue. A blue that seemed to pierce Jane right to her soul.

"*I bit you…and I want to do it again.*"

Her lips parted in surprise. She reached out to him once more.

"Don't touch me."

Her hand stilled, hanging in the air between their bodies.

"I don't want to hurt you." His voice was stilted. Not Aidan's. A stranger's. "And if you touch me…" That glow in his gaze just deepened. "I think I will."

They stood there, staring at each other, a cold and dark stand-off. Jane tried to figure out what to say to Aidan. Their lives were too twisted. They had to get everything straightened out.

But…as she stared into his eyes, she saw a beast staring back at her, a beast with the claws of a werewolf and the bloodlust of a vampire. Fear slid down Jane's spine. She'd trusted Aidan completely because she knew his control was always in place. Yet right then, she could see his control unraveling before her eyes.

And an Aidan without control…

He will be a monster.

She shook her head against the thought. No, no, Aidan was not a monster. He was hers. Her friend. Her lover. Her —

Jane made herself reach out to him. "We're going to be okay."

But Aidan gave a hard shake of his head.

Before her fingers could touch him, the scream of a siren broke the early morning silence.

Jane flinched at that sound, caught off-guard for an instant because she'd been so lost in Aidan. She thought the sound would die away after a moment, but…it grew louder. Her head turned and her heart kept racing in her chest as she saw the patrol car approaching.

Aidan swore and he turned his back on that car. She wondered if he was trying to hide his fangs.

Or maybe his claws.

The patrol car braked to a stop just a few feet away. The door opened and a uniformed cop leapt out.

"Detective Hart!"

She recognized the cop hailing her. It was Mason Mitchell, one of the more fresh-faced members of the New Orleans PD.

"Dr. Heider told me you were here." He rushed toward her, his breath panting out a bit. His eyes were wide, worried. "You would not *believe* the stories I heard circulating about you! Some people were even saying you were dead."

Aidan gave a rough laugh, but he didn't turn to look at the young cop.

"We have a problem," Mason told her. "A big one. I-I tried to reach you last night as soon as the call came in, but then that six alarm fire broke out—"

He was rambling. She'd worked a few cases with Mason before and she knew that when he got nervous, he rambled. "Mason." She said his name with a hint of warning.

He blinked. "Right." He licked his lips. "I'm…I'm sorry to tell you, Detective Hart, but there was an incident at the Hathway Psychiatric Facility yesterday."

Jane shook her head. No, no, this could *not* be happening. There had to be a limit to the amount of absolute shit that a person could deal with during a twenty-four hour period. She was at her limit, thank you very much.

"Your brother…he attacked the guard that Captain Harris had left with him and he—Drew Hart escaped."

"No," Jane snapped out the denial. "He's not out. He can't be out."

Mason nodded. "I'm sorry…but he is, ma'am. We've got a search going for him. But, considering that he attacked you and, ah…" His gaze cut to Aidan's tense back. "Mr. Locke over there, I thought you two would want to take precautions."

Jane pressed a hand to her chest. Her galloping heartbeat hurt. *Drew won't stop. If he's out, he'll be coming for me and Aidan.* "What happened to the guard?"

"Drew used a chunk of broken mirror to slice his throat and stab him in the stomach. The guard survived the attack, though I sure as hell don't know how," Mason admitted starkly.

He survived because he's a werewolf, and werewolves are harder to kill than humans.

"You want to help with the search?" Mason pushed. "Captain Harris…she's on her way to the station. She radioed me and asked me to bring you in."

Right. Going back in. Hunting Drew. Another day…

Another nightmare.

"Go, Jane," Aidan said, still not turning to look at her.

"But what about Paris?" She didn't want to leave. He would need her. He would —

"He's my pack. I'll take care of him."

Her gaze shot to Mason. Had he heard Aidan? Heard the word "pack" spoken so easily?

But…no, Mason was just standing there, waiting patiently. He didn't look suspicious or scared. That was good, right?

She hoped it was good.

"You could be in danger, Mr. Locke," Mason said. The guy was so earnest it was almost cute. "Do you want a protective detail? Do you — "

Aidan laughed and finally turned to face the younger man. Jane was relieved that his claws and fangs were out of sight. And his eyes…they only shone a little bit. Just enough that his gaze was unnerving. "I want the bastard to come after me."

"Uh, sir?" Mason swallowed. His Adam's apple bobbed. "I don't think that's a good idea. I mean, I heard that the scene at the college was crazy when he was firing, but that the guy was aiming for *you* — "

"I want him to come," Aidan said again, "because I want to end him."

Mason straightened his thin shoulders. "You can't talk like that, Mr. Locke. People can't take justice into their own hands. People can't — "

"Stop."

Jane shivered. That one word had been infused with power, the deep, twisting, sinister power of an alpha werewolf. The power to control a human. Completely. "Aidan," Jane began.

"Drew Hart tried to kill Jane. To me, that gives him a death sentence. Family or not." Aidan's gaze cut to Jane. "If he comes for me, I will fight back."

I will kill him. She knew what he was saying and she also knew—Drew *would* be coming for Aidan. Her brother had so much hate and rage twisted up inside of him. He wasn't going to stop.

And if Drew faced off against Aidan…her brother will die.

That's why I have to find him first.

Before the blood started to flow.

"I'm coming with you," Jane said to Mason, rushing toward him.

He nodded, but then his gaze dropped to her neck. "Detective Hart, I think you're hurt."

Aidan cursed.

Jane shook her head. "I'm fine."

"You're bleeding. We should take you to a doctor—"

"Just give me the keys to your car." Because there was nothing a doctor could do for her. He tossed the keys to her and Jane caught them.

Before she jumped into the patrol vehicle, she looked back at Aidan. He was standing there, his arms crossed over his chest, his eyes on her. Once upon a time, she'd asked him to promise *not* to kill Drew.

He'd refused to make that promise.

"Don't let your heart make you weak, Jane." Aidan's voice easily reached her. Mason was already in the vehicle, so she hoped he didn't hear the words. "Your brother doesn't see you as human. You're the enemy. He won't hesitate to kill you."

She knew he was right.

"So you shouldn't hesitate, either," Aidan said.

Jane slid into the car.

And she *hated* that Aidan was right.

CHAPTER EIGHT

Aidan watched as the cop car sped away from the scene, then he turned on his heel and headed back into the old BDSM club. The place reeked. It fucking reminded him of hell, and his best friend was chained up in that place?

This can't go on.

He marched to the back of the building and found Annette still crouched beside Paris. The voodoo queen was whispering softly to him, and Aidan could have sworn he saw the spark of magic in the air.

At the sound of his approaching footsteps, Annette whirled around. Fear flashed on her face as she stared at him. "No!" Annette yelled. "You said you wouldn't kill him! You said —"

"I'm not here to kill him." Aidan strode toward her and he stepped over the line of dirt she'd carefully cast on the floor. "I'm here to help him." Yeah, they could sit there all day, twiddling their thumbs and waiting on Vincent's witch to arrive, and with every moment that passed, Paris would get worse or…

Or we can try to fix him. "When he had my blood before, Paris had a moment of clarity. I *saw* it."

"You mean the moment when he asked you to *kill* him?" Annette cried.

Yeah, that fucking moment. "He wasn't a blood-crazed monster then."

"He was a suicidal fool!"

"He needs more clarity." Clarity equaled strength, right? "He needs more blood. My blood."

"Aidan…"

"I keep a supply of my blood on hand for any injured wolves. He's injured." In the worst possible way. "I'll call Garrison and get him to bring it here. The blood can help him." It had to help him. "And that blood…it isn't tainted."

"Tainted?"

Aidan swallowed. "The blood I have stored at the werewolf compound was taken before I gave Jane my blood." He paused and had to starkly confess, "And before I took hers."

He heard the sharp inhalation of her breath. "You've been drinking from Jane?"

He knew that Annette had seen more paranormal creatures and events than most people could imagine. And, well, if anyone could help him…

My money isn't on Vincent's witch. I'll always bet on the voodoo queen. He smiled at her, baring what he knew were vampire fangs.

She backed up a step.

"Seems I've developed an appetite for blood." No denying it. No pretending. "But I'm still an alpha werewolf." The change at the ME's lab had proved that. Only an alpha werewolf could shift into the form of the beast. Other werewolves got some nice bonuses — increased strength, claws — but they couldn't fully shift. That gift was reserved for alphas alone.

Gift, curse…all in the way you look at it.

When he'd been younger, Aidan had thought it was a gift. When he'd met Jane…

Curse. Because being an alpha had just been another reason for them to stay apart.

"You're definitely not a full-on vamp," Annette mused as she cocked her head, studying him. "If you were, you could never cross the dirt of the dead."

Maybe but… "Darkness is growing within me." He could feel it. "I'm not sure how long I'll be able to hold it in check." One thing was for certain — he knew an alpha wasn't ever meant to be a vampire. Not even some fucking partial vamp like he seemed to be. "It's like the two halves are battling inside of me." *Tearing him apart.* "And I don't know which side is going to win."

Fear flashed on her face, and he knew Annette wasn't afraid of many things. "Aidan…"

"I think the fire was the tipping point for me." For him, for Paris. "Jane thought she saved me, that she got me out in time…"

But…

The fire was eating my flesh. The pain was destroying me.

Her hand reached out and her fingers lightly feathered over his shoulder. "But you died, didn't you?"

He just stared at her. "Wherever I went," and he wasn't going to touch that, "Jane brought me back."

"Aidan…the things that are happening…they aren't natural."

He had to laugh as his gaze cut once more to his friend. "Like any of us have ever been *natural.*" Aidan turned from her. The bloodlust had built within him again. It was there now, almost constant. But he was fighting it. He was controlling it.

For the moment.

How long will my control last?

"Werewolves are natural. You weren't made, you were born to be a wolf," Annette said softly.

His lips twisted. "By that logic, Jane was born to be a vampire." The bullshit line that Vincent had once told him.

"Yes." Annette nodded. "I think she was. But then Jane met you and everything changed."

He looked back at Paris. His friend was still out cold. "He didn't want this change. It should never have happened to him." Rage pushed inside of Aidan. "I want you to scry, Annette. Go back to the fire. See everything — see what in the hell happened to him." Because death alone — no, that wouldn't have changed Paris. Something else had.

Someone else?

Annette gave a bitter laugh. "If only I could." Then she pointed to a few broken chunks of black glass. "Those are all that remain of my mirror. I can barely see the danger around us, much less look into the past. That's why I arrived too late to help Paris." Her voice thickened. "If there had been a way, if I'd known what was coming, I *never* would have let him have this end."

This end…The end.

Aidan exhaled slowly. "I'll get Garrison to bring the blood for him. It will tide Paris over, for the time being. Maybe he can become coherent enough to tell us what the hell happened to him."

Aidan whirled and headed for the door.

"You…are a good friend to him."

He stiffened at her words. "Bullshit." Aidan glanced back over his shoulder. "A good friend would have done what he asked. A good friend would have ended his torment." He gave a bitter laugh. "I'm just the selfish bastard who doesn't want to lose the only true brother he's ever known. I won't give him up, not without a fight."

And he wouldn't give in to the darkness growing inside of him, he wouldn't lose his fucking self. He'd fight, for as long as it took.

He'd fight.

***

There was blood staining the floor at the Hathway Psychiatric Facility. Jane paced in what had been her brother's room, but her gaze kept darting to that giant stain of red.

I broke the mirror. I gave him a weapon.

And he hadn't hesitated to use it.

"It's a miracle the guard is alive," Mason said.

Jane glanced over at him. They'd been briefed at the station, and then they'd rushed over to the psychiatric hospital because Jane had wanted to see the scene firsthand. With her enhanced senses, she'd thought that maybe she'd discover something the crime scene techs had overlooked.

"A wound like that," Mason continued, his gaze on the blood stain, "it should've killed him."

If the guard had been human, it would've killed him.

Mason's gaze rose to hold hers. "Lucky him, huh?"

There was a faint edge to his words. Jane's eyes narrowed. She'd brought Mason with her because the kid genuinely seemed to have strong instincts, but there was something about his voice, his body language…

Does Mason know? Had he realized just what was really happening in this city? Aidan hadn't exactly been subtle during their last chat. Jane cleared her throat. "I doubt he feels particularly lucky. I mean, the guy's throat was sliced open and he was left for dead. I doubt that will go down as his best day ever."

She paced toward the bathroom. The broken shards of the mirror were all gone now. No doubt, they'd been carefully bagged and tagged. She'd already read the report about Drew's escape. He'd attacked the poor guard, nearly killed him. Then Drew had used the guard's keys to gain access to the man's locker. Her brother had stolen the clothes from that locker right before he'd vanished.

Drew was clever, she'd give him that.

Clever and quite possibly insane.

"So how'd you turn out so normal," Mason asked as Jane crouched down to study the floor of the bathroom. "And your brother is…well, not?"

She rose. "Don't be too sure I'm the normal one." If only. Dammit, there was nothing to see in that room. No new clue for her to pounce on. Jane headed for the door.

But then she stilled. For just an instant, she could hear her brother raging at her again.

I didn't leave you! When the vampire had you in our basement. When he was burning your skin and you were crying, I didn't leave you. I got you out of there. I saved your life.

"He wasn't always a monster," she whispered. Once, he'd been a hero, but that had been very, very long ago.

Mason's footsteps shuffled closer to her. "In my experience," he said quietly, "no one is born a monster. Folks just…they become monsters. They can't deal with the world around them. They change. Not always for the better."

She looked back at him. Mason had been involved with several of her cases. She could still remember the way the poor guy had vomited when he'd found a young woman's body on Bourbon Street. He'd been so horrified. "Why'd you become a cop, Mason?"

He gave her a quick, nervous smile. "Because I want to save the world."

She stared at him. Hard. Looking for the truth, searching for lies.

"I know it's stupid," he continued, running a nervous hand over his jaw. "But…I do. I want to help. When my parents were killed, cops helped me."

Jane blinked. "I'm sorry, I-I didn't know about your parents."

"I was sixteen." He spoke without emotion. "We were all in the bank — my dad's payday. He was cashing his check and then we were going out for dinner. We did that, you see. Had our weekly family dinners. They were mom's idea. Said they gave us quality time." That smile of his was bittersweet. "No one could have predicted the bank robbery. Or the security guard who panicked. No one knew that the guy in the ski mask would start shooting. No one knew my parents…they'd be the first ones hit."

He spoke with so little emotion, but she saw the grief in his eyes.

"The cops came before anyone else could be hurt. They came in there and they saved me. They killed that shooter — and you know what, Detective Hart?"

She shook her head.

"He was a teen, just like me. Beneath that ski mask, he was a kid." His lips pulled down. "He was crying when he died. And I was crying when I buried my parents."

Okay, Mason was making her heart *hurt*.

"Monsters come in all shapes and sizes," he murmured. "You should remember that."

Jane's brows rose.

"Humans…" He inhaled deeply. "I think we're the worst of the lot."

Did he know? Or was he just—shit, was he just speaking in general?

"So, that's why I'm a cop. Because I know how dangerous the world can be and I want to protect people. I want to help." His head cocked as he studied her. "What about you?"

I'm a cop because I saw the monsters in this world when I was just eleven. And, believe me, Mason, humans are not the worst ones out there. The worst ones out there were the vamps who ripped out the throats of their prey or the werewolves who lost their sanity and slashed their prey into pieces. While working in New Orleans, she'd faced both of those monsters.

"Same reason," Jane mumbled. "I want to help." But she was helping no one by just standing there. Her brother had been far smarter than she realized—the guy had snuck away clean and vanished into the city. Had he fled New Orleans? Was he long gone? Or was he lurking around, planning an attack?

Jane's lips thinned as she marched out of Hathway. She paused just long enough to pick up her gun from the guard at the check-in desk. *Where the hell had the guard been last night? Why hadn't someone seen her brother slipping away?*

She secured her weapon and muttered her thanks as she exited. Her money was on Drew staying in the city, planning an attack. On her. On Aidan. Shit, as if she needed this extra pressure right then. Jane paused on the street outside. The light was too bright. Gleaming sunlight. Not that it hurt her. She wasn't yelling and burning to ash or anything weird like that. She just felt…weaker.

Jane lifted her hand, shielding her eyes, and when she did, her head tilted back. She found herself staring up at a small video camera. One that was perched on what looked like the second floor of the building across the street.

A building that *should* have been empty. There was a big FOR SALE sign in front of that building. But…

Mason gave a low whistle. "Security camera!"

So it would seem.

"Owners must have set it up to protect their investment," he said, voice excited. "Maybe they got footage of your brother leaving on there. We can at least see which direction he took!"

Protecting an investment, yes, that was one idea. But Jane hadn't exactly been having the best of luck with security cameras lately, and this…it just seemed like too much of a coincidence.

Her hand went to her weapon as she hurried across the street.

"Uh, Detective Hart?" Mason called. "Are we—are we going to contact the owners?"

She headed straight to the front door. A chain was in place there, and sure, she wasn't at her full vamp strength but…

Jane jerked the chain, a quick, hard tug that she hid with her body. "No need, it's open."

"B-but a search warrant—"

"You're right." Jane looked over at him and nodded once, decisively. "You don't have a search warrant. Stay outside."

He blinked. "Wait—what?"

"Stay outside." Her hand went to her holster. "I'll be right back." Her instincts were screaming at her. That video camera, perched so perfectly in order to catch the comings and goings at Hathway…

Someone has been watching me. Testing me. Is that same someone keeping an eye on my brother?

Jane had her gun drawn as she hurried up the steps. The building was deserted, as quiet as a tomb inside. Her heartbeat raced in her chest, and she kept thinking about Aidan and Garrison and Paris. They'd been searching an apartment, looking for her mysterious watcher.

And the place had been booby trapped for them. *That's why I told Mason to stay outside. I don't want him getting pulled into this mess. I don't want him getting blown to hell and back because he's following my lead.*

When she reached the top of the stairs, three doors waited…but all of them were wide open. Jane peered inside the first door and saw nothing. An empty office space. The second door also led to a vacant room, one covered with a layer of dust. But the third room…

Jane walked inside. And her breath froze in her lungs.

The floor of the third room was covered in spray paint—a big, looping design. A red paint image of the Greek letter Omega.

The same symbol that had been burned into her right side so many years before.

Jane crept into that room, her gaze darting from the spray paint design to the surveillance camera that was attached to the window.

The watcher did this. He was keeping an eye on me and on my brother.

But why? Why the hell was she so important to him? And who the hell was he? Jane paced closer to the window. No green light glowed from that camera. It was off now…because there was nothing left to watch? She needed that camera bagged and tagged. Maybe the crime scene techs could find some evidence on it, something that she could use. Something that…

A phone was ringing.

Jane stilled. Her gaze darted to the right, to the far corner of the room, and she saw a small phone on the floor. It vibrated, shaking against the wooden floor as it rang again.

Her breath blew slowly from her lungs. Was this another trap? She inched toward the phone. If she picked it up, was the place going to blow up? Would *she* blow up? For all she knew, the whole building could be wired to explode and the cell phone was some sort of detonation trigger. Just in case…

Jane raced toward the phone, moving with her vamp speed — or as much of it as she could muster right then. She snatched it up and rushed out of that building in mere seconds. When she left — she slammed into Mason because he'd been lurking far too close to the building's entrance. She drove the breath from him with that impact. Jane heard the loud *oof* he gave as he slammed to the ground.

She jerked him up and hauled him away from the building, her hand still tight around the phone. Jane glanced back. The place hadn't blown…yet.

"You were, um, sure moving fast," Mason blurted.

The phone had stopped ringing.

"Get some techs out here," Jane ordered him. "And some bomb sniffing dogs, too."

His eyes widened. He nodded once, then whirled away as he ran back to the patrol car.

The phone in her hand began to ring again. Since she was clear of the building, Jane answered. "Who the hell is this?"

Laughter. Deep. Rumbling. "Are you missing something, Detective Hart? Or maybe…someone?"

She nearly shattered that phone in her tight grip. "Yeah, I'm missing you. Some jerk who thinks it is funny to play with people's lives."

"You're not a person. We both know that."

Her shoulders hunched as she paced away from Mason. "I get it. You think I'm some unholy beast that needs to be put down, right? Some big, bad monster that has to be stopped, huh? Then come out—stop me. *Stop me.*"

"I know where your brother is."

Jane stilled.

"And I'm going to tell you…because I do like to watch you work."

You are a sick bastard and I will end you.

"It's not you he hates so much, is it? It's your lover." A sigh slipped over the line. "Poor Jane. You thought you'd found a happy ending. You don't even realize what you've done."

Jane spun around, her gaze searching the street. "Are you watching me right now?" Because she thought he was. After all, that phone had rang right on cue, just as she'd entered that room upstairs and then again—right when she'd cleared the building. He'd left her a burner phone—one that she was sure was going to prove untraceable—and the SOB was hiding in the shadows. Watching her.

"I've discovered that I rather like watching you, Jane. More than a job, it's a downright passion now."

His voice…it was distorted. Why? Why distort the voice unless…unless he thought she would recognize him.

"You should hurry, Jane. Your brother is going to strike soon. This time, I'm not the one you have to worry about."

Then he hung up. Sonofabitch.

***

Garrison handed the bagged blood to Annette, his gaze darting nervously around the old club. "Is he…is Paris really a vamp?"

Annette took the blood—the bags were cold because Garrison had just pulled them out of an ice chest. Nausea rolled in her stomach, but she fought it down. Now wasn't the time for fear or squeamishness.

She didn't answer Garrison as she turned away and stalked to the back room. The place seemed to whisper to her, dark and twisted secrets spilling from its walls. There had been pain in this place, and not just the kind that was *invited* at a BDSM club. The building had an old history, as did most of the places in New Orleans. Ghosts lingered. Pain and heartbreak pierced the air.

Those ghosts wanted to talk to her. She could feel them pulling at her, and, normally, she'd listen to them. Maybe she'd even try to help them.

Not today. Today wasn't for the dead.

Today was for Paris.

She shoved open the door to the back room. Aidan was there, staring down at his friend. Paris was rousing, blinking his eyes. His fangs were already out.

"Give me the blood," Aidan ordered darkly. "Then you'll need to get back."

It wasn't as if she *wanted* to get bitten, so that plan sounded pretty good to her. Annette crept closer, then she put one bag of blood in his outstretched hand. She set the others nearby, then backed up.

"Paris." Aidan said his name, his voice rumbling with the cold power of an alpha wolf.

Paris looked up at him...and then he was snapping his fangs. One instant, Paris had been slumped on the floor, and in the next second, he'd lunged up, going right for Aidan's throat.

But Aidan was fast — deadly, wickedly fast. Paris missed the alpha's throat and instead, a bag of blood was shoved into his mouth. His fangs punctured the bag and blood began to trickle out of his mouth.

But he's drinking it. I can see him swallowing.

Annette wrapped her arms around her middle as she stood there. Paris sucked that bag dry and he didn't vomit the blood back up.

That was good…wasn't it? Or was it very, very bad?

Aidan shoved another bag at Paris's mouth. Then another…another…Paris drained four bags of blood before his body sagged back against the wall, his hands hanging limply in the chains that bound him.

The ragged sound of Paris's breathing seemed to fill the room.

Aidan stared at him, and the alpha's face was impassive.

Paris had closed his eyes.

Annette inched forward. *Come back to us, Paris. Just come —*

His eyes opened — and his golden stare locked straight on her. Hunger flared in his gaze. Lust. And…shame.

Annette's lips parted in shock. "Paris?" Was he really coming back to them?

"Get…her…*out*." His words were a growl.

Pain iced her heart.

"No," Aidan fired right back. "Annette isn't going anywhere. You need her. I need her."

Paris squeezed his eyes shut. "You…were…s-supposed…to —"

"Don't even start that kill me shit right now," Aidan blasted. "You have no idea what I'm dealing with, got it? And I will *not* lose you like this. You're talking to me. You're sane again, you're —"

"Feel it…clawing at me…" Paris gasped. His eyes flew open. She could see the battle in his bright gaze. "Can't…hold…back…"

"Then we'll get you more blood," Aidan said. "We'll get you whatever you need, but you keep fighting, understand?"

"Werewolves…k-kill…vamps…"

"Don't tell me the rules," Aidan snapped at him. "I'm the alpha. I fucking *make* the rules."

Yes, he did.

Annette tip-toed closer.

"How the hell did this happen?" Aidan demanded. "How did you change? You didn't have Jane's blood. You didn't even have my blood in the days leading up to this shit. You—"

"Ambulance," he rasped the word. His gaze slid to Annette, and Paris licked his lips. The terrible burns on his body were finally starting to fade, "G-gave…blood…m-made…drink…"

"*What?*"

Annette shivered at Aidan's voice. So quiet. So cold. So deadly.

"Man…r-remember…" Each word seemed a struggle for Paris. His teeth snapped together again.

My, what sharp fangs you have.

The better to drink his prey dry.

And he looks at me as if I'm the prey he wants.

"H-he was there…poured blood…down…throat…" Paris yanked at the chains that held him, giving a guttural cry.

Annette jumped.

"It *hurts!*" Paris screamed. "R-ripping me apart! I feel it! *Inside – ripping me apart!*"

"I know," Aidan said, his voice dipping so low now that Annette had to strain in order to hear him. "I feel the same fucking way." His hand clamped on Paris's shoulder. "You fight, you understand? You keep fighting. You —"

Paris went for his throat again, the moment of sanity seeming to fade.

But once more, Aidan dodged those biting teeth. He shoved another bag of blood at Paris. "Tell Garrison we're going to need more," he ordered. "A whole lot damn *more.*"

Annette stared at the two men, her heart aching. *Breaking.* Paris had come back, but only for a few moments before the madness claimed him again. She stumbled away, gave the order to a dazed Garrison for more blood, then she stood there, a dull buzzing filling her ears.

Garrison rushed to get more blood. And she…

Annette lifted her hand to her cheek. Why was it wet? She didn't cry. She never cried. She didn't let herself feel enough to cry. She always hid her emotions. You had to hide when you cared. Because if others found out what she cared about…

They'd destroy what she loved.

Only…

Another guttural cry seemed to echo through the building.

The man she'd secretly started to love…he was already being destroyed. But…by his own words, someone had done this to him. Paris had said that someone had given him blood. Some bastard out there…some fool she didn't know…

He'd dared to fuck with the voodoo queen. With someone who was *hers.*

She was going to find the bastard. And she'd make him pay for that crime with his life.

CHAPTER NINE

Jane rushed toward the old BDSM club, her heart racing. She was sick to her stomach and she hated the fear that iced her veins. *Aidan. Get to Aidan. Get to —*

The door to the building opened and she nearly slammed right into Garrison. His eyes widened as he grabbed her arms. "Jane?"

She pushed him to the side and ran inside. She saw Annette, the woman was swiping at her cheeks. *Annette — crying? Oh, that is so not good.* "Where's Aidan?" Jane demanded.

Annette jerked to attention. Her hand lifted — oh, crap, her fingers were shaking — as she pointed toward the back, toward the room that housed Paris. Jane ran forward, then stopped at Annette's side. Her hand reached out and curled over Annette's shoulder. "What happened?"

Tears gleamed in Annette's eyes. "What's the use of all the power…if you can't save the one who matters most?"

Jane sucked in a sharp breath. "Annette…"

"I looked into my mirror hundreds of times over the years. People came to me — vampires came to me. Werewolves. Humans. They were all so desperate. And do you know what most of them wanted?"

Jane shook her head.

"To save a loved one. I…" Her head lowered. "I pitied them. Swore I wouldn't ever be like them. Because when you are willing to offer up your own life for someone else…that just means the fates *will* make you pay the ultimate price."

Jane didn't know what to say. Annette was hurting and the fault…*it's mine. I'm the one who didn't save Paris. It's on me.* Because she didn't know what to say in order to ease Annette's pain, Jane just pulled the other woman close in a tight hug.

Annette stiffened in her hold. "What are you doing?"

"It's called a hug, Annette."

Annette stayed stiff. "You'd better not bite me…" Her words were grumbled but her body slowly relaxed. A moment later, Jane risked a look at Annette's face, and saw that the tears had left her eyes.

For the moment.

"When did you start to love him?" Jane asked her.

Annette's chin lifted. "Does the when matter? Do you remember the exact moment you started to love that beast of yours?"

No, she just…had.

Jane slipped back from Annette. Her beast was in danger, and they had to be prepared for Drew. But before she could go to him, Annette caught her wrist in a tight grip.

"We have to find a way to save them both," Annette whispered.

"Trust me, that's what I'm trying to do."

But Annette's gaze didn't leave hers. "What will you trade?"

That answer was simple. For Aidan's life? "Everything."

Annette's hand slipped from hers. "I was afraid you'd say that." Her laughter was bitter. "Just like all the desperate fools who came to see me…wanting to save others…and losing themselves along the way."

Jane shivered as she hurried toward that back room. Annette followed behind her, so quietly, and when Jane stepped inside that room…

Paris was sleeping. Empty blood bags littered the floor around him. Aidan stood over the other man, his hands clenched, his head bowed.

Jane hesitated. "Aidan…"

His shoulders tensed. "You didn't do this, Jane."

Yes, she had. Guilt was a weight pulling at her ankles as she crept toward him.

Aidan turned to her and the fury on his face nearly stopped her heart. "Someone gave him tainted blood, Jane. *Deliberately.* While Paris was helpless in an ambulance, some bastard forced him to take vampire blood."

That wasn't what she'd expected to hear.

"He *told* me. My blood gave Paris a few moments of sanity. He remembered." Aidan's hand rose and she saw that his claws had broken from the tips of his fingers. "I will find the bastard who did this to Paris. He will *pay.*"

Because there was always a price in this world, just as Annette had said. A price for good deeds. A price for darkness. As she stared at Aidan's face, Jane could only see darkness. A rage that went soul deep and promised the harshest vengeance. She was staring into the eyes of the man she loved, and, Jane knew without any doubt in her mind, she was also staring straight into the eyes of a killer.

***

Jane had taken the phone with her. He'd rather suspected she would. After all, Jane was so desperate to protect her lover, she'd run straight to him.

And I was able to follow.

The old building wasn't the hiding spot he'd anticipated for Aidan Locke. But then, Aidan wasn't really the one who was hiding.

Paris Cole was hiding. Or, rather, being hidden.

He lifted his lens up so that he could focus on that building. He wasn't getting too close, even with the special lotion he'd used to hide his scent. Jane had run into that building, and she'd nearly knocked over a redheaded man in her haste. The redhead was familiar — he'd seen the guy a few times before.

Another werewolf. One who should have burned in the explosion he'd set, but Jane had saved his mangy hide.

The redhead didn't matter to him. He needed to see Paris. Needed to find out just what was happening to that werewolf. Had he changed? Was he a vampire now? Mindless, desperate? Or…something more?

Jane hadn't come out. He'd wait for her. After all, that was his job. To wait and to watch. He'd been paid so well for that job. For so very long.

And Jane had never even had a fucking clue. She'd thought she left her demons far behind her when she first moved to New Orleans. She'd been wrong. All along, they'd been right with her. She'd trusted the wrong people. She was *still* trusting the wrong ones.

She never even saw the threats coming.

But that was the thing about family and friends. They could blind you to their faults so perfectly. Blind you, trick you.

And in the end…kill you.

***

He had to hunt. Aidan's claws were out and his beast wanted to take over. The thinnest thread of control held him back from a full shift. What he'd learned from Paris…

Someone did this to him. Someone made Paris this way.

It fucking enraged him.

His gaze shifted to Annette. "He gorged on the blood so he should be sated for a few hours, but I…I can't leave him alone."

She immediately shook her head. "He won't be alone."

"It isn't safe to have other werewolves around him, not yet, so I can't send any of my pack here." He forced his back teeth to unclench. "Are you sure you can handle him?"

She gave a light, mocking laugh. "I told you before, alpha, I know how to handle the dead." Her own gaze gleamed with a barely leashed rage. "Go find the one who did this to him. Bring him back…*to me.*"

She thought to get her own vengeance? Ah, not happening. The voodoo queen would need to get in line. Once Aidan was done with the guy, if there was anything left of the bastard, Annette could have the scraps of his soul to torture.

When he turned to leave, Jane immediately stepped to his side. "I'm coming with you."

Not a good idea. Not when his control was so close to shattering. Aidan shook his head—

"That wasn't a question," Jane said quickly, breathlessly. "I'm coming. That freak watcher called me a few minutes ago—he said that my brother was on your trail, Aidan. We've got enemies closing in, and I'm not about to let you face danger alone."

His eyes narrowed as his gaze raked over her face. "You're afraid I'm going to kill Drew." Hadn't she asked him—more than once before—to promise he wouldn't take her brother's life? He would do many things for Jane, but that bastard…

He's a dead man.

Blood wasn't always the strongest bond.

"No," Jane snapped back at him. "I'm afraid he'll get more silver bullets and come after *you.* We're getting threats on all sides, Aidan. Know what that means?" She caught his clawed fingers with her own. Then she laced their fingers together. "It means we're stronger together."

That was what they'd always said. He looked down at her hand. So small and fragile and soft within his grasp.

Jane.

His Jane.

He wouldn't lose her. Not to anything. He *couldn't.* Aidan wasn't sure if his sanity would survive without her. That thin thread of control that was holding in his mind? It was there because *she* was there. An anchor inside of him, a light pulling him back from the darkness that Aidan could feel threatening to swallow him whole.

"We'll do it together," Jane whispered.

His gaze slid to her throat. He could see her pulse racing there, could almost taste the blood beneath her skin. He'd had such a small sip from her before.

He needed more.

He would have *more.*

His hold tightened on her. They left that hell, and he glanced back at Paris. Annette had knelt beside him, just beyond the line of dirt that she'd cast around his body. Paris hadn't been able to cross past that dirt, not yet. Even when he'd lunged to attack Aidan, he hadn't gone beyond the line. Aidan had crossed it in order to get to Paris, but his friend…

He was trapped.

Caged.

Beasts hated to be caged.

Am I different because I'm an alpha? Has Paris already lost his wolf completely? It would seem so. No wonder the bloodlust was hitting Paris so hard. He had no defense against it. Aidan's wolf was still battling, refusing to give up…

Tearing me apart in the fight.

Aidan sucked in a deep breath. He *would* find a way to fix of all of this. He wouldn't give up. He couldn't.

Aidan and Jane slipped outside. His gaze scanned the street, looking for threats. The cemetery waited nearby, and he could see the statues and the mausoleums creeping above the heavy stone wall. His nostrils flared as he pulled in the scents around him. Humans. Perfume. Wine. Cigarettes.

"He left this phone for me." Jane pulled it from her pocket. Her shoulder brushed against his chest. "The bastard had another surveillance camera set up, only this time it was in front of the Hathway Psychiatric Facility. He'd been watching my brother. When he called, he said that Drew was going to strike soon. That I had to get to you."

"And you came running." His words were rough and the hair on the nape of his neck rose. His gaze scanned the street. He looked back toward the cemetery and…

Light. Glinting.

Aidan didn't say another word. He just took off running. He went straight for that cemetery wall. Jane yelled after him.

Aidan leapt over the wall. His knees didn't buckle when he touched down on the other side. He rushed ahead, catching sight of a man's dark hair.

"Aidan!" Jane yelled.

He glanced back just as she cleared the wall. That was his Jane. *Strong.* He turned back to face his prey — the fool wasn't getting away.

The light glinted. He was watching us. Peering over the wall. Staring at us through —

Aidan grabbed the bastard.

And the device the man had been holding — a big, black camera — fell to the ground, shattering.

"*What the fucking hell!*" the man screamed. He turned on Aidan, swinging his fist. Aidan took the blow even as he caught sight of the dark lines of tattoos on the man's wrist and forearm. Aidan laughed at the weak impact of that hit, and then his claws flew toward the fool who had thought to —

Jane jumped between him and his prey. "Aidan, stop!"

A sea of red was before his eyes. He didn't want to stop. He wanted the bastard to *bleed.*

And I'll drink his blood. I'll drink him down. He'll beg and bleed and —

"Aidan?" Jane stared at him, worry flashing in her eyes. "Are you okay?"

Aidan drove his claws into the nearby mausoleum. Chunks of stone flew into the air around him. Rage was choking him, and he *knew* the way he felt was wrong. He tried to breathe, to get past the rage.

"Jane!" It was his prey talking—the guy was reaching for Jane, staring at her with *familiarity.* And Jane was—Jane was shielding the guy. Some human who was covered with tattoos, with piercings running up the side of his left ear, and who...

I know him, too. Fuck. He'd seen this guy before, back at Jane's old apartment. When a paranormal fire had swept through the building, this asshole had been there. Jane had gotten Roth to safety and then, when an ambush happened on the streets and bullets started flying, Roth had run for cover. *And this asshole just left Jane to protect herself.*

"Roth!" Jane looked back at the guy. "What in the hell is going on?"

Roth, Roth Sly. The name clicked for Aidan. *Fucking bastard.* He hadn't seen Roth since the night he'd gotten Jane away from her old apartment. He hadn't even given a second thought to the jerk since that time.

Obviously, my mistake.

"I don't know what's happening!" Roth yelled back. "I was minding my own damn business and this guy flew at me!"

Aidan tried to shove down his rage, for the moment. *Think. Focus.*

"I was taking some pictures—you know how fucking important my art is to me, Jane," Roth said, his words tumbling out. "Then this freak just came hurtling over the wall and *attacked* me."

"It's okay, Roth." Jane's voice was flat. "Everything is under control." She stared hard at Aidan. "Isn't it?"

His hands slowly slid from the stone. "For the moment." Maybe. Barely. He glared at the guy. "Roth. I remember you."

"Oh, shit," Roth whispered. "Why do I feel like you mean that in a bad way?"

Because I do. I fucking do.

"You lived on the bottom floor of Jane's building," Aidan's voice was a rough rumble. He couldn't manage more than that. "The night I met you, your sorry ass hid behind a street sign when bullets started flying. You left Jane out in the open, vulnerable. You saved your own hide."

Roth's eyes bulged. "She is a cop, man! She knows how to take care of herself!" Roth was nearly as tall as Aidan and the guy was muscled, but in a match of strength, Aidan knew the fool wouldn't even come close to his level. "I didn't want to die! So, hell, yeah, I ran and hid! That's what sane people do!" His gaze fell to the shattered camera. "Look what the hell you did…" He grabbed for the camera.

Aidan grabbed the bastard, snagging his wrist. The guy had a black raven tattoo that covered his inner wrist, and a snake was poised to bite that bird…*its prey.* "Do you like attacking those who are weaker than you?"

"Aidan!" Jane snapped. "He wasn't attacking. You did that."

"You were watching her." He knew it with utter certainty. "You were out here, taking pictures of Jane." He'd seen the glint of light that reflected off the guy's lens. Jane was being followed, watched, and this SOB had just randomly appeared? He wasn't about to buy that coincidence. No way.

"I was taking pictures of the street! Of the light coming over the buildings. Of *the dead.*" Roth's breath heaved out as he straightened his shoulders. "I'm an artist. This shit is what I do!"

Aidan didn't believe him.

Jane had bent to pick up the guy's broken camera.

"Jane, look, he's your boyfriend, right?" Roth said, his voice a bit frantic. "I mean, I remember when he came out of the fire at our old building. Calm him down, okay? Whatever weird-ass rage he's on, calm him down."

Jane slid closer to Aidan. She put her hand on his shoulder. For an instant, he did feel calm and then…

"Aidan, compel him to tell the truth," Jane said.

Surprise flashed through him. Jane hated it when he manipulated humans. She—

"I don't believe in coincidences," Jane continued quietly. "So ask Roth why he was here."

Hell, yes. Aidan smiled at his prey.

Roth blinked and the guy started to sweat. "Compel me? What's that shit supposed to mean? Is this some weird threesome thing? Because I'm flattered but I am not down—"

"Dumbass, I never share Jane." Aidan slammed him against an old crypt. "Compelling means you tell me exactly what I want to hear…because you don't have a choice." He could feel power pouring through his body. "What were you doing in this cemetery?"

Roth's face went slack. His eyes seemed to glaze over.

"What were you doing?" Aidan snarled.

"Taking pictures…for my exhibit. Life and Death, the thin line between…"

"Shitty title," Aidan muttered.

"Aidan," Jane said, a warning note in her voice.

He kept his tight hold on the human. "Why were you taking pictures of Jane?"

"Because Jane's beautiful." The answer rolled from him. "I saw her coming from that building and I had to take her photo, to add to my collection."

That answer had Aidan's wolf howling. Aidan took a slow breath. Then another. "What collection?"

Roth smiled. "I like beauty. I collect it when I can."

Behind him, Jane swore. "I do *not* like where this is going."

Humans could hide so much with their easy words and quick lies, but when Aidan had them under his compulsion, they had to reveal the secrets they kept deep inside.

"How do you collect beauty?" Aidan demanded.

Roth laughed. "With my art. I take pictures. I paint. I own the beauty. It becomes mine."

Aidan thought about just slicing the guy's throat open right then and there. "This dick is a serial killer in training," he told Jane.

"Maybe, but I don't think he's the guy who's been testing me."

No, maybe he was just a freak who seemed to be stalking Jane…and other women. Aidan cocked his head as he studied the other man. "Have you taken pictures of Jane before?"

Roth smiled. "Lots of them." That smile dimmed. "But most burned in the fire. So this was a good chance to get new ones."

A growl rumbled in Aidan's throat. "I really want to kill you right now."

Jane's fingers curled around his shoulder. "But you won't. You'll let him go, and I'll call the PD and give them a tip to watch this guy before he turns into even more of a perv." He felt the bite of her nails in his skin. "He…hasn't already hurt anyone, has he?"

Aidan stared into Roth's eyes. "Have you hurt a woman before?"

"No woman. I told you…" Again, that smile flashed. "I like beauty. I capture it."

"You won't *capture* anything else of Jane's, do you understand?" He forced as much power as he could into that command. "You won't even fucking look her way again, got me? You'll stay away from her. Because if you don't, I'll give you a real up-close experience for that thin line between life and death bullshit exhibit of yours."

Roth paled. "I…won't look her way."

"You won't fucking stalk *any* woman, got it?" This slimy bastard was pissing him off.

Roth nodded.

"Send him away," Jane whispered. "He's not the one we want, and I don't like us just being out in the open like this."

Because neither of them had exactly experienced the best of times in that particular cemetery.

"Get out of here," Aidan ordered. "And as soon as you clear the cemetery gates, you just keep walking, asshole. You won't recall much about our little chat, but you *will* remember to stay the fuck away from Jane."

Roth nodded. He reached for the broken camera. Aidan laughed. "Tough luck. You don't get that back, either. Now get out of here."

Roth stumbled away. He looked back, once, at Aidan, but his gaze didn't so much as dart Jane's way.

Aidan kept his gaze on the bastard until the man was out of the cemetery. Then he turned and stared at Jane.

His Jane.

"I lived in New Orleans for over a year with that asshole as my downstairs neighbor," Jane said, shaking her head. Her dark hair slid over her shoulders. "He was weird, yes, but I never thought…" Her gaze trekked toward the cemetery's heavy wall. "What happens when you can't trust anyone anymore?"

He wanted to tell Jane that she could trust him. That she could *always* count on him, but the words wouldn't come. Because he couldn't be sure they were true. Not with the changes going on inside of him.

The rage was still there, he hadn't stopped it. Rage that blasted through his very veins. He stared at Jane. That bastard had been taking her picture. What else had he been doing? Living in the same building, he would've had so much access to Jane. "I should've fucking killed him."

Jane shook her head. "No, then you'd be—"

"Baby, I am the monster." And right then, part of him gloried in that fact. He caught her hand, pulled her close. "And I wish I'd ripped out his throat." For daring to stare at Jane, to lust for her—oh, yeah, the bastard had fucking lusted. Aidan had smelled that scent in the air. The fool had wanted Jane.

He'll never have her. No one else will. Jane will always be mine.

The darkness stretched more inside of him, threatening to swallow the man he'd been. Threatening to take his sanity.

"For a minute there," Jane said, her voice husky. "I thought you were going for his throat."

If she hadn't been there, he would have. Aidan didn't speak as they left that cemetery. Back on the street, his gaze swept the area once more. More humans were out, filling the sidewalks. No one seemed to be paying him and Jane any attention.

But appearances were so often deceptive.

Aidan pulled out his phone. He called Vivian, even as his gaze kept searching for threats. The police captain answered on the second ring.

"What's happening?" Vivian's voice was tight. "Aidan, I've been trying to reach you – "

"Paris isn't dead."

"What?"

"I need you to find out who was working on him at the scene of the fire. Any EMTs, anyone who was near him — you fucking bring those people to me, got it?"

"Aidan, how did he survive? There was no pulse." Her voice was shaking. "I checked! I swear, I did. I would never let a pack member — "

"Bring them to me, Vivian." She'd always been a loyal member of his pack. He knew he could count on her. "I'll be at Hell's Gate." And he *would* get his answers.

"It's going to take some time." He heard her quick, indrawn breath carry over the phone line. "But I'll get anyone I can find, I swear it."

Aidan ended the call, then he curled his hand around Jane's. His claws were gone, but his beast was about to break free. Time to get off that street. Time to get back to his lair.

And time to claim what was *his*.

*****

Roth Sly stumbled down the road, blinking blearily. He glanced at his hands. They felt…empty. As if he should be holding something. Doing something. He stopped at the street corner, just staring as others hurried across the crosswalk.

Why the hell was he on that street?

He touched his head. His temples were throbbing like a bitch.

Someone bumped into him from behind. He realized he was just standing there, holding up the damn line. Muttering an apology, he turned to the man who'd nudged him. "Sorry…I just…" Roth gave a rough laugh. "I must have pulled one hell of an all-nighter." A hangover, that's what he had. That's why he felt weird and couldn't remember exactly what the hell he'd been doing. He'd had blackouts before, usually after he drank himself into a sweet oblivion. But…he hadn't drank like that in a very, very long time. Not since he'd started his last job.

The man who'd bumped him smiled. "No problem. We've all been there." It was a friendly smile. Easy going. "There's a coffee shop around the corner. Some caffeine might help you out, and they've got great beignets there."

"Right. Yeah, thanks, man." Roth turned away, rubbing a hand over his jaw and feeling the faint sting of a five o'clock shadow. He hurried around the corner, and, sure enough, down the way just a little bit, there was a coffee shop waiting. It was about thirty feet away. His left hand shoved into his pocket. Did he have any money on him?

Footsteps tapped behind him. He looked back, and that guy was there. The friendly dude from the crosswalk. Roth blinked. Was the fellow following him?

No, no, he was just being paranoid. That happened after he drank too much, too. Another unwanted side effect.

Roth pushed open the door of the coffee shop. The bell above his head jingled. He spotted an empty booth in the far back and he bee-lined for it. He sat down on the broken seat cushion, exhaling in relief.

And then, two seconds later, that same damn guy slid into the booth with him. "What the hell…?" Roth began.

The man shoved a thick, brown envelope across the table. "Where's Jane?"

Jane.

Roth started to sweat.

"I know you were following her today," the guy continued. He leaned forward. "I *paid* you to follow Jane. So where the fuck is she now?"

CHAPTER TEN

Hell's Gate was dead silent. Aidan marched across the club and went straight to the bar. Jane paced behind him, but stopped in the middle of the cavernous room. She watched as he grabbed a bottle of whiskey and poured it into a short, thick glass. He downed that whiskey in one gulp and then poured more. "Aidan…" Jane began, edging a bit closer. His mood was volatile — hell, that was a serious understatement. The whole bar felt heavy and tense, a tenseness that was emanating from Aidan.

He drained the second glass and set it back on the bar with a thunk. "That didn't help." His gaze locked on her. His eyes were so bright. "I'm still thirsty."

Something was different about Aidan. Darker. His features seemed harder and when he looked at her, the expression in his eyes was almost desperate.

His gaze slid over her face. Down to her throat. And that stare of his seemed to burn even more.

"I need a taste, Jane," Aidan whispered.

"A taste?" Her own voice came out too high pitched.

He put his hands down on the bar, then leapt right over it. He stalked toward her. *Stalked.* Definitely the right description for his slow, steady movements. "A taste of you."

Jane shook her head. "Captain Harris will be coming soon. She'll—"

"Not yet, she won't. It's just you and it's me." His hand rose and his fingers curled along the column of her neck. "I need a taste." His words were growled. And when he spoke, she saw his fangs.

Vampire fangs.

He pulled her closer. Her breasts brushed against his chest. All kinds of warnings were going off in her head as she stared up at him. *Handle with extreme care.* At the cemetery, she'd been aware of just how fragile his control had been. If she hadn't been with him, Jane feared he would have killed Roth. Sure, the guy was an asshole, but did Roth deserve to have his throat ripped out for that crime?

His fingers stroked her neck. "Let me taste you, Jane."

"Aidan…"

His head bent. His lips brushed over hers. It was a careful kiss. She hadn't expected that care. His mood was so volatile, his darkness so close to the surface, that she'd expected a rough claiming from his mouth. Hard. Domination.

Not seduction. But he was seducing her. With his mouth and his tongue. His kiss was so careful, so tender, and Jane found herself leaning toward him. This was Aidan. Her Aidan. Fate kept trying to tear them apart, but Jane wasn't going to let that happen. He was the one thing that had always felt right in her messed-up world.

He was the one person who made her feel right.

His mouth feathered over her jaw, then slowly moved down her neck. Jane's head tipped back and a moan slipped from her throat. He always knew just how to touch her. Always knew *exactly* –

His fangs sank into her throat. There was no pain, just pleasure, a white-hot lash that had her whole body tensing. Her hands rose and curled around his broad shoulders, but she didn't push him away. Her nails sank into his shirt as she pulled him even closer.

He was drinking her blood. He was tasting her…

And she loved it.

Her breasts tightened as need spiraled inside of her. Not some soft, gentle need. *Lust.* Dirty, hot lust. Her sex ached and her panties got wet. She rocked her hips against him, wanting to be closer.

His bite — it was doing something to her. She was rubbing her body against his like a freaking cat in heat, and Jane couldn't stop herself. She wanted her clothes gone, and she wanted him to fuck her. Right then. Right there. She didn't care where they were. She didn't care if anyone walked straight in on them. She needed Aidan.

Her breath panted out. *"Aidan!"*

He locked his hands around her hips and lifted her up. He whirled and put her down on top of the bar, then he pushed between her spread legs. His cock was full, shoving hard against the front of his jeans. Her trembling fingers jerked at the button on his jeans and she pulled down the zipper. That hiss was loud in the bar, but not as loud as the frantically drumming heartbeat that echoed in her ears.

Want him. Need him.

Her own fangs were out. Her breasts were tight peaks. She wanted Aidan to lick them. Wanted him to lick her — everywhere.

Pleasure. No more pain. That was what she wanted with him. Always with him.

Her hand curled around his cock. It was thick and hot in her hand. She squeezed him and —

"Jane." He'd pulled his mouth from her neck. He stared down at her, and she lost her breath as she stared at him. Aidan looked as if he wanted to devour her.

Staring into his eyes, she stroked him again, a long pump from the base of his cock to the head of his erection.

His jaw tightened. "I'm going to fuck you."

"Good." She needed him inside her. She needed—

"I'm going to own you." His voice was dark and rough as he grabbed her shirt and wrenched it up. His claws sliced through her bra and his mouth locked on one aching breast. Jane's head tipped back as she gave a wild cry.

In me. I need him in me —

"Just as you own me," Aidan rasped against her. Then his hand was at the snap of her jeans. He moved fast—that wonderful paranormal speed—and she was suddenly naked on the bar top. He pulled her closer, and he smiled at her.

But…

That smile was more beast than man.

His fingers pushed between her legs. "Wet for me."

She was *dying* for him right now. His bite had sent her body into an overdrive of yearning. She was about to start clawing at him if he didn't thrust inside of her. The ache was constant. She needed him to fill her. She needed him to fuck her into oblivion.

The desire wasn't normal. In some distant part of her mind, she knew that. Too intense. Too fast. Too consuming. But—

Screw normal.

Aidan yanked her to the edge of the bar. It was cold and hard beneath her and Jane squirmed—but her movements stopped when he bent over her and he…

He licked her. Kissed her. Stroked her sex and just fed that mad need that was about to rip her apart. Her hands slapped down on the bar as her body trembled.

"Fucking delicious," Aidan whispered. He looked up at her with his bright blue eyes. "Fucking *mine.*"

And he was hers. Soul deep. Good and bad. Always…hers.

He positioned his cock at the entrance to her body, and he sank deep. A hard thrust that stole her breath and was *exactly* what she wanted. In the next instant, he'd pulled her right off the bar. He held her easily in his arms, so damn easily, and her legs locked around him. She rose on him, sank down, again and again, going wild with the feel of him inside of her. His mouth pressed to her throat once again. His fangs sank into her and as he tasted her, she felt his cock swell even more inside of her.

It was too much—his bite, the deep thrust of his cock into her—Jane's orgasm hit, driving her over the edge and she screamed his name. It wasn't some blast of pleasure, it consumed her. Shaking her, trembling through her whole body.

She squeezed her eyes shut, she fought to get a breath, and the pleasure lashed against her.

Her sex squeezed him, hard and tight, and she felt him erupt inside of her. The hot splash of his release that just fueled her own climax. His grip hardened on her, he kept drinking from her, and Jane was utterly lost — taken.

His completely in that moment, just as he was hers.

She tried to get her heartbeat to slow. Tried to get her breath to ease. But…

I still want him. I want more. The need — that dark, twisting need that he'd awakened in her — wasn't gone. He licked her throat and then his head lifted. Jane forced her lashes to rise as she stared up at him.

He was still hard inside of her. He'd come, but, like her…

He wants more.

He gazed down at her, not speaking. Jane licked her lips. Her mouth was so dry. Just how much screaming and moaning had she been doing?

He slowly lowered her to the floor and pulled out of her. She gasped at that withdrawal, hating it because…

I wasn't done.

"Don't worry, baby," His voice was a rough rasp that just made her ache more. "I'm not done."

She couldn't look away from his gaze. *I can see his darkness. I can feel it all around me.*

But…Jane wasn't scared.

"Turn around," Aidan ordered.

She turned around, moving to face the bar. A mirror was behind that bar, reflecting her image back to Jane. Her cheeks were flushed, her dark eyes gleamed, and her hair was tousled around her head. She could see her breasts, the pink tips were thrusting forward, still aroused. Still desperate for more.

"Put your hands on the bar."

Her hands flattened on the bar.

"The vamp in me had you his way." His voice was so rough. So deep.

*The vamp in me…*He'd just admitted what he was. She should say something. Do something—

"Now…" He caught her hair in his hand and pulled it to the side, baring the curve of her right shoulder. He pressed a kiss there and she felt the hot caress of his breath on her skin. "Now it's the wolf's turn."

Her breath hitched. She felt his cock against her ass.

"Lean forward more," he told her.

She leaned forward. His hand slid around her body and his fingers stroked her breast. She arched into his touch, wanting so much more.

"Spread your legs."

She did.

"Wider."

She loved the dark rumble of his voice. Her gaze was on the mirror. On him, on *them,* as he leaned over her.

His hand slid down her body, moving to her sex.

"So ready, soft and slick." His breath feathered over her once more. "Do you know…what it means when a werewolf marks his lover right…" He kissed the spot where her neck and shoulder met. "Here?"

Jane shook her head. She couldn't look away from their reflection in that glass. He'd bit her there before. Had that been a marking?

"Biting here means the werewolf has his mate. It's a claiming. A marking. One that goes far beneath the skin and straight to the soul."

Jane swallowed. His cock pushed against her. His fingers slid over her clit, stroking her arousal to a fever pitch once again.

"You already have my soul, Jane." He pressed a kiss to her skin even as his fingers kept stroking, harder now, and Jane rose onto her tip-toes with a gasp. Another climax was building, so close. So—

"You have my soul, my heart, and every fucking bit of darkness in me." He nipped her. Not a vampire bite. Different. Rougher. A flash of quick pain caught her off-guard. Her eyes widened in shock as she stared at his reflection.

His head lifted and he stared at her in the mirror. A smile—slightly cruel and wolfish—curled his lips. "Can you handle me? *All* of me?"

Before she could answer, his hand slid away from her clit. She was left on the edge of her orgasm, every muscle in her body tight and quivering. "Aidan!"

He lifted up her hips and he drove his cock into her sex, plunged balls deep. Her hands fisted over the bar top. "Can you?" Aidan demanded, voice nearly that of a stranger. Too rough.

She kept staring into the mirror. Staring at him. "I can…" Her breath panted. "I can handle everything you've got."

He smiled.

Then he bit her. No, *marked* her. Because this bite was different. His teeth clamped over the curve of her shoulder as he withdrew, then thrust deep. He took her frantically, driving fast over and over, and Jane wasn't on the edge of her orgasm any longer. The climax slammed into her, rolling through her whole body and she shuddered again and again.

Her sex contracted around his cock, but he didn't come, didn't slow, didn't stop. If anything, his thrusts became harder. He was growling behind her, rough, animalistic sounds. And when his hands slapped down on the bar near hers—when he caged her there with his body—she saw his claws.

The beast was out. And he was claiming his mate.

Only fair. I'm claiming him, too.

Her hands grabbed his. Locked with his. And Jane was stunned to see claws burst from the tips of her fingers. "Aidan!"

He slammed into her, lifting her up with the force of his thrusts. Her orgasm kept sweeping through her, and every thrust just had the pleasure surging hotter. Her body was so sensitive now, so completely tuned to his.

They were moving together, a rhythm that was too wild and fast but somehow seemed utterly perfect. She wanted that moment to last forever, for the pleasure to never end, but Aidan plunged into her once more, a thrust that took her completely off her feet, and then he roared her name as he came.

This climax hit her harder, sharper, and Jane gasped as her body fell forward. Her head sagged and her drumming heartbeat echoed around her.

She licked her lips, swallowed twice, and finally managed to say, "Aidan?"

He nuzzled her neck.

She stared at their hands. Her claws were gone, his weren't.

"I love you, Jane." His voice was still rough, slightly ragged at the edges. But it was definitely the voice of a man, not a beast. "Whatever happens, whatever comes…remember that."

She lifted their entwined fingers to her mouth and pressed a kiss to the back of his hand. "I love you." She didn't like those "whatever happens" sort of talks. They usually meant bad things were coming.

Something so bad that it would tear them apart. Her eyes squeezed shut, as if she could hide from the truth, for just a moment. "Nothing bad is going to happen." The words slipped from her, almost like a child, trying to fight the dark.

A low laugh rumbled from him. "Oh, sweetheart, don't you see? I am the bad thing."

Ice brushed across her heart.

***

Annette sat on the old, dusty floor. Paris was just a few feet away from her, sleeping now, but still chained. Bags of blood—Aidan's blood—were in the ice chest at her side.

"Uh, Ms. Benoit?" Garrison shifted nervously from foot to foot. "What else can I do to help?"

She glanced at him. "You didn't attack Paris when you arrived. I figure that's more than enough help." And he'd brought the blood back. A definite good deed that she would see he was rewarded for completing. The redheaded wolf had just found his way to her good side, though most folks swore she didn't actually *have* a good side.

She did. It was just well hidden most days.

"I don't…I don't want to attack him."

His words made her head jerk toward him. Garrison rubbed his throat. "His scent…it's been changing since I got here. He doesn't smell like other vamps anymore."

That was good, wasn't it? A sign that Aidan's alpha blood might be helping Paris? "What does he smell like?" Because she had no clue. All she could smell right then was the scents of blood and mildew.

Garrison inched a bit closer. Did he know that she had a gun loaded with silver bullets in her bag? If he was lying to her and the guy was about to go for Paris's throat, she *would* be stopping him.

No one was going to take Paris away.

The force of her attachment to Paris was…frightening.

"He smells…like Paris."

Her brows rose.

"The scent of the wolf is there," Garrison mumbled, frowning. "Woodsy, wild. There's another scent clinging to him, now, too, though." He inhaled deeply. "Apples." He shook his head. "Jane always smells like apples. And lavender."

Annette stiffened. *Jane always smells like apples.* She shoved her hand into her bag and brought up her knife.

"Wh-what are you doing?" Garrison stammered. "And what the hell all do you have in that bag?"

Everything I need. Paris was out cold, so she grabbed his wrist and sliced him.

"Stop!" Garrison shot toward her. He caught her hand and pulled her away from Paris. "Don't you hurt him!"

She wasn't going to hurt him, not anymore. "I got what I needed."

"For him to bleed?" Garrison's cheeks were nearly as red as his hair.

"Yes," Annette said simply. Then she handed him the knife. "Take this to the ME, Dr. Bob Heider. Make him run his tests on the blood. Tell him I know he ran a test when Paris first woke, but he needs to examine *this* sample." Because if Paris's scent was changing, then maybe other things were, too. She thought quickly, then said, "Get him to compare this blood to Jane's." Because she knew he kept samples of Jane's blood on hand.

Jane's blood.
Aidan's blood.

Carefully, Garrison took the knife from her. "Shouldn't I like…bag this or something?"

Annette rolled her eyes. "This isn't a crime show, wolf. I don't have freaking plastic bags on me." They weren't included in the *everything* she had contained in her oversized purse. The purse was for her weapons and her magic. She generally left science to others. "Just be careful with the knife. Move as fast as you can and get that blood to Dr. Heider."

Garrison nodded and made his way to the door, moving with slow, mincing steps.

Her breath huffed out. "You can go a bit faster than that!" Her gaze stayed locked on him until he left the back room and then...

Awareness slowly edged up her spine. Her gaze slid back to Paris. A very *awake* Paris.

Oh, damn. Annette glanced at the floor. The line of dirt still circled him. Good. She would just make absolutely sure not to pass that line again. *When I sliced his hand, I passed it. Foolish mistake.* But she'd had to know...

His nostrils flared and his gaze slowly slipped over her face. When his lips parted, she caught sight of his fangs.

"Don't even think about it," Annette whispered. "I'm not on your menu."

But he smiled at her. "Love, you *are* the menu." Then he leapt to his feet and charged right at her. The chain that fed into the top of the wall broke—the stupid chain that had been manacling both his wrists—as he lunged to attack. *So much for the new chain Vincent had brought to use.*

In the face of Paris's attack, Annette didn't move. She didn't flinch. She didn't back away. She waited.

Paris slammed into the invisible force field created by the dirt of the dead and by her power. He howled. The sound was very, very wolf-like. *So his beast is still there. Good to know.* She'd been afraid that his wolf was dead.

Not so.

"What…is…happening?" Paris yelled. He shoved his hand against a wall that was there — one he couldn't see.

"You're being restrained," Annette told him simply. "Until you're more…yourself."

He snarled.

She picked up a bag of blood and tossed it to him. The blood sailed right over the line of dirt. "Drink up," Annette urged him. "Because I need *my* Paris back."

Greedily, he grabbed the bag. He tore into it with those razor sharp teeth and started to guzzle the blood. He guzzled and guzzled and… "Don't watch me," Paris whispered.

She stiffened.

His gaze held hers. "It…shames me."

That *was* her Paris talking. He was coming back. Bit by bit. "You don't need to be ashamed with me." She reached for another bag and tossed it toward him.

He caught it. Still stared at her.

"It's going to be okay," Annette whispered to him.

But Paris gave a sad shake of his head. "No…now I'll never be good…enough for you."

Her heart *hurt.* "You are good enough. Monster or man, it doesn't matter to me." It had never mattered. "But next time, don't be so slow making your move, got it? You want something, you want *someone,* you act." Because life was too fragile. Too quick. And even her magic couldn't stop all the bad things in the world. "Paris…" Annette sighed his name. "I won't let you go." That was *her* shame. That she needed him so much, that she'd come to care for him so much, that she would make any deal, use any dark trick, to keep him with her. *I won't lose you to death.*

No matter what it took.

***

Garrison rushed into the ME's new lab, and when the doc saw him—

Dr. Heider jumped to his feet and put his hands into the air. "Don't hurt me!"

Garrison frowned at the guy, but then he realized Heider was staring at the bloody knife he gripped in his hand. Humans. "The voodoo queen told me to bring you this." He dropped the knife onto the doc's desk. "It's got Paris's blood on it, and she wanted you to test it."

Heider inched closer to the knife. "Test it? I ran exams on Paris's blood earlier. The results were clear…the guy's a vamp."

Garrison's jaw hardened. "Run new tests. Using *this* sample."

"It's probably contaminated to hell and back." Heider sniffed. "I mean, you were just running around town with the sample…"

Garrison growled. He might not be an alpha, but he was still a wolf. "Run the tests."

"Right, tests." Heider nodded. "But it's not like the results will change. Not like someone can go *back* from being a vamp." Hider pulled on a pair of gloves.

"Annette also said…" Garrison cleared his throat. "She wants you to compare the results to Jane's blood."

Heider hesitated. "Got to say, at this point, I'm surprised Paris actually still *has* a head. I would've thought the guy would be well on his way to the afterlife by now."

Garrison growled once more. "Careful, doc. That's my pack member you're talking about. But, yeah, he's still got his head." And Garrison wanted the guy to *keep* it. He liked Paris. Paris was his friend, and Garrison didn't have enough of those.

Heider's gloved fingers gingerly picked up the knife. "A vampire killed your family," he said as he turned away from Garrison. "Shouldn't you hate them all?"

"I *do* hate the vamp who took my parents." Rage would always twist in him when he thought of that bastard. "But that guy is nothing but ash now. He can't hurt anyone."

Heider was taking some samples from the knife.

"I don't hate all vamps." The words just seemed to slip from Garrison. "I don't hate Jane." He couldn't hate her. As for Paris…"Like I told you, Paris is pack."

Heider was silent as he ran his tests. Garrison just stood there, shifting a bit from foot to foot and glancing at the body bag to his left. Why the hell would anyone want to work with the dead all day?

"You haven't felt the urge to attack Paris?" Heider's voice drifted to him.

Garrison rubbed the back of his neck. "At…at first, I could feel my beast and he *wasn't* happy but…but the more blood that Paris took, the better it got."

Heider glanced up from his microscope. "Blood?"

"Yeah, he's been drinking the bagged blood that Aidan had. I think the alpha's blood is really helping him," Garrison added. "He looks better and he…seems saner."

"Alpha blood." Heider peered back through the lens of his microscope.

"It can cure anything," Garrison murmured.

But Heider stiffened. "No, it can't cure *anything.*" He looked over at Garrison. "Where is Jane now?"

"With Aidan."

"Of course, she is. Because Jane doesn't see the danger with him. She thinks she can trust him…" Heider made a long *hmmmp* sound. "Will she still be trusting him when he tries to rip out *her* throat?"

"That's not going to happen!" Garrison glared at the guy. "Aidan loves her." He'd seen the way his alpha looked at Jane.

"Love and obsession can often be confused, especially by someone like Aidan."

The doc was pissing him off. Garrison's hands fisted and he took a menacing step toward Heider.

"Easy, wolf," Heider spoke quickly. "I'm not the enemy."

"Then who the hell is?" Garrison demanded. "I need to know. We all need to know exactly who we're facing." So they could take the bastard out. He advanced on the doc. "What do you see in his blood? Can you figure out which vamp it was that changed him?"

He saw the doc's Adam's apple bob. "Yes, I think I've figured that part out."

Garrison waited.

The doc didn't say more. He did pull out more slides and put them under his microscope.

"Uh, want to clue me in? Who's the enemy?" Who did Garrison need to kill? Because he was more than ready to fight in order to protect his friends.

Dr. Bob took off his glasses and set them — very carefully — on the table. "Jane." His voice was soft, and his expression had turned ashen. "It's...Jane." He stared at Garrison in growing alarm. "I think she'll be the end of you all."

CHAPTER ELEVEN

The water poured down on Jane as she stood beneath Aidan's shower. He'd carried her up the club's stairs. A sweet, but totally unnecessary gesture. She hadn't stopped him, though, because if the guy wanted to carry her...

Why not relax and enjoy the ride? He'd been so tender as he eased her into his shower. His hands were careful on her skin. Even now, he stood just behind her, lightly smoothing soap and lather over her arms.

"Did I hurt you?" His voice was quiet.

She smiled as she turned toward him. Her body was slick and her skin slid against his. "Not even a little." But...was that the truth? When he'd marked her, it had stung. A sharp flash of pain that had caught her off-guard. The pain had only lasted a moment, and then there had been so much pleasure.

His hands slid down her arms.

And he stepped away from her.

Jane stayed beneath the warm spray of the shower, watching him as he slipped out and quickly toweled off. He knotted the towel around his waist, and her gaze drank him in. Those wash-board abs, his powerful shoulders.

Sexy. So very sexy.

"I...died in the fire, Jane."

It took a moment for his words to register. She shook her head, and even managed a quick laugh. "No, you didn't. I got you out. I saved you, Aidan."

Steam drifted in the air around her.

And Aidan shook his head, just once. *No.*

The warm water was suddenly chilling her. Jane's hand flew out and she turned off that water. The *drip, drip, drip* that followed seemed way too loud to her sensitive ears. She stepped out of the shower, standing on his lush mat and dripping all over the place, but not really caring about that.

More important things were happening. "I saved you," Jane said again.

He pulled out another towel. Big, fluffy, white. With the same care he'd shown her before—as if he were afraid a touch would bruise her—Aidan carefully dried her skin. Then he wrapped the towel around her body.

"Aidan?" Jane prompted.

His hands fell away from her.

"I burned and I died, Jane." Stark. Cold. "My last thought was of you. I can remember that. The flames were eating my flesh, I hurt so much, and all I wanted…it was just to see you again."

Tears stung her eyes. "You — you were breathing. I got you *out*."

He started to speak, but then stopped. He turned from her and paced to the small closet in the bathroom. He pulled out a pair of faded jeans and yanked them on. Then he jerked a soft, black t-shirt over his head.

Jane stood there, wrapped in the towel, goosebumps covering her skin, and feeling more vulnerable than she'd ever felt before.

Aidan reached for her spare clothes. He offered them to her. "Dress…then we'll talk." His jaw clenched. "It's…too hard to focus when I can see you like this."

Then he turned his back on her and walked away.

Jane stood there a moment. The clothes were on the sink near her. And all she could hear was…

I died.

She dressed with shaking hands and hurried out of the bathroom. Aidan was standing in front of his desk, with his back to her. She wanted to run to him and wrap her arms around him, but something held her back.

That something? It was fear. Plain old fear.

"I was changing before the fire," Aidan spoke without looking at her. He was running his fingers over the top of his desk, as if tracing something there. "I knew it. I started to crave blood and…my instincts changed."

His instincts. "You mean the urge to kill every vamp on sight?"

Finally, he looked back. "Yes." There was a pause. "And the blood that I craved the most? Jane, it was *your* blood." He swallowed. "And I still crave it." The words seemed to be a warning.

She wasn't in the mood for warnings. She moved closer to him.

"I died in that fire. You were my last thought. But…I came back."

"Vamps don't rise that fast," she whispered. *He'd died violently, with a vampire's blood in his system. Okay, yes, technically, that might make him change but —* "Werewolves aren't supposed to become vampires."

"I did. Paris did. I think we can just screw that 'supposed to' shit straight to hell."

Jane flinched.

"I came back. I woke up burning and I woke up…" His gaze slid down to her neck. "Hungry."

She had to touch him. Jane's hand pressed right over his heart. "You woke up as *you*. You came back totally —"

"Vivian had seen to it that I was given blood before I even opened my eyes, Jane. Plenty of it. Vivian wanted to make sure I was strong so she did what she thought was best. She didn't even realize that she was strengthening a vampire, but that was what she did. *That's* how I held onto my control. But my control is getting weaker. There's a darkness growing in me, and I feel it becoming stronger every single second."

His heart thundered — too fast — beneath her touch.

"I'm worried about what I'm going to do."

"You aren't going to *do* anything wrong!"

He smiled at her. "The wolf in me didn't stay dead, Jane. It came back, too. A wolf and a vampire living in one body…and they're trying to tear me apart."

Her breath seemed to freeze in her lungs.

"I'm afraid I'll hurt you," Aidan said.

"You won't."

But his hand slid over her neck, moving down to brush over the mark he'd left on her. The mark that, even with her new healing powers, hadn't faded. "I already did."

"Aidan…"

"You are mine, Jane. And I can't let you go."

Had she *asked* to be let go?

"I worry about what I'll do…when you finally run from me."

That — that was crazy. "Do I look like I'm running?"

"Not yet."

But you will. She could practically hear those words whispering in the air between them.

"No," Jane fired back. "I'm not going to—"

The phone rang, shrilling loudly on Aidan's desk. He glanced at it, his eyes narrowing, and she thought he'd ignore the call because, you know, they were in the middle of important shit. But then he reached for the phone. "Locke," he growled.

Jane could hear the caller all too clearly. It was Vivian, and she said, "Aidan, I've got one of the EMTs, Sharon Lawson. She swears that Paris was alive when she first brought him in her ambulance, but something happened…she blacked out for a moment and when she woke up, he was dead. His neck was broken and Sharon is swearing to me that wasn't the case before she passed out."

Fury darkened his face. "Why the fuck didn't she say something to someone before?"

"Because she's a human," Vivian said, her voice soft. "And she's terrified. She has vague memories of a man climbing into the back of the ambulance with her, but considering that her patient died on her…Sharon is blaming herself. I found her in a damn bar, just down from you on Bourbon Street. She's trying to drink herself into oblivion."

"Drag her ass out of oblivion and get her here. I'll make her remember."

"On the way, alpha," Vivian responded. The phone clicked when she hung up.

Aidan slanted a fast glance at Jane.

"We aren't done with our conversation," she warned him.

"What more do you want me to say?" His smile was bitter. "I'm losing myself. I can fucking feel it. I'm drowning, and I'm afraid I'll pull you under with me."

"I'm not afraid of sinking."

His hand slid over her cheek. "I think I should tell you to run, while I still have some control. This beast that I've become…it wants you something fierce. Vamp and werewolf…a fucking abomination."

She caught his hand and held tight. "Then *I'm* an abomination. You know I have both wolf and vamp running through my blood, too. But I'm not going crazy. I'm not turning psycho and attacking everyone in sight. You won't do it, either! I know that you won't—"

"I wasn't born to be a vampire, Jane. You were." His expression was tormented. "Right the fuck now, I want to sink my fangs into you. I want that sweet blood of yours on my tongue, and I want my cock in you. I have a hunger for you that's not ending. It's getting stronger and deeper with every moment that passes."

"You think I don't want you just as much?" She remembered the wild need that had burned to life inside of her when he'd taken her blood. "Because to be clear, I do, Aidan. I do."

"You don't understand." The lines near his mouth deepened. "You aren't seeing the danger."

"Because it's you!" Jane nearly yelled. "There isn't any danger for me when I'm with you! Don't you get that, Aidan? You're my safe zone. My anchor. I'm not afraid when I'm with you." She stared into his eyes, needing him to understand this. Needing it to go bone deep. "I *won't* be afraid when I'm with you."

He gazed back at her.

Jane exhaled and turned away from him. "Let's go downstairs. I want to hear what that EMT has to say, too, and—"

"You will be afraid of me, Jane." His voice came out low, without any emotion. "Before I'm done, I'll terrify you."

***

Vivian dragged the blonde with her as they hurried down Bourbon Street. The woman was still clutching a hurricane in her hand, and her steps were weaving as she struggled to keep up with Vivian and not spill her precious drink.

"I want to go back!" Sharon called. "I need more drinks!"

Vivian rolled her eyes. "You need to get your ass sober, woman." She got it—she did. Sharon had been crying into her hurricane when she arrived. Sharon was convinced that she'd done something to cause Paris's death. *Like there isn't already enough guilt going around on that one.*

"I'm going to lose my job," Sharon mumbled. "When my boss learns that I passed out on a patient…he'll think I was drinking on the job."

"Yes, well, the fact that you've been chugging drinks all morning isn't going to help that case out any," Vivian retorted. She could see Hell's Gate up ahead. Good. Now to get Sharon inside and let Aidan work his magic.

"I wasn't drinking." Sharon jerked to a stop.

A stop? Now? When they were so close?

Sharon stared down at the drink in her hand. "I was trying to save him. I wanted to help. But when I-I opened my eyes…I was lying on top of him. My hands were at his throat. And his neck…it was broken."

Vivian snatched the drink from Sharon's hand. "I don't think you're strong enough to snap a man's neck."

Sharon blinked at her. "I…I lied." A stark whisper.

Does the woman even realize she's talking to a police captain? Vivian had identified herself earlier but…

"I told everyone on scene that he'd broken his neck during the fall. He didn't. It happened *in* my ambulance. It must have been me." She shuddered. "It was me. Me, *me* — "

"Stop that shit," Vivian ordered flatly. They'd already been through this guilt routine at the bar.

Sharon stopped. She blinked at Vivian.

"You want to know what happened in that ambulance? Then you come with me, right the hell now." She'd questioned Sharon for a while before and gotten the woman to mumble an admission about the man who'd appeared in the ambulance, then Sharon had clammed up. *Aidan will take care of that situation.*

"H-how can you find out the truth?"

"I have a friend who can help you remember what went down. Remembering things like that, well, it's his specialty."

Hope flashed in Sharon's gaze. "You mean it? He…he sounds like some kind of amazing friend."

Vivian steered her toward Hell's Gate. "Oh, yes," she murmured. "Trust me, he is." *Aidan's the kind of friend you don't want to piss off.*

***

Roth Sly stumbled into his apartment, and the soft footsteps of his guest followed him right inside.

"You were hired to follow Jane," the guy groused. "What the hell kind of screw-up are you pulling? If you can't do the work, I can sure as hell pay someone else for the job."

Jane.

Roth glanced to the right, to the images that he had pinned to his cork bulletin board. Shots of Mary Jane Hart were up there. Mary Jane with her gun drawn as she faced a thief. Mary Jane as she prowled through a cemetery. Mary Jane as she stood outside of Hell's Gate with that big, dangerous bastard Aidan Locke at her side.

Roth quickly glanced away from those photos even as he edged closer to the bulletin board. Without looking directly at the image of Jane again—for some reason, he just didn't want to do that—he reached out and grabbed the photos. He tossed them into the trash.

"What the actual fuck are you doing?" The man who'd followed him home demanded.

Before Roth could speak, the fellow had grabbed him and shoved him against the wall. The guy held him there, far too easily. And Roth found that he didn't want to look the fellow in the eyes, not directly.

Because…

Because I know he's not human, no matter what he might want me to think.

"You let Aidan Locke get to you," the man snarled. "I *told* you he was dangerous. That you could *never* get fucking close to him. I gave you the lotion to use in order to hide your scent from him. He wouldn't have known you were ever close…"

Roth hadn't wanted to talk to the guy at the coffee shop, and, honestly, he'd been kind of dazed when he first walked in the place. It had taken him a few moments to even recognize his employer of the last year.

The last year.

Yeah, he'd met the secretive asshole a long time ago, long before he'd ever encountered Mary Jane for the first time. The sly bastard had offered him one thousand dollars a week to watch her.

A thousand dollars? When he'd barely been bringing in anything with his art work? Hell, yes, Roth had jumped at the chance. Especially since Jane was just the type of pretty brunette he liked to watch, anyway.

And I'd gotten paid for the gig. I thought it was my lucky fucking day.

He wasn't feeling so lucky any longer.

"Aidan Locke is an alpha werewolf," his boss snapped. "He can play with your head and you wouldn't even know it."

Actually, he *did* know it. His temples were throbbing. Nausea rolled in his stomach.

"What did you tell him about me?"

"N-nothing," Roth said. That was the truth, he hoped. He hadn't told the guy anything about his boss. At least, he didn't think he had. The whole scene was kind of blurry in his mind.

"Why don't I believe you?" His boss dropped his hold on Roth and paced away.

Because you're not a very trusting bastard?

"Aidan could have made you forget every single fucking thing you said to him." The boss peered out of the blinds that covered Roth's windows. "He could be hunting me, even now. Dammit, I needed more *time*."

His boss was seriously pissed.

"Aidan won't forget you," his boss said. "He'll start digging into your life. He'll want to learn everything he can about you. And if he digs too hard into your world, he'll find me."

Roth's heartbeat was racing in his chest. The job had taken a far darker turn six months ago, and yeah, the money had increased to go along with the new orders. First his payment had increased to five grand a week, then to ten grand recently, and the money had been so good that he hadn't cared that some people were getting hurt.

When you went so long without money, getting it…well, it could change a man.

The boss's rage wasn't a good thing. It was very, very bad, and Roth tried to defuse the situation before it headed to hell. "I gave the other wolf the blood!" Roth said quickly. "Just like you said to do!"

"At least you did something right." A dark mutter.

Roth notched up his chin. "More than just something. I've been doing *exactly* what you told me, all along." Maybe the boss needed a reminder. "I-I broke into the ME's lab the night it caught on fire, remember? The night Jane changed? I snuck in there while Jane was still out cold on the ME's slab. Heider had samples of her blood and I took them, without him even noticing me." And one of those samples had been given to Paris. *See — I was following orders.*

"Yes," the man acknowledged. "That night, you did very, very well."

Roth blew out a low breath. *Damn straight, I did well.* "And when I gave it to the other wolf, to Paris, I was doing *exactly* what you wanted. I've always done what you wanted."

This time, a soft smile flickered over his boss's face. "You have."

Roth began to relax. This was good. He was going to be okay. "I've done all the tests, monitored Jane's progress exactly as you wanted." Hell, maybe by the time he was done talking, the boss would even give him a raise. "Look, I won't make the mistake of getting near Aidan Locke again, okay?" It had just been a screw-up that night. He'd taken pictures when he shouldn't have lingered. "I'll keep doing my job and no one will know what's happening."

His boss nodded as he came closer. "It is important for no one to understand what's happening. At least, not yet."

"I won't breathe a word—"

The boss's hand flew out and locked around Roth's throat. "I know you won't. After all, it's incredibly hard for the dead to speak."

Roth tried to fight him but…but the bastard was so much stronger than he appeared. He clawed at the guy's hold, twisting and kicking and—

"Thanks for all the hard work," his boss whispered. "Now consider yourself fired."

CHAPTER TWELVE

The big door at Hell's Gate swung open, and Jane glanced over at the entrance. Captain Harris walked in first, and her expression was grimly determined. She came in with her hand locked around the wrist of another woman, a blonde with a short, pixie hair-cut and mascara stained eyes.

"Aidan, Jane," Vivian murmured in acknowledgement. She shut the door behind her and her guest. "Meet Sharon Lawson, the EMT who was working on Paris the night he died."

Aidan was sitting at a table in the middle of the club. Jane stood at his side. As Vivian and Sharon approached, Jane could practically smell the human's fear. Sharon's gaze darted all around the club's interior. "Sh-shouldn't more people be here?" Sharon asked. "I mean, I know it's early but the other bars on Bourbon Street are already—"

"We're closed," Aidan murmured. "The bouncer I have out front won't let anyone inside, not without my approval."

Sharon licked her lips. "Are you the 'friend' that is supposed to help me remember?"

"I am." His hands were flat on the table. His claws weren't out. Jane figured that was a good thing. She was standing and not sitting because...

Because I feel like I need to keep a close eye on him. She *wasn't* scared of Aidan, but she also wasn't sure just how smoothly this little meeting would go.

She wanted to make sure he didn't cross any lines and, oh, say...hurt a human.

"Come closer," Aidan ordered.

Sharon looked as if closer was the last place she wanted to go, but when Vivian nudged her, she edged a few steps toward Aidan.

"Have a seat." Aidan's voice was calm. That eerie kind of calm that came right before a storm.

Sharon slumped into the chair across from him.

"Vivian told me," he began, body relaxed, "that you don't remember exactly what happened on the ambulance."

Sharon twisted her hands on the table top. "One minute, my patient was alive. The next..." She swallowed. "I was lying sprawled on his chest and my hands were around his neck. I don't remember hurting him, I swear, I—"

Aidan caught her hands. He stared at them, then he looked up at her. "You will remember."

"Wh-what?"

A shiver slid down Jane's spine. His voice wasn't so calm now. Now…he was more like the storm.

"You will remember what happened on that ambulance. You will tell me exactly what happened to Paris. Every detail. See it in your head right now. Tell it to me."

Sharon's hazel eyes seemed to glaze over.

Jane looked at Vivian. Vivian's focus was on Sharon.

This always makes me so damn uncomfortable. The idea that Aidan could force his way into someone's mind. That he could control that person completely…

I'm glad he couldn't control me. She never wanted to give up that kind of power to someone else.

"I was working on the patient," Sharon said, her unfocused stare seeming to see her past. "He was breathing. His vitals weren't the best, but I knew he was going to make it. How incredible. I'd just seen him fall from that second story window, but he was going to *survive.* Other people were still in the building and I had to work on him alone because my partner was needed to tend to the other victims. But then…" A furrow appeared between her brows. "A firefighter came to help me."

Aidan's head tilted toward her. "A firefighter?"

"Yes, he said he had training, that he could help." She gave a hard, negative shake of her head. "I told him I had the patient, I could take care of him, but…" Her hand lifted to her neck. She stopped talking, just touched her neck.

"Tell me what happened next," Aidan said.

Her eyes had gone wide. "He pulled out a needle and shoved it into my neck." Her fingers were rubbing along the side of her neck. "I couldn't even speak! Everything went dark. When I woke up, I was on top of the patient. His neck was broken."

"And I'm guessing the firefighter was long gone," Jane said, unable to stay silent any longer.

Sharon nodded.

"What did he look like?" Jane was betting the guy had been no real firefighter. Like her, he'd probably just taken a uniform so that he could hide in plain sight.

Was he watching me that night? Did he see me do the same thing?

Sharon frowned, but didn't answer Jane's question.

Jane sighed. "Aidan, keep doing your thing." She glanced down at him and saw — his claws were coming out. Crap.

"Describe the man," Aidan instructed flatly.

Sharon nodded. "Big. Wide shoulders. Tall…over six feet, I-I think. He had on his helmet when he came inside the ambulance but…but when he brought that needle toward me, I saw his wrist. H-he had tattoos there."

Jane stiffened. Tattoos?

"See the tattoos in your mind," Aidan said. "Tell me *exactly* what they looked like."

"A raven." Sharon's voice had gone breathless. "He had a raven flying on the inside of his wrist and a snake was reaching up to bite it."

Jane took a step back.

Roth? They'd *had* the bastard. They'd had him, and they'd just let him go.

Sharon's chair scraped across the floor as she shot to her feet. "That guy — he killed my patient, didn't he?"

Killed him…transformed him into a vampire. Same thing, mostly.

"Who is he?" Sharon demanded. Her frantic gaze flew to Vivian. "The cops have to find him! You have to arrest him! You have to — "

Vivian put her hand on the woman's shoulder. "Don't worry. We'll take care of him." Her gaze slid back to Aidan. "Won't we?"

He was already rising to his feet. "Hell the fuck yes, we will." He stalked around the table toward Sharon. He paused, staring into her eyes. "You never saw me today. You never came to Hell's Gate. The patient's death wasn't your fault and you know that. So go back to your life. Go back."

And forget the monsters in the dark. Jane bit her lip so that she wouldn't say those words.

A few moments later, Sharon walked out of Hell's Gate. Aidan watched her go, his clawed hands hidden behind his back.

Jane was on the phone, calling in favors at the PD and getting Roth's address. *Roth Sly.* The sonofabitch. Was he already in the wind? Running hard and fast?

The dispatcher came back and rattled off his current address to Jane. She thanked him, then hung up the phone. She looked over and saw that Aidan and Vivian were standing nearly toe-to-toe. Uh, oh, that couldn't be good. "Guys?" Jane cleared her throat. "I've got the address. We need go get the hell over there." *Before the guy clears town.* If he hadn't already.

Jane had learned one important lesson that day. Aidan's power had limits. Apparently, he had to be sure and ask the *right* questions. Because otherwise, some jackass like Roth could slip away.

Despite Jane's words, neither Aidan nor Vivian moved. Vivian just kept her stare locked on Aidan as she asked, "Where's Paris?"

"Safe." A clipped, rough answer.

"You're not going to tell me? *Me?*"

Jane paced closer. She grabbed Aidan's arm. "Come on."

But he kept gazing at Vivian. "I can't tell you, not yet."

Vivian's lips pressed together, then, after a tense moment, she said, "What did that bastard do to Paris in the ambulance? Something worse than death…"

Aidan nodded. "Yes, worse." Pain flashed on his face. "But I'm trying to bring Paris back. I just need more time. And I can't risk more pack members finding out just yet."

Vivian stumbled back, as if she'd just been stabbed. "You don't trust me?"

"You need deniability, Viv. Because if I go down, you're the only one who can keep this pack together. They have to trust *you*."

She held up her hands, palms out. "I'm no alpha."

"No, but you're the fucking closest thing, and they need you." He inclined his head toward her. "I will handle this." Then he looked at Jane. "I should have killed that bastard earlier."

Killing Roth wasn't the answer—they needed to question the guy. Find out what he'd given to Paris. Why. This time, they'd ask the right questions. She knew Aidan had gotten sidetracked earlier…*because of me.* His feelings for her had gotten in the way, and, dammit, *she* should have been the one to push for a deeper truth from Roth.

Instead, she'd been focused on making sure Aidan's control didn't explode.

Jane and Aidan hurried for the door but...Vivian snagged Jane's wrist, stopping her before she could leave Hell's Gate. Aidan strode outside, and she heard him talking to the bouncer/guard who was on duty out there. Jane had caught a glimpse of the guy when she and Aidan first arrived. Troy. Tall, muscled, a strong, fierce wolf with multi-colored eyes. She knew his job was to make sure humans received the message that Hell's Gate was closed — closed to all but a select few for the time being.

"What's wrong with Aidan?" Vivian asked, her voice hushed.

Jane's shoulders tensed.

"You think I can't see that something is going on? Jane...what is happening?"

She stared into Vivian's eyes. She wanted to tell her but...

"Jane."

Her head snapped toward the door. Aidan was back. He lifted his hand, offering her his palm. "We need to hunt."

Jane pulled away from Vivian.

"Watch out for him," Vivian whispered.

Jane's hand curled around Aidan's. Was the captain asking her to watch Aidan's back? Or was she telling Jane...

Watch out for Aidan's attack?

They walked outside and Sharon had been right, the rest of Bourbon Street was busy while Hell's Gate was absolutely dead.

When Aidan gave an order, it was followed. The nearby guard gave her a brief nod. She inclined her head toward him.

A wild, woodsy scent teased her nose — a scent *not* coming from the werewolf guard Troy — and she heard the rush of footsteps coming toward her.

"Aidan!"

They turned together and she saw Garrison frantically waving at them as he ran down Bourbon Street. He shoved people out of his way, muttering apologies as he went. "Aidan, I know what happened to Paris!"

So did they. Or rather, they knew *who* had happened to Paris.

Then Garrison was in front of them, breathing heavily, his cheeks flushed. "Annette…she gave me Paris's blood."

Aidan grabbed the guy and pushed him against the wall of Hell's Gate, moving them away from the humans who were eager for their drinks and parties as they strolled down Bourbon Street.

"She wanted me to take the blood to Dr. Heider and get him to run his tests." Garrison's words tumbled out so fast that Jane had to strain to understand him.

"Slow down, Garrison," she urged him. *So I can figure out what's going on.*

His gaze snapped toward her. "It was you."

Jane's brows shot up. "What?"

"Your blood and Paris's blood…the doc said they're showing the same characteristics. The blood that Paris was given was *yours.* That's why he changed. He had your blood in him when he died."

She could feel Aidan's stare on her. She looked at him and sure enough, that glittering blue gaze had locked on her. "I didn't give it to him," Jane said.

"I know," he gritted out. "Roth fucking did."

But where had Roth gotten her blood? And why had he given it to Paris?

Aidan rolled back his shoulders. "Garrison, go back to Annette and Paris. Stay there until you hear from me."

Garrison nodded. "Right. But, um, what am I supposed to do there?"

"Keep them both alive. If anyone comes gunning for Paris, you take them the fuck out, got it?"

The bright color faded from Garrison's cheeks. He stared at Aidan, and suddenly, the guy didn't look so young. "I got it, alpha. I got it."

***

He hadn't asked the right questions. That alone told Aidan just how far gone he was. Days ago, he never would have made a mistake like that. His mind was in damn chaos, and he'd screwed up.

And I put Jane in danger. I should have eliminated the guy when I had the chance.

Aidan leapt up the steps that would take him to Roth Sly's apartment. Jane was right in front of him, her gun was already in her hand.

He'd had Roth in his grasp, and he'd let the bastard go. *I won't be making the same mistake again.*

Jane thought they were going to interrogate the guy. That Roth would get taken into police custody when they were done with him. Just because he was human, did Jane seriously think Aidan was going to let the fellow live?

He hurt Paris. He's been stalking Jane. That fucker is going down.

They reached the landing. His nostrils twitched and the coppery scent that reached him stirred the vamp within.

Blood. A whole fucking lot of it.

When he heard Jane's sharply indrawn breath, he knew she'd caught the scent, too. They both ran for the apartment door on that second floor — the historic building only had two floors, and the bottom floor was a closed down book store. Aidan beat her to the apartment door and he kicked it in, making the wood splinter. He rushed inside, his claws out, his fangs ready to bite—and then he found his prey.

Roth Sly lay on the floor, a growing pool of blood beneath him. Jane rushed to Roth's side, slipping a bit in the blood. She put her hand to his neck—jeez, the bastard's throat had been cut nearly from ear to ear and the blood was pumping out of him fast.

"He's still alive!" Jane cried. She slapped her hands over his neck, trying to stop that wild flow of blood.

That scent…*So much fucking blood.*

Every muscle in Aidan's body tensed.

"He needs an ambulance!" Jane yelled. "Aidan, we have to get help!"

Help wasn't going to arrive in time for that guy. Aidan saw the truth clear as freaking day. Why didn't Jane see it, too?

"Who did this to you?" Jane leaned over Roth. "Look at me, tell me—"

But Roth was trying to frantically turn his head away from Jane, struggling weakly with his last bit of strength. *Because I told the bastard to not so much as look at her again.* Aidan surged forward even as he tried to stamp down the bloodlust that was rising within him. *Like a damn buffet in here. So much blood.*

His heart drummed in his chest. He bent next to Jane, right in that blood, and put his hands on top of hers. "Who did this?"

Roth's lips parted. He was trying to speak, but no words were coming out. Had his attacker severed his vocal cords?

Shit, shit.

Roth began to jerk beneath his hold. "He *isn't* going to make it, Jane," Aidan snarled. The human was going to die, any moment, unless...

Unless Aidan gave him blood. Alpha blood might just give the guy the strength to hold on a bit longer, but...

I don't know what my blood will do to him. Werewolf and vamp blood...straight to a human? Just what kind of monster would he make then?

"No, Aidan," Jane said as if reading his mind. "It's too risky. We don't know—"

A guttural cry broke through Jane's words. That cry didn't come from Roth—the guy was barely breathing. Instead, that choked cry of fury came from the man who'd just lunged through the broken doorway, a man with dark hair and eyes too much like Jane's.

Drew Hart had joined their little party. The bastard lifted his hand and Aidan saw the glint of the knife he held. "Found you," Drew shouted as he stared at Aidan. "Now I *end* you." He charged across the room, barreling straight for Aidan with that knife gripped tightly in his hand. Aidan was willing to bet the weapon was made of silver.

Jane leapt to her feet. "Drew, stop!" She ran at him.

Oh, the hell, no. Aidan had played this scene once before. It hadn't ended well, and he would *not* be repeating that nightmare. He grabbed Jane's arm and yanked her behind him even as Drew sliced down with the knife.

The knife slammed straight into Aidan's heart. And it burned. Smoke rose from Aidan's chest. *Right, knew it was fucking silver.*

Drew laughed. "I…just had to wait for my moment…when you were distracted…*got you, got…*"

"Aidan?" Jane's voice was broken.

He looked down at the knife in his chest. "Silver."

"Right, you bastard!" Drew yelled, spittle flying from his mouth. "It's—"

Aidan yanked out the knife. More smoke drifted up from the blade. "Stung," he allowed. "But it sure as shit didn't end me."

Drew's eyes widened in horror. "What? How? No! You're a werewolf! You told me—but I knew before, long before I set foot in this town—I was prepared for you! I was—"

Aidan lunged forward and he shoved that knife right against Drew's throat.

Jane's brother stopped talking. He barely seemed to breathe. The blade was pressed to Drew's skin. It would be so easy to slice that skin right open.

"I'm not just a werewolf any longer." Aidan bared his fangs. "So silver to the heart won't stop me." He considered the matter for a moment. "I'm not sure anything can stop me."

Drew paled.

"But I know how to stop you," Aidan said. And he was going to enjoy this. "I'm going to cut off your head. Cleave it straight from your body, and then you won't ever hurt me or what's *mine* again."

"Aidan…" Jane's voice. Still lost. Still…stunned. "Aidan, I—"

He didn't look back at her. He didn't hear Roth's wheezes any longer and he knew the bastard was gone. His gaze slid to the left. To the photos on the wall. Photos of *his* Jane, though some of the images had been ripped down. "What did you do?" Aidan asked Drew. "Kill the bastard and then just lie in wait for us?"

Roth had been the bait. And Drew—

"Mary Jane!" Drew cried out. "He's a fucking beast! Stop him! He's going to *kill* me!"

Jane's fingers curled around Aidan's shoulders.

"I'm your family!" Drew's voice was breaking. "I just…I wanted to help you! *I was protecting you! Always!*"

"No, you dumbass. You were the one killing her." Aidan let the knife's blade cut into Drew's skin and blood began to trickle down Drew's throat. "You killed her and you killed Paris."

Drew shook his head and that rough movement just made the knife slice deeper. "Paris? Like, Paris, France?"

"Like my *friend* Paris." The scent of the blood was getting to him. Bloodlust and rage were combining within him. *Why slice his throat? I can drain the bastard dry. I can make him beg for death. I can rip his world apart with one bite.*

"I don't know any Paris!" Drew yelled.

"You were working with Roth, weren't you?" Aidan snapped his teeth together. "And what…Paris was just in the fucking way? A distraction that you needed to make?"

Drew kicked him and raked his fingers over Aidan's face, drawing blood.

Aidan dropped the knife. It clattered to the floor.

Drew blinked, looked at the knife, then back at Aidan. "You—"

Aidan lifted his claws. "I don't need the knife." He would take the man's head all too easily without that weapon. His claws drove right for Drew's throat.

"*No!*" Jane threw her body into Aidan's, shoving him away so that his claws just raked over Drew, slicing deep into his jaw and neck.

Drew screamed in agony.

Jane and Aidan hit the floor. He roared as he pushed her to the side and leapt to his feet. *My prey. My fucking prey.*

"Aidan, stop." Jane had jumped to her feet, too. She stood in his path. Drew was running for the door and Jane was shielding that bastard. "Aidan…"

"*He dies.*"

That she would dare to stand there and protect Drew Hart…after all he'd done. *Jane's life. Her blood on the ground. And the fucker just went for my heart.*

The control he'd tried so hard to hold ripped away in that moment. The fire of his shift swept through him only…

Aidan didn't shift, not completely. His muscles seemed to double in size. His claws grew longer, darker, harder, and his fangs sharpened even more in his mouth. He let out a guttural roar.

Jane stepped back. "Aidan?"

Nothing stops me.

"Aidan, stop!" Jane grabbed his arm. "Something is wrong. You're not—"

He yanked her close. His fangs went for her neck.

"Aidan?" Now her voice was soft, scared.

Apples and lavender wrapped around him. *Jane. My Jane.* And his fangs were raking at her throat. He was about to savage her.

My Jane.

He tore from her and rushed for the door.

His prey was already on the stairs. Did Drew think he was going to get away? To have the chance to run again and attack Aidan once more? To try and take out Jane?

No. It ends. The end is here.

Aidan was Drew's fucking end.

He grabbed the banister.

Drew was on the ground floor. He'd grabbed the knife, tricky bastard. Like that was going to do him any good.

Aidan leapt over that banister and shot straight down. His feet touched the floor even as Drew yanked open the building's main door.

"Aidan!" Jane's desperate shout followed him. "Aidan, *wait!*"

He wasn't going to wait. He was going to rip Drew Hart apart. Aidan's shirt was stained with blood — his blood — but the wound had already healed. He could feel the tightness of the skin. He'd never healed that quickly. Never had such strength pulsing through his body.

I can do anything. No one will stop me.

He chased Drew outside. There were other humans on the street, but they were far away.

"Help me!" Drew screamed.

The fool was begging for help? After what he'd done?

"Help—"

Aidan grabbed the bastard and hauled him into the alley, then he slammed Drew against the stinking wall there. "No one's going to help you," Aidan told him. "You're going to fucking die right here."

The long slashes he'd made on Drew's jaw and neck dripped blood.

Blood. So much blood.

"She'll hate you!" Drew yelled. "You do this…*you will lose Jane!*"

The fool dared to talk to him about Jane? When Drew had been the one to set this nightmare in motion? Aidan's fangs flew toward Drew's throat.

"Stop." A soft voice. Feminine.

And Aidan found himself freezing. Not because he wanted to stop. Not because he wanted to spare the SOB before him. But because magic held his body immobile.

"He's strong," that same feminine voice said, a bit breathless now. "I can't hold him for long so if you want his prey to live, you'd better do something *now*."

Aidan wanted to look toward that voice, but it was as if his whole body had locked down. His wolf—the beast that hadn't shifted fully before—

was clawing at his insides, desperate to get out. To attack this new threat.

Footsteps rushed toward him and Drew was yanked out of his grasp. Drew was yelling and screaming and —

"Quiet." Not a woman's voice, not this time. A man's voice — deeper and *familiar*.

Using every bit of his strength, Aidan managed to slowly turn his head — a few precious inches — and he saw Vincent Connor with his hands clamped around Drew's shoulders.

"I'm saving your ass," Vincent snapped at the screaming man. "So cut out the damn noise before *I* decide to bite you."

And Jane was right behind him, staring with horror at the scene.

Staring with horror at me.

"I'll take him back to my building," Vincent said.

The old damn BDSM club.

"Don't worry, Jane. I'll keep him alive until you come." Vincent nodded toward Aidan. "Try to calm down your beast. If that's even possible." Disgust beat in his voice. Then, in a flash, he was gone.

And he'd taken Drew with him.

Aidan erupted. "No!" He howled his fury into the night.

"Can't hold him any longer." It was the other woman's voice again. Sounding even weaker. "Never felt power…like his."

And the magical force that had held Aidan in check broke. He lunged forward but Jane grabbed his arms. She put herself right in his path, between him…and the woman with long, pale blonde hair. Blonde hair and green eyes that glittered in the darkness.

"Aidan, calm down."

There was blood on Jane. Roth's blood. The scent just drove him wilder. *No control. No restraint. The darkness is taking over.*

"We have to talk, Aidan," Jane said quickly. "We have to figure things out. We have to—"

"Get. The. Fuck. Away."

Jane's eyes widened. "What?"

"Get the fuck away." His words were guttural. He could barely force them out. The blood scent was driving him crazy. *Get away before I hurt you.* Because he was afraid he'd crossed a line, there was no going back. He was being swallowed by the darkness. Consumed. And…

I like it.

"Aidan, let me help—"

He grabbed her and shoved Jane against the wall of that alley. That filthy, disgusting wall. His fangs snapped down to her throat and hovered there. He wanted to bite her. He wanted her blood, but if he tasted her right then…

Will I stop?

His head slowly lifted. He stared into Jane's eyes and saw her fear. He could smell her fear.

Jane should never fear me. I should be the one who protects her, always. But something was wrong.

He was wrong.

"I'm sorry," he whispered. And then he jerked away from her. He raced toward the entrance of the alley, feeling the shift hit him. The beast hadn't come out before — the vampire within him had dominated up in that apartment — but the wolf was emerging right then, and nothing could stop it. Fur burst along his skin. His bones snapped. He howled at the pain because it was an agony far deeper than he'd felt with a shift before. And when he left that alley…

Aidan wasn't a man any longer.

CHAPTER THIRTEEN

What in the hell just happened? Jane pushed away from the alley's wall, aware that her knees were shaking. Aidan had been going for her throat—and not in the sexy, lover-like way he'd done back at his club.

He'd been out for blood. Hers.

"I'm guessing he isn't always like that." The feminine voice drifted to her, a little weak.

Jane looked at the woman who stood a few feet away. The blonde who'd just appeared with Vincent. The lady was taller than Jane, probably around five foot ten. She wore jeans and a t-shirt, with small, black boots on her feet. She looked utterly normal right then, but Jane knew the woman was packed with magical power. After all, Jane had seen what the blonde did to Aidan.

"No," Jane murmured as she approached the newcomer. "He's not." Her gaze swept over the woman. The blonde wore thick, gold bangle bracelets around her wrists. "You're Vincent's witch."

The woman took a step back. "Is that what I am?"

She was so not in the mood for games. "Lena," Jane snapped out. "Vincent told me your name."

"What else did he tell you?" Now Lena seemed vaguely curious.

"That you were strong." Jane took another step toward her. "That you were the reason the guy can pretty much vanish in an instant, a little trick that I don't know of any other vamp performing."

"Umm…" Lena smoothed back her hair, even though it was already perfectly in place. "He does owe that trick to me."

Jane moved to walk around her, but Lena side-stepped, blocking her path. Jane's brows shot up. *Oh, sister, you do not want to be doing that.*

"You shouldn't go after him right now." Lena's voice had dropped. "He's…he seemed rather dangerous, and I do believe he told you to get the 'fuck away' from him."

"Aidan needs me."

"I think the guy needs a whole lot right now," Lena muttered.

Jane's eyes narrowed on her. "Why didn't you stop him from fleeing?"

"Because the guy is strong — too strong for me to hold for long." But Lena actually seemed...happy...about that fact. "Didn't anticipate that power. Bet Vincent didn't, either."

Jane moved to the left.

The witch moved, too.

"Seriously, get the hell out of my way, *now*," Jane ordered. "I don't want to hurt you."

"And I don't want to be hurt anymore." Sadness flashed on Lena's pretty face. "But we aren't always given options. If you follow Aidan tonight, you will lose him."

"What? Did you look into a scrying mirror and see that?"

"A scrying mirror?" Lena shook her head. "Never used one. I don't see the future, just the present, and I can see that right now...that man is fighting for his sanity. No," she rolled back her shoulders. "I think he's fighting for his soul."

And Jane was just standing in an alley, talking shit with a witch she'd just met. "All the more reason for me to *get to him*."

"If he hurts you, he's lost, and he knows it." Lena's gaze swept over Jane's face. "Go to him now, and he'll cross a line that will send him straight to hell."

Okay, enough of this crap. "Move...or I'll move you." She wasn't afraid of a witch's power.

Lena stared at her a moment longer. "The end, Jane. Do you see? It's all been leading to this moment. For so many centuries, everything has been building up to this."

"To this?" A dark, smelly alley? The lady wasn't moving so Jane just grabbed her—and moved her. "This moment is me choosing to follow Aidan. Me *choosing* Aidan. I know he's suffering, I can see it—"

"The darkness is swallowing him. His two halves…wolf and vampire…they were fighting for supremacy within him. Didn't you *see* that?" Lena demanded.

Jane marched to the edge of the alley. Lena rushed behind her.

"The wolf took over when he left!" Lena's voice was breathless. "The beast doesn't reason. It just reacts. I know, I've seen more than my fair share of alpha werewolves during my time on this earth. But right now, Aidan Locke is like an alpha on serious steroids. Even his mate can't calm the beast in him."

Jane had Aidan's scent, and she knew she could find him, no matter where he'd gone. She looked back at the witch. "Want to bet?" She didn't wait for an answer. She turned to the left, locked on Aidan, and she ran after the man who mattered most to her.

When he'd had her against that wall, it had been as if she were staring into the eyes of a stranger. There had been no tenderness, no love in his blue gaze. Only rage. Bloodlust. He'd looked at her as if *she* were his prey…

And she'd been afraid. Of him. Of what was happening to them both.

There were so many people on the streets. How the hell had they missed a giant black wolf rushing past them? Were the people on Bourbon that drunk already?

Jane's pace quickened as she tried to catch up to him, but even though his scent drifted in the air back to her, Jane couldn't see Aidan.

Maybe no one could see him…maybe he's moving too damn fast for human eyes to notice him. That would explain why the humans weren't screaming in the streets.

An alpha on steroids. That was how the witch had described him.

Oh, shit, but this was going to be one hell of a night. Jane ran forward and she tried not to think about the brother that a vampire had taken away, the brother who wanted her dead.

***

"Why…are you with me?" Paris's voice was a weak rasp.

Annette shrugged. "Someone has to keep you safe."

He laughed. "I'm not…the one in danger." His golden gaze dipped to the line of dirt around him, then back up to her face. "You are. Isn't that why…you have me caged?"

He was making more sense when he talked now. Seeming a bit…saner. That was good. He'd drained more bags of blood and his bloodlust appeared sated, for the moment. She could talk to him again. Talk to Paris.

"I have you caged," her voice was nearly as soft as his, "because if you come for my throat, I'll have to stop you. Kill you. And I don't want to do that."

His lips twisted in a mocking smile, one that flashed his fangs. "Because my life matters to you?"

She wasn't in the mood for mockery. "Yes." A simple, true answer. "You do matter."

He tensed. "Why didn't you tell me that…" His words were growled. "When I was still alive?"

She held his gaze. She'd always thought he had such beautiful eyes. "Because I was waiting on you to make the first move." Waiting on him, while she fell *for* him. Paris Cole. The true blue werewolf. The most loyal of the pack. The man of courage and honor.

The man who'd stolen a voodoo queen's heart without even really trying.

"Too…late for a first move now." His gaze fell from hers and his hands fisted in his lap. When they'd hauled him out of the ME's lab and transported him to that old club, Aidan had made sure the guy was given fresh clothes—jeans and a t-shirt. He looked almost…normal. "The last thing you want is to be tied to whatever the fuck I am."

"No, the last thing I want…" She waited for his gaze to rise and meet hers once more. "The last thing I want is to be in this world without you."

Surprise flashed on his face.

"I've waited a long time for you, Paris. You'd better be worth the wait."

And his eyes seemed to lighten. Some of the terrible tension left his face. He wasn't a blood-crazed monster. He was…Paris. Her Paris. Coming back to her. Fighting his way back and she thought they'd have a chance together, she thought—

Footsteps raced behind her. She grabbed her gun and jumped to her feet. But when she turned around, she saw that the guy who'd been racing toward her was just Garrison. He ran toward her, but his gaze flew around the room, searching for threats.

"Garrison! What's happened?"

Tension rolled off the guy. "Aidan sent me." His eyes were still searching every corner of the room. "I'm here to protect you two."

She laughed.

He glared at her.

"Garrison, trust me, I can protect Paris just fine." She didn't need the junior-wolf taking over the job.

"Alpha's orders." Garrison threw back his shoulders and suddenly didn't look quite so young or reckless. "Paris is my friend, and I will protect him. No one is going to get to him on my watch."

A chill slid over her. "Who's coming to get him?"

But Garrison just locked his jaw. Did that mean he didn't know? Or he wasn't telling her?

"What did you find out about the blood?"

"His blood is the same as Jane's. Doc said the cells had transformed the same way. He thinks…he thinks the blood Paris was given belonged to Jane."

"Someone is making new monsters." The gravel-rough words came from Paris.

Her gaze slid toward him. He lifted his hand, showing the claws that had sprouted from his fingertips. The claws of a werewolf, even though he had the fangs of a vamp. "And I guess I was one of their experiments."

She'd never needed her scrying mirror more. Annette felt as if she were walking blind. Who was the enemy? Where was the threat coming from?

And what was going to happen next?

CHAPTER FOURTEEN

"I need a doctor!"

The scream came from the front of building, jarring Annette. She had been trying to scry in the chunks of glass she had left, but she'd seen *nothing*. Paris had been silent and watchful behind her and Garrison...

He'd been a guard dog. She wasn't even sure how long the guy had been pacing the perimeter around her and the frantic scream had her crashing back to reality.

At that scream, Garrison lunged out of the back room. She rose, about to follow.

"Don't." Paris's rough voice. "Stay with me."

She looked back at him. He still seemed sane, so maybe the blood he'd taken had turned the tide for him. Perhaps it was her imagination, but he just *appeared* better to her. She hoped it wasn't just wishful thinking.

"I'm *bleeding!*" The plaintive voice cried out. "Take me to a hospital! Take—"

She grabbed her gun and made sure it was hidden behind the loose skirt of her dress. Then she took up a position in the middle of that room. Anyone coming through that door would have to go through her before getting to Paris.

A few moments later, she also saw their guests.

"I'm back," Vincent Connor said, flashing her a tired smile as he sauntered into the back room. "And I've brought friends."

He had his hands clamped on the shoulders of a man with dark hair and dark eyes, a man who seemed familiar to Annette though she'd never met him in person before, she was sure of it. Deep gashes covered his neck and jaw, obvious signs of a wolf attack.

Just which wolf had the guy pissed off? And why was he *there?*

Garrison was glaring at the injured human, but not attacking. Not yet, anyway.

And there was a woman in the little group, too. A woman with pale, blonde hair and bright green eyes. Heavy gold bracelets—bands?— curled around her wrists.

"Just what friends are these?" Annette murmured. She made sure to keep her position in the middle of the room, and Garrison hurried to her side.

"This…" Vincent's hold tightened on the bleeding human. She was surprised he hadn't decided to take a bite with all that tempting blood flowing. "This is Drew Hart. The human who has been fucking everything up for us."

"Vampire bastard!" Drew cried out. "You let me the fuck go, right now, you—"

"Lena…" Vincent sighed out the name. "Make him stop talking."

The blonde waved her hand toward Drew. Instantly, his lips clamped together and he stopped speaking.

"Thank you." Vincent didn't look the blonde's way. His gaze was on Annette. "How's our wolf? Still rabid?" Then he made a show of glancing around her.

She bristled. "No, he's—"

"*Not* freaking rabid," Paris muttered from behind her.

Surprise flashed on Vincent's face. "He speaks…and with sense, too."

Lena inched forward.

"Where's Aidan?" Annette demanded. Her hand tightened on her weapon.

Vincent glanced over at Lena.

Sadness flickered on her face. "When I saw him last, the darkness had taken him over. He'd lost the battle and was running wild into the night."

What? No, no way. He—

"Aidan had two beasts inside of him, a werewolf and a vampire." Lena's voice was so soft that Annette had to strain in order to hear her. "That's not the way things were meant to be."

Paris is carrying two beasts.

"They ripped apart his sanity. Only bloodlust and rage are left in him now." Lena shook her head. "I tried to warn Mary Jane Hart, but she wouldn't listen to me."

Drew frantically shook his head. Blood dripped from his wounds.

Vincent's teeth snapped together.

"Mary Jane went after him." Lena's shoulders fell. "But I'm afraid that when she finds Aidan, he won't be the man she needs. He may not even be a man at all."

Paris was dead silent behind Annette and tension seemed to be rolling off Garrison.

"I tried to tell Jane." Vincent shoved Drew down onto his knees before him. "She wasn't meant to be with Aidan. The consequences of their mating would be disastrous. Now, she'll see for herself just what I meant."

Annette backed away from him. Her gaze fell to her broken scrying mirror. Those precious chunks…

And for just a moment, she saw something. A quick flash.

Of Hell.

***

Hell's Gate. Jane followed Aidan's scent back to the club on Bourbon Street. His haven. The place where it had all started for them.

She'd met Aidan just outside of Hell's Gate while working her first case as a homicide detective. A woman's dead body had been dumped near the club. Of course, that particular victim hadn't stayed dead, not for long. And Jane's world had quickly spun out of control.

Slowly, she approached the entrance to Hell's Gate. The guard stood as she neared. "Ms. Jane…" Troy looked over his shoulder at the closed door. "You shouldn't…I don't think you should go in tonight. Something isn't right."

Troy had claw marks on his stomach. She'd smelled his blood from a block away. Jane swallowed. "Aidan did that to you?"

He nodded.

Shit. "When I go inside, lock the door behind me. Then go back to the werewolf compound and get that wound treated, okay?"

But he didn't move. Troy's eyes — one blue and one green — stayed locked on her. "It isn't safe for you."

"I can handle him." She sounded way more confident than she felt. "But everyone else needs to stay away for now." Until she had *her* Aidan back. And she would get him back. There was no alternative for her. Whatever she had to do in that place, she'd do it. Jane wasn't about to lose him. They'd already been through too much together. She wouldn't give him up now. "Lock the door behind me," so they wouldn't get any unexpected visitors, "then go," Jane ordered.

He hesitated but, after a moment, Troy stepped out of her way. Jane's hand curled around the door handle and she opened it slowly, the hinges creaking. She stepped into the club, and it was dark inside, a cavernous darkness.

It was a good thing she could see so well in the dark.

She advanced a few feet and the door swung shut behind her. The locks turned, a loud, distinct click of the tumblers. She listened a moment and heard Troy's footsteps fading away. Now…now she was alone with her beast.

Jane knew Aidan was there. She hadn't spotted him, not yet, but Jane could feel him. Watching her. The hungry stare of a predator.

Was he a wolf?

Or a man?

Both?

She rubbed her hands on her jeans. She still had blood on her — Roth's blood. She wanted to go back to his place, to search for clues, to get his damn body taken care of but…

Aidan came first.

He mattered. Because Jane was very afraid that Aidan was slipping away from her.

She walked into the middle of the club. Her gaze swept over the ground floor of Hell's Gate. "Aidan?"

A low growl had the hair on her nape rising. Her gaze shot upward, toward the second level of the club, and she saw his hulking form.

He wasn't a wolf, not any longer.

Her breath expelled in a relieved rush and a wide smile curved her lips. "Aidan, you're okay!"

He began walking down the stairs, a slow, steady glide. His eyes glowed a bright blue in the darkness.

He was…bigger. The guy had always been muscled, but this was different. His arms were bigger, his shoulders far wider, his height even a few inches taller.

An alpha on steroids.

Jane licked her lips. "You're okay," she said again but it sounded as if she was trying to convince herself of that fact.

He didn't speak. Jane retreated a step, then stopped herself. She forced her shoulders to straighten as she waited for Aidan to come to her.

They'd made love in this same place just a little while before. Aidan had said that he loved her, and she knew he'd meant those words. He loved her.

She loved him.

They were going to get through this madness.

Some way.

She could practically feel the threat in the air around her. It was instinctive, the way a hunted animal could sense the predator closing in.

Aidan was before her and the hard, dangerous expression on his face clearly said Jane was his prey.

He lifted his hand and his dark claws came toward her face.

***

"The alpha won't hurt Jane." Garrison was adamant. "He loves her."

Annette bent to get a better view of her broken mirror chunks. She could see fire and hell. Blood and death and…

Jane.

"He won't kill her," Vincent agreed. "Because I don't think he can. Beast, man, or vamp…he still thinks of Jane as his. But when the chips are down…" He exhaled slowly. "I'm afraid Jane won't have an option. She'll have to stop him before he turns on innocents."

Annette stared into her glass. "The end." That was what the burn mark on Jane's right side symbolized. She looked up at Vincent.

"Yes," he said. "Jane will be his end."

Drew was straining in Vincent's hold. Straining and still bleeding.

Paris growled.

Instantly, Annette straightened. She pointed at Drew — a still bleeding Drew. *That blood scent is just going to make Paris wild.* "Get him out of here! Paris might not have been able to keep human blood down, but that doesn't mean the scent won't screw with his mind!" She gave a hard negative shake of her head. "He isn't like you, Vincent. Paris doesn't have centuries' worth of strength to hold his hunger in check."

Vincent nodded. "No, he isn't like me. I was born to be this way. He wasn't." He hauled Drew to his feet and yanked him toward the door. "Another end."

No, nothing is ending for Paris.

Lena stared at Annette.

"I'll secure him in the other room," Vincent called. "Jane is going to want to see her brother when she gets here."

He was confident that Jane would be arriving but…what about Aidan?

"He thinks Aidan will die tonight," Lena whispered.

Annette eyed the woman.

"He doesn't get it," Lena added. "The man Aidan was…he's *already* dead."

Garrison took a lunging step toward her. "*Liar!*"

Annette put her hand on the young wolf's shoulder. "Easy." Too much was happening, too fast. She needed to figure things out. Paris was eerily silent behind her and she was almost afraid to look back at him.

Aidan, get your hairy alpha ass back here and help out your pack.

"Aidan is the strongest wolf I know," Garrison said, his pride in Aidan obvious. "Nothing takes him down."

"Jane will." Lena seemed certain. "That's what she was meant to be, don't you see that? The end. *His* end. The end for them all."

"Witch," Annette muttered. "I'm really not liking you."

Lena's eyelids flickered. "Why do people keep calling me that?" She sauntered around the room and her toe brushed against a chunk of broken black glass. "Bet you wish that was still working, don't you?"

Suspicions swirled within Annette. She knew there were lots of powerful paranormal beings out there but Lena…

"Lena!" Vincent roared. "I need you! Come to me!"

Lena offered Annette a faint smile. Then she turned away.

Power seemed to pulse in the air behind her as she left them.

"You need to call Police Captain Vivian Harris!" Annette shouted after her. "Drew should be in her custody! She can help us!"

Another growl built from Paris's throat. Annette looked back at him. His eyes were darkening with emotion.

With...bloodlust.

"Here we go again," Annette whispered and she felt her heart break a bit more.

CHAPTER FIFTEEN

Aidan's claws slid over her cheek, his touch as soft as a whisper, not so much as scratching her skin.

Jane's breath eased out on a ragged sigh. "I'm afraid."

His nostrils flared. "I can smell your fear." He smiled at her as his claws slid down her neck. "I like that scent."

She caught his hand, held tight. "No, you don't. You hate it when I'm afraid."

Aidan just stared down at her. Such a cold, empty stare.

"You love me," she told him. "You don't ever want me to be afraid."

His brow furrowed.

"I know you're in there." Jane tightened her grip on him. "And I'm going to get you out. I'm—"

He lifted her up and they seemed to fly across the club. In the next instant, she was sitting on the bar, and he was standing between her legs.

He'd grabbed her wrists, and he'd pinned them to the bar top, one on either side of her body.

Jane stared at him and remembered him making love to her. Right there.

But when he looked back at her, his gaze was that of a hunter, one who was about to devour his prey.

"Aidan…" Jane began.

And he bit her. He moved so fast that she didn't realize his intent, not until it was too late. Jane had still thought that she could reach him. But he sank his fangs into her throat and the white-hot sting of his bite stole her breath. He drank from her, seeming to glory in her taste. Because this was Aidan—her Aidan—her body responded to him. Her breasts ached, her sex yearned.

He licked her neck. "I like that." His voice rasped against her. "I'll take more." His fangs raked over her skin.

"Stop!" She yanked her wrists from his grasp and slammed her hands against his chest.

His head lifted.

"Aidan…" Chill bumps were on her arms. "Say my name."

His eyes narrowed.

"Say my name," Jane ordered again, frantic, desperate. Because he was gazing at her as if she were a stranger and that scared her most of all. Whatever was happening inside of him, Jane needed Aidan to remember her. To remember them. To remember what they were to each other. "Do you even know who I am?"

His fangs flashed. "Yes." A hiss. "I know…you're mine." His head came back toward her, lowering over her neck.

He was going to bite her again.

"No!"

Jane shoved him, hard. Hard enough that he stumbled back and slammed into a nearby table. Her breath sawed out of her lungs as she jumped off the bar. "Aidan." Now she snapped out his name. "*Aidan,* get your shit together and get it together *now*. Because this isn't you."

He'd shattered the table and fallen to the floor. He glared up at her, snarling, and he shot to his feet. He swiped out at her with his claws, but Jane jumped back, dodging the attack.

"What are you doing?" Jane yelled at him. "Don't make me hurt you." That wasn't what she wanted. She never wanted to hurt Aidan. She loved him too much.

That love was why she was standing there right then, why she was so desperate to reach him. To get past the darkness and find her lover.

"Hurt me?" He laughed, and it was a guttural, brutal sound. *Not Aidan's laugh.* "Come try." He opened his arms to her, spreading them wide. "Nothing can hurt me. No one. I'm a fucking alpha."

Her chin notched up as she began to circle him.

"I like the way you smell." He turned, keeping his gaze on her as she moved around the bar. "Like the way you taste even better."

"Aidan, *stop this*." Because the tension was getting worse. She could feel it thickening in the room. He was going to attack, she knew it. And when he did… "I don't want to lose us."

He smiled at her, flashing fangs. "I think I'll like the way you fuck, too."

He is a stranger. Where is my Aidan? "Trust me, you love the way I fuck." She grabbed one of the broken chair legs. Held it tight. "But that's because you love me, and you need to remember that, right now. Because if you do anything to me…oh, Aidan, it will destroy you once you get past this darkness. The guilt will eat you alive." She knew it. "I matter too much to you."

He leapt at her. Jane hit out, swinging with the chair leg, but he just ripped it from her hand. He shattered that wood with a careless grip, then he was holding her, shoving her back against the wall and caging her with his body. "I don't think…" he whispered. "You matter much at all."

Pain knifed through her. White-hot agony because it was a blow straight to her heart. "No, you remember me…somewhere inside, I know you do. You remember everything. You said I was yours…because you know I am. Just as you're mine. You came to Hell's Gate because this place is your haven. You came here because you wanted to be safe. You—"

"You have my mark on you." His claws slid down and rested in the spot where her neck curved into her shoulder, the spot he'd marked before. "I can *feel* it. That's how I know you're mine."

She searched his eyes, wanting more than an animal instinct of recognition. "And this place? You came back to Hell—"

"My scent was all over this building, so I know it's mine, too." Once more, he gave that rough laugh. "This whole town will be mine. I'll take *everything*. I'll destroy the humans in my path. I'll make the cities fucking red with blood. I'll show them all the power I possess."

A tear slid down her cheek. "This isn't you."

"It's very, very much *me.*"

"I did this," Jane whispered. "My blood. Mixing with yours…the wolf and the vamp were battling inside you, but in that fight, something happened to the man you were."

Aidan nodded and he gave her that cold smile. "He died."

"No—"

But his fangs were coming at her again.

***

Annette stared down at the biggest chunk of black glass. The image of hell had faded and now she saw Aidan. He stood alone in a cemetery, with his hands clenched at his sides. Grief ravaged his face. Torment. She could feel his pain. It was ripping him apart because…

Jane was gone.

A massive mausoleum waited in front of Aidan. The doors were chained. Aidan took a step toward that desolate place —

"Ms. Benoit?" Garrison poked her shoulder. "You okay? You've been staring at that glass for a while."

She blinked and rose to her feet. Dizziness rolled through her, but Garrison steadied her with his strong grip. "Aidan."

"He's not here yet," Garrison spoke softly. "Shouldn't he be here? What's taking him so long?"

Annette tried to pull in a deep breath. Her lungs felt empty. "You need to get to him."

Alarm flashed on Garrison's face. "Why?" His gaze dipped down to the mirror. "What did you see?"

Aidan is going to hurt Jane. "Go to him. He's in Hell's Gate." That was why she'd seen hell. Sometimes, her visions weren't literal. "Stop him."

Garrison nodded and surged away from her, but then…

He stopped.

Garrison turned back to face her, his hands clenched. "I…I can't."

She cast a quick look at Paris. He stared at her with a ravenous gaze. She licked her lips then dragged her gaze back to Garrison. "Why not?"

"My alpha gave me an order." Garrison marched toward her. "He told me to protect Paris, and that's what I'm going to do. I won't break my alpha's command."

Are you freaking kidding me? "Even if your alpha suffers for it?"

Garrison bit his lip, but…nodded. "I swore to protect Paris, and that's what I'm going to do."

Oh, hell. Now he was going to be a rule follower. "You damn well better protect him." She jabbed her finger into Garrison's chest. "And do *not* cross that dirt line until I get back." She was actually starting to worry about just how much longer that dirt of the dead would work. It hadn't stopped Aidan and the more time that she spent with Paris…

He doesn't seem like just a vamp to me. He had werewolf claws a bit ago. Aidan's blood and Jane's blood…they're mixing in him now, changing him. And it just might be enough of a change to fool the magic she'd put in place.

They were running out of time, she knew it. Annette had to act. She wasn't going to leave that building, but she would go get Vincent. If anyone was strong enough to stop the alpha, it would be him.

Garrison would never stand a chance against Aidan anyway.

Annette left her bag and rushed out of that back room. It was eerily silent in the long hallway. Where was Vincent? He'd taken Drew away earlier, but she had no idea where they'd gone. She ran by several empty rooms and then, through an open doorway, she saw them.

Drew was on his knees. Vincent's hands were locked around Drew's throat. "I snapped your sister's neck," Vincent said, his face twisted and angry. "Just like I'm—"

"What are you doing?" Annette yelled at him.

Vincent stiffened. Then he shoved Drew away from him.

Lena just stood there, a few feet to Vincent's right. She was watchful, silent.

"Were you about to kill him?" Annette marched closer to him, her gaze sweeping the room. Drew's lips were still pressed tightly together. "Why the hell haven't you called Captain Harris? She should be handling him."

"I didn't hear you coming." Vincent slanted a quick glance at Lena. "Why didn't I hear her coming?"

Lena just shrugged.

Annette glanced between the two of them.

Drew threw his body forward and tried to crawl toward her, but Vincent caught him and jerked him back.

This is wrong. "Captain Harris should be here," Annette said as she edged back a bit. "She handles the paranormals."

"I can handle him." Vincent smiled at her. "I'm trying to understand why he hates vampires so much. I mean, his father was a vamp. Shouldn't he be *grateful* to our kind? This hatred…this determination to kill paranormals is unnatural."

Drew's gaze fired fury at the vamp.

Lena just watched them.

Annette found her gaze dipping to the bracelets around Lena's wrists. There was something familiar to her about those golden bangles. Something that nagged at her mind.

"You won't be a threat to Jane any longer," Vincent assured Drew. "You won't be a threat to anyone." He bared his fangs and Annette knew he was about to rip out the human's throat.

"Stop it!" Annette yelled. "He's her brother!"

"A murdering bastard of a brother." Vincent glanced over at Annette. "You do realize, of course, that he came to this town with the express purpose of killing paranormals?"

Annette hesitated.

"Think about it," Vincent said. "When he shot Jane at that college campus, he was armed with a gun that contained *silver* bullets. Humans don't just pack silver bullets by chance. He knew what Aidan Locke was. He knew about werewolves. He was here to kill them. *And* to wipe out any vamps who got in his way."

"How would he have known?" Annette asked.

"Because he had hired a man to follow Jane around town. A bastard named Roth Sly." Vincent paced closer to her. "That's what I've been able to learn so far. Drew hired Roth to watch and to report back on everything that he learned. Roth was his eyes and ears but…" His shoulders slumped. "He killed Roth tonight. That's where Lena and I found this bastard…at Roth's apartment. The whole building reeked of blood and death."

Her heart thudded too fast and hard in her chest. Annette inched back another step. "Drew Hart hasn't said a word."

Vincent lifted one perfect brow. Such a handsome face. So charming.

"You had Lena stop him from talking earlier. His lips…they're still sealed together." She could see it. Drew was straining hard to talk but it was as if his mouth had been glued shut.

Vincent shrugged. "He was talking a moment ago, I assure you. Just ask Lena. Lena…" He threw a quick glance her way. "Tell the voodoo queen that Drew was talking."

"If that's what you wish…" Lena's voice was mild, but there was just the faintest emphasis on that last word.

Wish…

Annette's stare jerked to the gold bracelets. *Oh, shit. We are all so screwed.*

"He was talking plenty," Lena murmured. "Telling us how he hated paranormals. How he wanted us all to die. He came to New Orleans with those silver bullets to take out paranormals. He won't stop until we're all dead."

Vincent nodded, looking satisfied. "See? That's why it just makes sense for me to kill the bastard right now."

Drew frantically shook his head. More grunts and moans came from behind his sealed lips.

"After all…if I don't end him, he'll just attack Jane and Aidan again. They're your friends." Vincent appeared pained. "You don't want your friends to die, do you?"

Her throat had gone desert dry. "No, no, I don't want them to die."

And she didn't want to die, either. So Annette was going to have to play these next few moments very, very carefully…

Because she'd just realized she was standing in the room with a devil.

***

Darkness was choking him. His head throbbed, his heart raced, and a ravenous hunger for blood had his whole body aching.

She was in front of him. The beautiful woman with the dark hair and the deep eyes. The one that he looked at and just knew...

She's mine.

She was crying and that was wrong. His hand lifted and he caught one of her tears on his claw.

"Aidan, come back to me."

He was Aidan. He had trouble thinking. Everything was slow and muddied by the dark. And by his hunger. He wanted to attack. To rage. To destroy.

But the woman was there.

And she was his.

The scent of her fear was still heavy in the air. But there was something more there, too. Apples. Lavender.

Those light scents were familiar, just as she was familiar to him. He wanted to pull her close. To hold her. To kill her.

And he wanted to fuck her. Hard and deep. Endlessly. Until she submitted to him, completely, totally.

He wanted to drink her blood and gorge on it. He wanted...

I want to get away from the darkness.

"How can I reach you?" She put her hand on his chest. "You're not just a wolf. You're not just a vamp. You're a man. A good man. That part of you has just been pushed down, deep inside. You weren't born to the bloodlust." She rose onto her toes, staring up at him. "I want you back. I'll *have* you back."

Then she was pulling his head down toward her. Her mouth took his in a kiss that was soft and sweet, gentle and searching.

It was all wrong. He didn't want soft. Didn't want sweet.

He wanted rough and wild and consuming. That was what his beast demanded. Her sex. Her blood.

Her…life?

No, not her. She's mine.

She's…

Jane?

The name was there, whispering through the chaos of his mind. He tried to grab it and hold on to it, hold on to her, but in the next instant, it was gone.

He was gone.

"No." Her hands clamped tightly around his shoulders, her nails biting into his skin. "I *felt* you. You were back, just for a moment. You were with me."

He growled.

"You want me?"

He was on fucking fire for her.

"I want you. *My* Aidan. My lover. The man who would take any pain to protect me. The man who loves me more than anyone ever has before." Her breath shuddered out. "Because that's the way I love him."

His chest burned.

"I love him…I love *you,* good and bad. I don't care about the darkness that you *think* is taking you over. I can deal with the dark. I can deal with the light. I can deal with everything…" And another tear leaked down her cheek. "Everything but losing you." She pressed her mouth to his. Her tongue slipped out, licking along his lips, arousing him even more. "I love you."

Inside of him, there was pain, so much pain. Tearing him apart. Gutting him. The dark was swallowing him whole and the pain was burning his insides but she…

She was still kissing him.

And his need for her pushed past the pain. Another growl tore from him. He caught her hair in his hand and he pulled back her head, giving him better access to her sweet mouth. His tongue thrust inside. He took and took and…

She gave.

There was such terrible pain but she felt right. Good.

And he wasn't going to let her go.

***

Annette schooled her expression as she stared at Vincent. "I need to get back to Paris."

A hard banging seemed to suddenly echo through the building. She jumped and her gaze flew behind her.

The banging — the knocking — came again.

Someone's here, at the door. Someone wants inside this hell-forsaken club.

"Lena," Vincent snapped. "See who the hell that is."

Lena's eyes closed. "It's the ME, Heider."

The woman could see something like that without the aid of a scrying mirror? Annette's suspicions about just what Lena was deepened…and so did her fear. She licked her lips and said, "Garrison was with him earlier. He must have told Heider we were here. Heider was analyzing Paris's blood. I'd — I'd better go see what he discovered." She'd stuttered. Oh, hell. She never stuttered. Mostly because she never allowed herself to feel fear. But the fear racing through her blood wasn't just for herself.

It was for them all.

Paris.

Garrison.

Aidan.

Jane.

We've been tricked. By a creature who is the most skilled at tricks.

She hurried from the room. "I'll go get Heider." *I'll give him a message. Get him to run and bring back Vivian.* Vivian and the whole freaking pack. Because they were about to enter a blood bath.

They were about to face the true end.

She nearly tripped in her haste to get to that front door. She pulled it open, the rusty hinges groaning, and Heider stood there, his tortoiseshell glasses in place, his hair standing a bit on end as if he'd been running his fingers through it all night. When he saw her, he took a quick step back. "Ah, Annette…" She heard the faint click as he swallowed. "Is, um, is Jane here? I really need to talk to her and Garrison said that—"

She grabbed his shirt front and yanked him close. "Go get Vivian." Her words were barely a breath of sound.

He stared down at the hand fisting his shirt. "Um, yeah, I need Jane. I have to tell her about the tests I did—"

Footsteps tapped behind her. Vincent was coming close. With his vamp hearing, had he picked up on her words to Heider? "Leave," she said, her voice even softer. "*Run.*"

Heider backed up. "Jane's blood was definitely given to Paris. And when I thought about it, I remembered that I'd had samples at my old lab. I'd taken them from her right before everything pretty much went to hell."

They were *in* hell. The guy was not getting the freaking hint and Vincent's steps were coming ever closer.

"I think someone stole her blood and gave it to Paris." He nodded, decisively. "They stole it from *me* and used it against Paris."

"Don't worry about Paris." They had another immediate concern. She could practically feel Vincent behind her.

"Maybe the good doctor could help patch up Drew," Vincent called out. His voice was mild, friendly. Non-threatening. *Clever bastard.* "Especially since you've said I can't kill him, Annette."

She caught the slight widening of Heider's eyes. Really—was he just *now* seeing the vamp closing in on them? "Go." This time, she didn't speak the words at all. She just mouthed them as she frantically conveyed her message. "Go*! Enemy. Get help.*"

Heider grabbed his phone from his pocket as he stumbled. "Oh, damn, I have a text from the office." He backed away, fast and looked down at the phone in his hand. "Another dead body. The dead just don't stop." Then he turned on his heel. "I'll be back with—"

Vincent tried to lunge past her and grab Heider, but Annette twisted her body and she threw herself against him as hard as she could, hoping to catch him by surprise. They slammed down onto the floor together. "*Run!*" She screamed at Heider but he was already running, not even stopping to look back.

She'd always known the man had a very high sense of self-preservation.

"You bitch," Vincent snarled.

She was on top of him, but she was hardly strong enough to hold down a vampire. He threw her off him, and Annette hurtled through the air. She expected to hit a wall. To feel her back break…

But someone caught her. Strong arms wrapped around her and held her close. "You're all right."

What the hell? Her head jerked to the left and she saw that her rescuer was Garrison. Garrison!

He eased her to her feet then pushed her behind him. She peeked over his shoulder and saw that Vincent had risen to his feet. Lena had closed in on their little group, but she just stood there, watching. Not helping Vincent but certainly not doing anything to stop him, either.

But then Lena caught Annette's eye. She lifted her hands, and the bracelets around her wrists gleamed.

If she's what I think she is…she can't help but she sure can destroy us.

Outside, she heard the sound of tires squealing. Heider had gotten away. Now, if he could just bring help—

"You'll be dead, voodoo queen, long before anyone comes back to you." Vincent flashed his fangs. "Figured it out, did you? Or maybe you just finally fucking saw the truth in your black glass? Lena said the truth could only hide for so long. The more blood and death that was shed, the more the truth would emerge." He didn't even sound worried. "I knew I was working against the clock."

That was why he'd come to see her at the Voodoo Shop. His little visit made sense now. He'd been trying to figure out just how much she knew.

Too little.

Too damn late.

"Go to Paris," Garrison told her. "I'll hold him back."

"You, pup?" Vincent laughed as he began to stalk toward them. "You can hold nothing back. You're worthless, useless. You should have died years ago when the vamps took the rest of your family." His disgust was obvious. "All of the fucking werewolves should be gone. They are nothing but animals, savages, and it's time for their end."

She held tight to Garrison's arm. If she left him, he'd die.

"I was always meant to be the end of the werewolves, I knew it," Vincent continued. "It just took me a while to realize how that end would come."

Annette glanced down the long hallway that would lead her back to Paris. Her bag was back there with him. Her weapons.

Shit.

"I was patient. I waited *centuries*. Then Lena saw Jane…I actually wished for Jane, and she was born. A perfect weapon. A perfect poison."

Jane's blood. That's what he's talking about. Her blood is the poison. Because her blood had transformed not one, but two werewolves. Turned them into something…else.

"I just had to make sure she was prepared properly. Had to take her away from her family…easy enough to do, I just sent one of my most trusted vamps to kill them. And to mark her. I wanted the world to know what she was."

The end.

The symbol that had been soldered into Jane's skin made sick sense.

"I'd hoped that she and Aidan would come together. When she became a police detective, I even arranged the first murder victim for her to find. I made sure the body was dumped at Aidan's place so that Jane would meet him. I know what happens when an alpha werewolf gets close to a female vamp-in-waiting." Smug satisfaction rolled off the bastard. "So I let nature take its course. I waited and—"

"You didn't count on Jane actually falling in love with Aidan." The words slipped from her but she knew they were true. "You thought she'd kill him."

He laughed once more. "Well, of course, she's *going* to kill him. She's killing him tonight. I told you, Jane is my poison. She's poisoned Aidan with her blood. There is no going back. He dies tonight." A beat of silence. "And so do you." He lunged for them and Garrison leaped to meet him, surging forward in a fierce attack.

CHAPTER SIXTEEN

Sanity was gone. There was only desire. Desire for blood. Desire for her body. Desire to take and take and take.

He'd ripped her clothes away. But she'd...helped him. She'd shoved out of her jeans. Kicked away her shoes and reached for him with her soft hands that slid like silk over his skin.

His fangs were hard and aching, as aching as the dick that wanted to sink into her.

She was in his hands, his to claim but...

Jane.

Again, the name whispered through the chaos of his mind.

Apples and lavender. Laughter and soft smiles.

His hands curled around her hips. He knew the grip was too rough, that he had to be bruising her, but he couldn't stop. Her back was against the wall, her legs were locked around his hips, and he was about to drive into her.

He'd take her body and her blood.

He'd take—

"Jane?" Her name tore from him and he held back. Sweat beaded his brow. His muscles trembled, but Aidan didn't move. Not so much as an inch. He held himself still and clawed to find the man he'd been.

The man worthy of her.

Why was she doing this? Why was she letting him touch her? Why was she kissing his jaw so softly, as if…

As if he were still the man she loved.

He wasn't. She knew he was a monster. He was so far gone—

"That's right," her soft whisper came to him. "I'm your Jane. And you're my Aidan and nothing or no one will ever come between us." Her head eased back and she gazed into his eyes. "Stronger together, remember? Strong enough to fight whatever is happening inside of you. Strong enough to find our way through the dark, as long as we're together."

"Get…away…from…me…" A hoarse plea, one that came from the depths of his soul.

"I can't. You're holding me too tightly."

And he was. Holding because he could *not* let go.

But Jane smiled at him. "And I want to be here. I want to be with you. I want to make love with you."

He wasn't making love. He was taking. Hurting, destroying—

"Kiss me again, Aidan. Kiss me like you mean it."

But he didn't kiss her. He eased her back to her feet and he stepped away. The agony inside of him got even worse, wrenching at his heart as if the damn thing would be yanked right from his chest.

"Aidan?"

He fell to his knees and his claws scraped over the floor. Jane's hand grabbed his shoulder.

"Aidan? What's happening?"

His head turned slowly and he stared at her fingers. So delicate. Just as she was. Didn't she see how close she was to destruction? His gaze lifted and slid over her body. Her curving hips. Her beautiful skin.

The scar, the raised white flesh in the shape of…

The end.

His gaze lingered on that scar. But then Jane sank to her knees beside him.

"I see you in there. I know you're coming back. Come back," she urged, "and stay with me."

He could only shake his head. It didn't feel as if he were coming back to her. It felt as if his whole body was splitting apart. His very soul being torn from him.

She pressed a kiss to his lips. Another tender touch to the beast. "I love you, Aidan Locke."

She shouldn't. She—

Jane pushed him back so that he fell on his ass. Then she crawled on top of him and wrapped her legs around him. They were sitting up, facing each other. Her sex brushed over his cock.

No, Jane, I don't want to hurt you! A roar from inside of him.

"We're going to make love, Aidan."

She kept saying his name, deliberately, he was sure. A hold on the man he'd been.

"We're going to make love and you're going to come back to me."

Then she took his cock and guided it into the entrance of her body. That warm, wet heaven, and when he sank inside of her, he lost the little bit of fucking sanity that had been there. It was too good. She was too good. Tight and hot and clamping down on him.

Heaven.

Hell.

His.

"Look at me."

His gaze jerked to her face.

"See me," Jane whispered. "The same way I see you."

Then she lifted her body up, pushed down. He snapped his teeth together because the urge to bite her was so strong, but he wouldn't do it. He *wouldn't*.

Sex. Fucking.

Love.

Jane.

His hands clamped around her hips and he moved her faster, pushed deeper. Her breath heaved out and she gave a little moan…the breathless cry had to be the sexiest sound in the world.

Give her pleasure.

The whisper came from deep within him.

Give her joy.

A command.

Give her everything.

He pressed his lips to her neck. Not to bite. Not to take. But to kiss because he remembered that was one of her sweet spots. Jane loved it when he licked her there.

He lifted her up, then made sure to plunge into her with a long thrust that took his cock right over her clit.

She loved it when he stroked her just like that.

He withdrew, then sank deeper. And suddenly, they weren't sitting on that floor. He'd pushed her onto her back, brought her legs up high so that he could go even deeper.

Because she loved that.

His claws were so careful, not scratching her skin. His fingers caressed her. Teasing her breasts just the way she liked. Then he was licking her nipples. Sucking her, getting her to arch against him and shudder as she called out his name.

Aidan.

She came around him. He felt the fierce clench of her orgasm and he couldn't hold back. Her release sent him right over the edge. He drove into her, over and over, pumping his cock into her and the climax slammed through him.

His heart thundered in his ears. His breath heaved in his chest. And Jane…*his* Jane curled her arms around his neck.

His head slowly lifted. He stared into her eyes.

Jane smiled at him. "I knew you'd come back to me."

He kissed her.

Come back? Hell yeah, he'd fucking walk through hell for her.

"Jane," Aidan rasped. "I love you."

***

Vincent's fingers curled around Garrison's neck and he lifted the wolf high into the air. "You're not even a damn alpha," a sneer curled his lips. "What the hell do you think you'll do against *me?*"

Annette backed up. She had to do *something*.

"I was…was thinking…" Garrison gasped. *"This."* Then he yanked a gun out from inside his jacket. *Her* gun, Annette realized. Smart, sneaky wolf. He fired that weapon, again and again. The blast of the gun had Annette's ears ringing even as blood soaked Vincent's shirt.

He staggered and dropped Garrison. "F-fucking…bastard…" Vincent spat.

Lena grabbed Annette's arm. "Silver won't stop him. The blood loss will barely slow him down. *Run.*" She pointed toward the main door. The way out of that building.

Run? And leave Paris?

Not an option.

"Run!" Garrison yelled at the same time. He kicked Vincent in the stomach. Clawed at him. "I'll hold him off—"

Vincent grabbed Garrison and sank his fangs into the young wolf's throat.

"Go," Lena whispered.

"You can't help me," Annette said.

Lena shook her head.

Garrison shoved Vincent back, but the vamp charged again.

"I know what you are." Annette backed away from Lena. "I know!"

Sadness flashed on Lena's face. "Then you know why you need to run."

No, she knew why she had to get to Paris, fast. "I wish you could be on my side," she said.

Lena's eyes gleamed. "So do I."

Annette glanced at Garrison once more. He was driving his fists into Vincent, again and again, but Vincent wasn't going down.

It took one hell of a lot to make a vamp like Vincent go down.

She turned and ran — not out of the building, but to Paris. She raced into the back room. He was on his feet, straining against the remaining chains that held him. Still inside her circle. She grabbed her bag, scooped up a chunk of her scrying mirror and —

"*Voodoo queen!*"

She looked back. Vincent was in the doorway. There was no sign of Garrison or of Lena. Vincent had blood dripping down his chin. He was blocking the only way out of that room.

There was only one place for her to go.

Annette leapt across the line of dirt. She threw her body right at Paris. His arms locked around her and held her tight.

Snarling, Vincent came after her. He tried to jump over that line and come at her, but he slammed into the invisible wall created by her magic.

He fell back on the floor, bellowing his rage.

"Sorry, asshole," Annette panted, "but the dead can't cross my line."

His eyes promised pain as he rose to his feet. He stared at her with fury in his eyes and then...

He laughed.

A chill skated down her spine.

"I can't cross and neither can he." Vincent pointed at Paris. A Paris who held her locked in his arms. "How long do you think it will be before he loses his sanity again and goes right for your throat?"

Like she hadn't already had the same fear.

"*I* was the one who ordered his poisoning. That's what it is, you see. A poison. Jane's blood...Aidan was a fool to give her his blood before her change. It just made the vamp power in her even stronger. So strong that now her blood can transform anyone, even a werewolf."

"You were the one watching Jane, all along."

He shrugged. "I hired a dumbass human to keep an eye on her...then to see how she was developing. I also used him to administer the poison to Paris there. After all, I needed a good test subject."

Paris's hold tightened on Annette.

"Paris has certainly proven that this little experiment is successful. Jane's poison can transform werewolves." He stepped closer to the line of dirt, but didn't cross it. "Do you know what that means?"

She did. "The end…of the werewolves." She clearly saw what he wanted, what he'd been aiming for all along.

Vincent nodded. "They'll become vampires. Werewolves will cease to exist. The fucking beasts that destroyed *my* family…werewolves…they'll be gone. Wiped from the earth never to appear again."

She felt the hot stir of Paris's breath along her neck.

"Unless you were born to be a vampire," Vincent murmured. "You have very little control. Paris was fucked from the word go. A lost soul, ready to turn the streets red with blood. Soon, I'll have an army just like him. Werewolf power and vamp bloodlust. We're going to change the world. Humans will live in fear and finally, *finally,* it will be the hour of the vampire. We'll dominate the way nature always intended."

It wasn't nature. It was his screwed up plan.

"It's not going to happen," she whispered even as Paris's teeth raked over her throat. "Help will come. Jane and Aidan will stop—"

"I saw Aidan, right before I came here tonight. He's the best part of this little plan, you see. He showed me what happens to an alpha. His beast is too strong to die during the transformation into a vamp…so the vamp and the beast fight inside of him, and from what I saw, that fight was ripping away the last of his humanity." He smiled at her. "Newly turned vamps often feed on those closest to them. Family members. Friends. Lovers. I *saw* Aidan. He was on the edge. And Jane, lovesick fool that she is…she ran after him." Vincent's head tilted as he studied Annette. "He'll try to make a meal of her, and Jane…well, she'll have no choice but to fight back. She'll kill him." He turned away. "Just as Paris is about to kill you."

She tried to slip from Paris's hold, but he just held her tighter. "What if Aidan kills Jane? Aren't you worried about *that?* Then you'll lose your precious poison! This will all be over and—"

"I have Paris now. He has Jane's blood mutation. He'll spread the poison. I'll give it to his whole pack. They will fall." He kept walking. "I hope it doesn't hurt you too much when he bites."

She felt the prick of pain as Paris's mouth opened wider on her.

Vincent paused at the door and looked back at her. His lips twisted. "Oh, who am I fucking kidding? I hope it hurts like a bitch, voodoo queen. I hope your last moments are agony and hell."

Then he left her.

She shoved her hand down into her bag, her hand fisting over the wooden stake inside. She didn't want to do this. Not to Paris. "Don't," she whispered.

*Don't make me end you. Please, don't. Not to you.
Not —*

But his teeth slid away from her skin. Once more, she felt the hot stir of his breath against her neck. "Not to you," he whispered, as if echoing her thoughts.

And he spun her in his arms so that she faced him. Annette stared up at Paris and she saw his clear gaze. Not filled with bloodlust, just…Paris.

"Had to make it…look good," he muttered.

He had, definitely.

"I'm me." He swallowed. "Don't know how long it will last…but I'm me."

Yes, *yes!*

"So, love, let's think fast," Paris said. "And figure a way out of this fucking nightmare."

CHAPTER SEVENTEEN

"Never do this shit again," Aidan whispered as he brushed a kiss over Jane's lips. They were upstairs in his office and she'd just dressed in the last spare pair of clothes he had for her.

Aidan made a mental note to buy the woman more clothes to keep on hand at his club—lots of them—because he seemed to keep ripping her outfits to shreds.

Jane turned toward him, one brow raised. "What shit? You'd definitely better not be talking about the sex…"

His hand wrapped around her waist and he pulled her close, bending to press a quick kiss to her lips. *Making love, sweetheart. You taught me that.* "I mean you, risking your life, when I've gone over the fucking edge."

"But don't you see, Aidan? I'd go over the edge with you, any day."

She would, she had.

He kissed her again. Then he put his forehead against hers. Time for some hard truth. "I lost myself." He knew it. "I was being ripped apart and I couldn't stop it. I wanted pain. I wanted blood. I wanted death." That shamed him.

"But you didn't kill anyone...though you will owe your guard a serious apology bonus for that slice you gave him."

Aidan winced. Dammit, he hadn't meant—

"You came back." Her voice was soft. "Whatever was happening on the inside, *you* beat it. You're strong and you're sane and you're here with me." Her smile made his heart ache. "Just the way it's supposed to be."

He could stare at her smile forever.

But....

Her smile slipped. "We have to go and talk to Drew. I have to settle things with him." She pulled from his arms.

And he felt colder. "I was going to kill him." Aidan wouldn't lie, a big part of him still wanted to kill that little bastard for all that he'd done. If Jane hadn't stopped him...

"I know," she said.

He looked into her eyes and realized that she did know—exactly how he felt. All of his secrets. With Jane, his soul would always be bare.

But that was okay because he knew her secrets, too.

"I need to question him. Find out just what the hell is happening. It just...it doesn't make sense to me that he'd hire Roth. And all those tests? Drew wouldn't do that. It doesn't fit." She turned and marched for the door. "The pieces aren't going into place. I'm missing something."

He followed her down the stairs.

She was halfway down the stairs when she froze. "How did Vincent know we'd be at Roth's?" Jane slowly turned to face him. "I didn't…everything was happening so fast that I didn't even question how he was there. I raced into the alley after you and he just…he appeared."

Yeah. "The vamp has a bad habit of doing that."

Jane licked her lips. "I can never detect his scent. He hides it somehow."

With magic.

"I don't know if he was there *before* we arrived," Jane said, her gaze sharpening with suspicion. "Or if he arrived when we raced outside."

Aidan stared into her eyes. "There was an awful lot of blood at that scene."

"Only there was no blood on Drew's knife. Or on him." Her breath came faster. "If he'd just cut Roth's throat, there should have been spray on him. There wasn't."

He strained, trying to remember. Had there been blood on Vincent?

"No blood was on Vincent," Jane said, a frown tugging down her lips. "But he could have moved so fast, used that vamp speed…he could have killed Roth and never gotten so much as a speck of blood on him."

While Drew wouldn't have been so fortunate. "Drew was following us." Aidan thought this through. "He could have been watching Hell's Gate and when we left, he tailed us." And Aidan had already been so fucking on the edge he hadn't even noticed the guy. "He was coming to kill us—"

"But Drew hadn't killed Roth." She spun around and raced down those last stairs. "He didn't do it but Vincent sure as hell could have!"

He'd never liked that damn vamp. They rushed outside and—

"Jane!"

And they saw Heider shoving his way through the crowd on Bourbon Street. The guy was huffing and puffing and appearing absolutely terrified.

Jane ran toward him, but Aidan beat her to the ME. He grabbed the guy, holding tight to his shoulders.

"You…won't answer your damn phone," Heider wheezed. "Neither will Captain Harris."

"I'm not answering because my phone was confiscated by you," Jane replied. "Remember, when you put me in a body bag? You got all my belongings and I didn't exactly have the chance to get them back."

Heider opened his mouth, closed it. Frowned.

"Heider," Aidan snarled.

The ME's frightened gaze shot to him. "Annette," his voice broke on the name. "Something is wrong. She needs help and the vampire — that scary ass freak Vincent — he was there."

Vincent.

"I tried to get the captain but she wasn't answering her phone, Jane wasn't answering — so I came here, to you." Heider lifted his chin and stared at Aidan. "You're alpha, right? That means you handle the paranormals in this town."

Aidan let go of the doctor and his fingers twined with Jane's. "*We* do."

"Good…then get to Annette. She needs you. Something bad is going down." Heider backed up a step. Sweat coated his forehead. "I mean, it has to be bad, right? If the voodoo queen is scared…"

If Annette was scared, the situation wasn't just bad.

It was a nightmare.

"Go to the werewolf compound in the swamp," Aidan ordered.

Heider immediately lifted his hands. "Hold on, hold on, I'm the *human* here — "

"Vivian will be there. She always loses her cell signal when she goes out there. So if she's not

answering her phone, she's still there. Get her
and the other wolves and tell them what's
happening."

Heider blinked. "What *is* happening?"

"We have a vamp who needs his ass put
down." *Finally. I've been waiting to kill that bastard.*
"And the wolves are going to war."

"C-can't I just keep calling her?" Heider
gulped and pulled out his phone. "I...I can just
keep trying. She'll get a signal eventually. I can—
"

"Bob." Jane said his name flatly.

He flinched.

"I know this is scary," Jane said and her voice
softened. "I know this is far more than you
signed on for—"

"I'm human," he whispered. "Not a
paranormal. I get involved in this war, and I'll be
dead."

"You're already in this war," Aidan said.
Didn't the guy see that? Heider had been
working for the wolves for years.

"It's okay to be afraid," Jane continued, firing
a fast frown at Aidan before focusing on Heider
once more. "But we need you. *I* need you.
Vincent is trying to destroy us—not just wolves
but I'm afraid he's out to destroy anyone in his
path. We need to stop him."

Heider swallowed and managed a weak nod.

Jane's hand squeezed his shoulder. "Go out to the werewolf compound. The wolves know you, they'll listen to you. Get them back to town. Get Vivian."

"And then bring them all to us," Aidan said. "We'll be at the old club near the cemetery."

Heider swiped his hand over his forehead. "You assholes really need to get better cell service out at that compound."

Aidan stared at him.

"I'm going!" Heider snapped. "I'll find the wolves and you just—you make sure that bastard doesn't hurt the voodoo queen, okay?" He turned away. "I...I like her, too. Dammit, you paranormals have got to stop growing on me..." His footsteps rushed away.

Jane gazed at Aidan. "Are you ready for this?"

Ready to destroy the vampire who'd tried to take Jane from him? Ready to stop the bastard who'd thought to attack his pack? "Hell, yes."

It was Vincent who wouldn't be ready for them.

***

They made a pit stop before they headed for the confrontation with Vincent, a fast little stop by the Voodoo Shop. Jane picked up some needed supplies and then they raced to the site of what she knew would be her last stand against Vincent.

Jane stood outside of that little building. The old BDSM club. When she'd first become a vampire, Vincent had brought her there. He'd chained her up, he'd given her blood, he'd acted as if he were helping her but…

All along, just what was your master plan, Vincent?

She and Aidan could have gone in there, fangs bared, claws out, but…

Vincent would have expected that. He'd been playing them all along, so now, it was time for her and Aidan to play *him.*

So she lifted her hand and she pounded on the door. She didn't kick it in, in a giant show of force, but, oh, she was so tempted. Kicking it in would reveal that she knew Vincent's game. Playing the scene another way…that would give Jane the chance to get killing close to Vincent.

The door opened a few moments later. Only Vincent wasn't the one who greeted her. Lena stood there, her gaze oddly sad. "You shouldn't come inside," Lena murmured.

There was something about that woman…Jane couldn't decide if Lena was as evil as Vincent or if she was another victim.

"Where is Aidan?" Lena asked as she looked over Jane's shoulder. "You two…you're stronger together."

Goosebumps rose on Jane's arms. That was something that she and Aidan only said to each other. For that woman to know… "You're not a witch, are you?"

Lena gave a barely perceptible shake of her head.

"What are you?"

Footsteps pounded toward them. "Jane!" Vincent's bellowing voice.

"Imprisoned," Lena breathed back. Then she stepped away.

Vincent ran toward Jane, a broad smile on his face. What she was doing was a huge gamble. But Vincent wouldn't know that Dr. Bob had found her. Especially if she came in, playing it cool and…

Jane started to cry.

Grieving.

The tears weren't hard to summon. After all, when she thought of how close she'd come to losing Aidan, pain knifed right through her body. It had been a near thing, all because of the asshole who was staring at her with his own fake emotion — concern.

"Jane?" He reached for her shoulder and pulled her inside. Pulled her close to him. "Jane, what happened?"

She looked down at her hands. They were shaking. Rage would do that to a woman. Make her shake. "I…killed him."

He sucked in a sharp breath. His arm wrapped around her and he pulled her close. "I'm so sorry."

No, you're not.

"He was b-beyond reason," Jane stumbled over the words. "Trying to take my blood, trying to attack with his claws…" She blinked back her tears and stared up at him. Saddened. Grief-stricken. "What happened to him?"

Lena shuffled away from them. Jane could hear the faint rustle of footsteps in the far back room — was that Annette and Paris? And where was Drew — was her brother even still alive?

"I don't know what happened," Vincent replied. "Such a terrible situation."

Liar.

Jane's hand slipped beneath her jacket. Her fingers curled around the wooden stake that she'd brought with her.

"It's going to be all right, Jane," Vincent assured her as he pulled her even closer. So close that she could feel his heart beating. "I'll help you."

Oh, I don't think you will.

Since she was close enough to feel his heart beat…that meant she was more than close enough to kill. Sometimes, you didn't see your enemy coming, not until it was too late. Vincent had taught her that. "I-I need to see Paris and Annette. I have to tell them—"

His head lifted and he stared down at her with a solemn expression. "I'm sorry, Jane."

Are you? Are you really?

"Paris attacked Annette. He…he went as crazy as, well, as I think Aidan did. She got too close to him, she made the mistake of trusting him, and…he ripped out her throat."

Jane didn't move.

"He came for me, then," Vincent said, his jaw hardening. "And I had to stop him, Jane."

She kept staring at him, as if she were shell-shocked.

Lena waited in the shadows, just a few feet away.

Jane's fingers were itching to take that stake and plunge it into his heart but the cop in her…the cop that always demanded justice, the cop that never took on the role of judge, jury, and executioner, she hesitated.

"I lied," Vincent suddenly confessed.

She let her brow furrow.

"I do know what happened." His lips twisted down in sadness. "Werewolves…their beasts aren't meant to transform. It drives them mad. Aidan had *your* blood, Jane. Your blood is what drove him over the edge. It mutated his cells, changed him. Destroyed him."

Her skin was absolutely icy right then. And the hand hidden beneath her coat had a death grip on the stake.

"Alphas keep their blood on hand for their pack, right?" He was speaking quickly, as if he'd just figured something out. "Aidan must have given his contaminated blood—contaminated because of you—he must have given it to Paris. That's why Paris changed." Horror flashed on his face. "The whole pack could be changing. If they got the contaminated blood, they could all become mindless predators. But don't worry, I'll help you stop them." He nodded decisively. "We'll put them all down. We'll—"

"End them?" Jane cut in, finishing for him.

He smiled. "Yes, if that's what we must do…"

Sick sonofabitch. "I'm going to end someone," Jane snapped. "But it's not them."

Lena gave a fast, warning scream.

But it was too late. Jane yanked up her stake and drove it right at Vincent's heart.

Never saw that coming, did you?

***

Aidan slipped through one of the old, broken windows in the BDSM club. Silently, he made his way to the room that Paris had been chained inside. He didn't worry about his scent giving him away. Yeah, Vincent had an enhanced sense of smell, but Aidan and Jane had picked up a potion to disguise that scent.

And since he already knew how to walk soundlessly…

Jane will keep him distracted. I'll get my pack mate and the voodoo queen. And we will fucking destroy Vincent.

A simple enough plan.

Stronger together.

He slipped into that back room, but when he saw Paris, Aidan stilled. Paris had his arms locked around Annette and the guy's fangs were bared right over her throat, as if he were about to gorge on her blood.

Shit! No! I can't let him —

Aidan leapt forward, a roar ready to burst from his lips but—

Someone else screamed. A high, quick scream of warning. The cry didn't come from that back room. It came from what sounded like the front of the building.

Where Jane is.

But at the cry, Paris's head whipped up. His eyes locked on Aidan and Paris stared at him not with a mindless, bloodlust filled gaze, but…

"It's Aidan." Paris's lips curved into a grateful smile. "That's who I sensed coming, not Vincent. It's just Aidan."

His hands fell away from Annette.

Aidan frowned.

Annette bent and brushed away the dirt near her feet. "Finally, alpha. Shit, do you know how nervous I was getting?"

Nervous…or scared?

Aidan's stare swept over Paris as his friend yanked at the manacles on his ankles. "Had to…act like I was still…deranged." Paris ripped away the manacle from his left foot. Then his right. He shot a quick glance at Aidan. "You're sane, too, right? Because Vincent was telling us you were destined to go over the edge."

"I did," Aidan said flatly. "But Jane pulled me back."

The scream had faded away. It hadn't been Jane's scream, he knew that. Vincent wouldn't kill Jane, he couldn't. The bastard needed her. She was his end.

"It was Vincent all along," Annette said quickly. "He hates wolves. He wants to eradicate them all. He's using Jane's blood to do it — he says it's poison to wolves."

Not exactly. Dangerous, but not lethal.

"Jane is taking care of the bastard," he told them. "Distracting him while I get the two of you to safety."

"I'm not fucking leaving," Paris threw back. "I owe the bastard, I owe—"

Blood.

The scent teased Aidan's nose. His head turned as the sound of footsteps shuffled closer.

"Ah, Aidan," Annette began, her voice shaking a bit. "There's something you need to know about Vincent…and Lena…"

Vincent appeared in the doorway. Blood soaked his shirt. One of his arms was locked around Jane's neck and his other hand…it gripped a bloody, wooden stake. He had that stake pressed to Jane's chest.

"*Jane.*" Vincent said her name with fury — with betrayal. "You lied to me. *Aidan still lives.*"

Aidan's claws were out. His beast was now fully under his control — beast and vamp — and both were ready to tear into Vincent.

"Yeah, well," Jane didn't sound even a little afraid. Just pissed off. Brave. *My Jane.* "You lied to me from day one, so I figure that makes us even." Her gaze jerked toward Annette. "I drove that stake into his heart and he didn't go down. Why the hell not? Want to enlighten me on what I've missed here?"

Before Annette could speak, Vincent laughed. "You've missed plenty, Jane. You all have." His mouth brushed against Jane's cheek. "Ever wonder how your brother knew to fire silver bullets when he attacked on that college campus? *I* was the one to give him the gun. I was the one to visit him and tell him there were dark, dangerous threats out there…that there were creatures he needed to fear, not just vampires."

"He wouldn't have listened to a vamp," Jane's voice was strained. "Not Drew—"

"He didn't know what I was. I made sure of it. Just as I made sure that Aidan's little compulsion trick wouldn't work on your brother."

How the hell could he do that?

But…

Lena had crept up behind Vincent. Aidan's gaze darted to her.

Magic. Fucking magic.

"I visited your brother often over the years. Never when you were around, of course." Mocking laughter slipped from him. "I guess you could even say I gave him poison, too. A slow poison of hate that ripped into his mind. Humans can be so easy to manipulate."

Jane yanked against his hold, but Vincent's grip didn't falter. And the stake kept pressing right over her chest.

"Lena…" Vincent called.

The blonde stepped closer to him. She always seemed to be in the shadows, waiting for Vincent to call her up.

"I do wish you'd eliminate those three," Vincent ordered, his voice bored, as if he'd just told Lena to take out the trash. "Aidan Locke. Paris Cole. And not-so-great voodoo queen, Annette Benoit. I wish you'd get rid of them right now."

Like he gave a shit what Vincent wished.

"I'm sorry," Lena said. She lifted her hands. The gold around her wrists gleamed.

"Fuck me," Annette whispered. "We are so dead."

Not yet. Not by a long shot. Not—

"She's a djinn," Annette told them, turning desperate eyes on Aidan. "There shouldn't be any of her kind left, but he has her bound to him…I think that's what those bracelets are— they're chains for her. She has to do exactly what he says and—"

And Vincent had just wished for Lena to end them.

A blue smoke drifted from her fingers and it came right at Aidan. He opened his mouth but…

Aidan started to choke.

"*No!*" Jane screamed.

"I'm sorry," Lena whispered as she slipped by Jane and Vincent.

Aidan couldn't breathe. Annette was coughing next to him. Choking. She hit the floor first and Paris tried to grab her to pull her into his arms. Paris lifted her up and tried to run, but the strange blue smoke just tightened around them.

"A death cloud," Vincent called. "One of my favorite tricks…"

Each breath just brought more of that blue cloud into Aidan's lungs. So…

He stopped breathing. He rose to his full height. He could hold his breath a long fucking time.

He'd always been able to do so.

And he'd do it now, for as long as it took.

Vincent was staring at him, his expression becoming bemused, and behind the bastard…

A new enemy waits.

Because Aidan had just spotted Drew Hart. The bastard's lips were clamped tightly shut and he had blood covering him. He was creeping forward, a human completely outmatched but Vincent wasn't looking back to see that new threat. He was too busy holding tight to a fighting Jane. He didn't see…

Aidan smiled at Vincent. The vampire bellowed his rage. "You should be fucking *choking* to death, wolf!"

Screw you.

And Drew Hart attacked. He jumped on Vincent's back, clawing at him with his fingers, going for his eyes. Vincent let go of Jane.

She snatched the stake from his fingers and shattered it in her grip.

Vincent sank his teeth into Drew's throat. He ripped, he tore, and blood flew—

Aidan grabbed Jane's hand. They needed to get away. His blood was throbbing in his veins. His heartbeat thundered in his ears. Paris and Annette were on the floor.

"It's her!" Jane yelled, pointing at Lena. "We have to stop *her!*"

Drew's body fell to the ground. He twitched as blood pumped from his throat. Vincent was still crouched over Drew's body, as if he'd attack again. "Worthless," Vincent snarled at him. "Just a human…one in the way. You shouldn't have taken Jane out of that basement so long ago. You should have left her so that Thane and I could finish what we'd started…*you were always fucking in the way!*"

Aidan grabbed the bastard by his shoulder. He swung Vincent around to face him. "Guess who's in your way now?" He drove his claws into Vincent's chest, sinking them in as deep as they would go. "I am." The blue smoke drifted into his lungs. *Burned.*

Vincent screamed, a cry of rage and pain. But then…he looked down at Aidan's claws in his chest and he started to laugh. "You can't kill the unkillable. You're going to fall, and I'll be alone with Jane. Soon enough, I'll get her to see things my way. Soon enough—"

"Hey, asshole!" Jane called.

Vincent's head whipped toward her. Jane had grabbed Lena and she had one hand locked around the nape of the woman's neck. "Let's level the playing field, shall we?" Jane glanced at Lena. "Sorry, this will hurt…" And then she rammed Lena's head into the nearest wall. Lena sank to the floor, sprawling, unconscious.

The blue smoke immediately vanished.

Aidan sucked in a deep breath. *Game the fuck on.*

He yanked his claws from Vincent and attacked again. Faster. Harder. The blood flew, the vamp stumbled back, but he didn't go down.

How in the hell did Vincent keep standing? Keep living?

"I don't think he can die!" Jane shouted. "I drove my stake right into his heart—and the bastard just yanked it back out!"

Vincent stood in the middle of that room, blood soaking him. Aidan was in front of him, Jane had just circled behind him, and Paris was to his left. Annette stood to Vincent's right, staring at him with eyes gone even darker with the swirl of her power.

Never count out a voodoo queen.

"Can't be killed," Annette said, her voice weak but her spine straight. "His djinn must have given him that power, the darkest of all gifts."

And, once more, Vincent laughed. "She did! You fools, did you really think I'd come at the wolves and *not* have stacked the deck in my favor? You can stake me, and I won't stop. You can take my head, and I'll still come back. I'll always rise…again and again. I'm immortal. Eternal. There is no end for me."

"*Annette,*" Jane suddenly snapped. "Step to the side. *The freaking side, now!*"

Annette looked down at the floor. Understanding flashed on her face a second before she jerked to the side.

And Jane shoved Vincent — she shoved him hard to the spot that Annette had been in just moments before.

Then Annette and Jane were both on the floor, on their hands and knees, scrambling to push the line of dirt closed so that it circled around Vincent.

Vincent's face tightened with his fury and his hand flew toward them. Aidan surged forward but —

"The dead can't cross my line." Annette leaned back on her haunches and glared up at Vincent. "So take that, you bastard."

Vincent roared his rage. He threw his body forward, but he seemed to slam straight into an invisible wall.

He was caged.

Jane heaved out a rough breath. "That should hold him, for now." She rose to her feet. Aidan grabbed her and pulled her close. She smiled at him. "You okay?" Jane asked.

Jane was alive — hell, yeah, he was okay. But...

Horror flashed on her face. She shoved Aidan to the side even as Vincent bellowed his rage again. But Jane didn't run toward Vincent. Instead, she ran to the fallen form of her brother.

The left side of his throat was ripped open. His eyes were wide, terrified. His lips were still clamped together and weak moans came from him.

"Drew?" Jane fell beside him. She grabbed his hand. "Drew!"

He was struggling to speak, but no words emerged.

"*Djinn!*" Annette bellowed.

And Aidan saw that Lena was slowly rising to her feet. Blood trickled down her temple.

"I know the rules." Annette jerked her head toward Vincent's enraged form. "Vincent has something of yours, right? What the hell is it? How does he control you?"

Lena touched her chest. "He has my heart."

"Uh…" Paris shuffled a bit closer to Aidan. "Tell me she doesn't mean that literally."

Aidan was afraid she might. He had no clue how to deal with a djinn—he'd actually thought those creatures were just myths until about five minutes ago.

"Where is it?" Annette demanded. "Where's your heart?"

"*Lena!*" Vincent shrieked. "I control you! I *own* you—kill them! No, no, make them kill each other! Get them to turn on each other—rip each other apart!"

Lena took a swaying step forward. "I...have to...obey..."

Screw that shit. Aidan took a menacing step toward Lena.

"I don't want to hurt that woman," Paris's voice rumbled. "But I will. I will kill her if I have to do it."

It was looking as if they would. It was...

It—

He saw the gleam of gold around Vincent's neck. Aidan's eyes narrowed as he stared at the small gold chain...a chain that he'd noticed on Vincent before. The vamp was hardly the sentimental type...

"Annette, can I still cross your line?" Aidan demanded. But he didn't wait for her to answer. He surged forward—

And hit an invisible wall.

Sonofabitch. He'd feared that after his battle with the darkness, he'd altered. Now he was wolf and vampire. Beast and undead.

And he couldn't get past the line. *Fuck.*

Vincent started laughing, that cold, twisted laughter of his. "Realized what I carry, didn't you alpha?" He jerked up the gold chain. A ruby hung from that chain. "You locked me in here, but that means you locked yourself out. No one can get to me...and I'll keep control of my djinn. I'll have her kill you all, then free me and then—"

Annette flew over that line of dirt.

Paris bellowed.

She grabbed the ruby, snapped the chain and threw the prize to Aidan.

Annette gave them the heart even as Vincent grabbed her in his arms and sank his teeth in her throat.

"No!" Paris cried. His fists drove into the invisible shield, again and again.

Aidan's fingers curled over the ruby. "Djinn," he said, staring at Vincent with fury hardening his heart. "You're free."

There was a clatter. From the corner of his eye, he saw that the bracelets that had circled Lena's wrists had fallen to the ground.

"Voodoo queen...*to me.*" Lena suddenly ordered.

And invisible hands seemed to rip Annette right from Vincent's grasp.

"Fucking bitch!" Vincent roared.

Lena's expression never altered. She waved her hand at Drew. "A brother can speak…"

Drew gasped. "Jane…s-sorry…so…s-sorry…L-love…"

He didn't get to say any more. Not because of a djinn's curse. But because he'd just taken his last breath. Jane's shoulders hunched. Her grief seemed to fill the room and then she leapt to her feet. She ran toward Vincent— "Undo your spell on him, Lena! Your spell, your magic, whatever the hell it is!" Jane shouted. "Take away his power so he can *die!*"

But Vincent licked his blood-stained lips and raised his hand. He shook one finger at her. "That gift, once given, can *never* be taken away." He leaned closer to Jane, stepping right up to the line that caged the dead. *And the undead.* "You'll never be free of me. Long after your lover is ash on this earth, I will still be here…waiting, for you, Jane. Waiting for us to bring about our end."

Jane shook her head. "No, no—"

"Yes," Lena said, voice rasping and sad. "I'm sorry but…that gift doesn't go away. He *cannot* end. Cut him into a thousand pieces, and he will regenerate. Burn him, and the ash will merge to produce a man. It's the darkest gift, I warned him of that…the gift that requires the highest price. He wanted to be a creature that *couldn't* ever be banished from this world, so he became a monster with no soul. That was his price…"

Aidan curled his arm around Jane and pulled her back against his body. *Your lover will be ash.* "You still don't understand what you've done, do you, Vincent?"

Jane's brother was dead.

The djinn was free.

Paris was holding tight to Annette.

And Jane…

Aidan and Jane were still standing.

"I've already died once," Aidan told Vincent, keeping his eyes locked on that soulless bastard. "And I came back. Your brilliant plan to *end* werewolves? It backfired. I'll get Heider to run all of his tests, but I know what he'll find…just like Jane, I've stopped aging. Death isn't standing over me, waiting, because I've already defeated that bitch once. So I won't be going anywhere. I'll spend forever at Jane's side. I'll watch her back and I'll love her. And you will *never* hurt those we care about again."

Vincent's face crumpled. "No! *No! She was the end* — "

"We saved Paris, too. Now that he's stronger, we know how to keep werewolves who transform sane…they just need enough blood, fast enough. Werewolf blood. You didn't destroy the werewolves. You just made us stronger." Now it was Aidan's turn to smile. "And my whole pack will be here soon…"

"Doesn't matter." Vincent shook his head once, hard. "I can't be destroyed! I can't — "

"A stake might not take you out, losing your head might not even stop you, but…" Jane said, cutting through his words, "but you can spend an eternity in hell."

Vincent stilled. "Wh-what?"

"I hope you're ready for the end," Jane told him. "Because for you, it's coming." She turned in Aidan's arms and stared up at him.

Yes, they were thinking the same damn thing. He could see it.

They couldn't kill Vincent…

But they could stop him. They could contain him.

His end. It was fucking at hand.

CHAPTER EIGHTEEN

New Orleans Homicide Detective Jane Hart stalked through the cemetery. The heavy stone mausoleums rose up around her and the statues seemed to watch every step that she took. It was long after midnight, and the cemetery *should* have been deserted…

Jane turned right.

And found a voodoo queen waiting for her. A bandage covered Annette's neck. "It's done," she said simply

Paris curled his hand around Annette's shoulder and she settled back against him.

So, yeah, they're definitely a couple now. Jane was happy for them, and really damn curious to see how that relationship would work. Considering that Jane and her beast were now bound to happily-ever-after forever style, she was one hundred percent sure the voodoo queen and the werewolf-slash-vamp would make an incredible team.

"Are you sure he's out cold?" Jane asked. She crept closer to the group assembled. Paris,

Annette, Aidan, and Lena were all standing in front of a crypt that looked positively ancient.

"Vincent couldn't be destroyed," Lena said in her soft, husky voice. "But he can sleep. I put him under and he won't be waking up."

Jane stared at the entrance to the crypt. Wolf carvings were on the stone doors and a heavy, thick chain locked those doors closed.

"He's unconscious, and he's trapped inside a stone coffin," Aidan rolled back his shoulders. "Werewolf guards will keep patrolling this cemetery, just in case, and Annette will scry to be sure the vamp won't have any chance of escape."

Jane slowly exhaled. This was the plan they'd come up with—imprisonment. Locked away, Vincent wouldn't be able to hurt anyone else.

"We could have kept him awake," Lena said, tilting her head as she studied those stone doors. "That way, he would have felt every moment of his imprisonment."

That was…inhumane. And there was still too much humanity left in Jane for her to do that. But…her gaze took in the lines of strain near Lena's mouth. "How long were you with him?"

"Five centuries." Lena's head turned so that she met Jane's gaze. "And every moment was hell."

So…Lena really was a djinn. Or a genie. Or whatever folks were calling her kind these days.

Though from what Lena had said, she was the last of her kind.

She could grant wishes. Could wield enormous power, but if anyone possessed her heart…

They controlled her. Completely.

Five centuries was a very long time. Jane could see why the woman would want her share of payback.

But we have to be the good guys. We can't let the darkness take us over. Because as she'd seen with Aidan, the darkness could be far too powerful, once it got a grip on someone. "It's better this way," Jane said. "He won't hurt you again. You're free."

Lena smiled at her, a real smile, one that lit up her green eyes. "Yes, I am."

Paris cleared his throat. "So…what does a djinn do…when she's free from five centuries of hell?"

Lena tossed back her head and laughed. "Anything she wants." Wind seemed to swirl around her. "Anything…" Her body shimmered. But then she stared at Jane. "I said he was asleep…I never said I wasn't going to give the bastard bad dreams. I hope he chokes on the nightmares."

Then…she vanished.

"I think I like her," Annette said. "She has style."

Style and the ability to kill with a thought. *Scary.*

"Even if a…nightmare…were to somehow wake him…" Annette laced her fingers with Paris's. "Vincent wouldn't go anyplace. Before the crypt was sealed shut, I took the liberty of making a circle around his coffin. He's not getting out." She brought Paris's hand to her lips. "Time for us to go, love. Cemeteries…they're just not that sexy to me."

He laughed. "Time to go."

Annette and Paris had taken just a few steps when the voodoo queen hesitated and glanced back at Jane. "It could have ended differently."

A chill skated over Jane's spine.

"The bond between you and Aidan could have been weaker…we could have all lost everything." Her gaze darted to the crypt. "And someone else could have been inside there."

"Who?" Jane asked.

Annette just gave her a sad smile. "It's nice to know that fate isn't always determined. We can change things. If we love enough, if we fight hard enough." Her breath expelled in a soft rush. "I'll see you again, soon, Mary Jane Hart."

Jane watched Annette and Paris walk away, her friend's words still rolling through her mind. *If we love enough, if we fight hard enough…*

Maybe people just had to fight harder for the ones they loved.

When she couldn't see Annette and Paris any longer, she sidled closer to Aidan and cleared her throat. "I stopped by to see Dr. Bob." He'd hugged her until she'd thought she might pass out from the pressure of his grip. Apparently, the man had been *very* glad they'd all survived another battle. "He confirmed your suspicions…your cells aren't aging any longer. You're…you're like me that way."

His hand curled under her chin and he gazed down at her. "So that means I have forever, with you."

"Yes."

He leaned forward and pressed a soft kiss to her lips. She rose onto her toes, loving that gentle touch. Loving *him.*

"So, my Jane," Aidan murmured. "What do you want to do with forever?"

She stared into his eyes. Her family was gone—her brother buried. Had Drew changed his mind at the end? Realized that what *she* was, it wasn't so bad? Jane liked to think that he had. He'd saved her, for a second time, and the last word he'd spoken…

It had been *love.*

The girl she'd been so long ago still loved her brother, despite everything.

And the woman she was…she loved the man before her. *More than anything.*

"What do I want to do?" Jane asked. She smiled at him. "I was thinking maybe we'd take a vacation."

He blinked.

"Go someplace…far away from death. Take a break from murder." Her hand pressed over his heart. "Get naked and make love as often as possible."

"Sounds like a fucking fine plan to me." His words were a rumble.

It was time for them to get away. They'd fought their battles, good had won and now…

Forever was about to begin.

There would be no end for them. There would just be life — good and bad and everything in between. But during those long days and nights, they'd be together.

Happy.

Living their life. Loving each other…with a bond that was stronger than blood. Stronger than death.

One that was soul deep.

Vampires and werewolves didn't have to be enemies. Sometimes, they could be perfect mates.

Jane and Aidan walked out of the cemetery, and they left the dead behind.

The End

###

If you enjoyed the Bitter Blood, keep reading for an excerpt from THE WOLF WITHIN, Purgatory, Book 1.

THE WOLF WITHIN
(PURGATORY, BOOK 1)

FBI Special Agent Duncan McGuire spends his days — and his nights — tracking real-life monsters. Most humans aren't aware of the vampires and werewolves that walk among them. They don't realize the danger that they face, but Duncan knows about the horror that waits in the darkness. He hunts the monsters, and he protects the innocent. Duncan just never expects to become a monster. But after a brutal werewolf attack, Duncan begins to change...and soon he will be one of the very beasts that he has hunted.

Dr. Holly Young is supposed to help Duncan during his transition. It's her job to keep him sane so that Duncan can continue working with the FBI's Para Unit. But as Duncan's beast grows stronger, the passion that she and Duncan have held carefully in check pushes to the surface. The desire that is raging between them could be a very dangerous thing...because Holly isn't exactly human, not any longer.

As the monsters circle in, determined to take out all of the agents working at the Para Unit, Holly and Duncan will have to use their own supernatural strengths in order to survive. But as they give up more of their humanity and embrace the beasts within them both, they realize that the passion between them isn't safe, it isn't controllable, and their dark need may just be an obsession that could destroy them both.

THE WOLF WITHIN - CHAPTER ONE

Special Agent Duncan McGuire raced around the street corner, chasing his prey even as his heartbeat thundered in his ears. Duncan's partner, Elias Lone, was just steps behind him. No damn way were they letting the killer escape.

The twisted bastard had already murdered four women in Seattle. Slashed their bodies. Torn out their throats. This nightmare was ending.

Duncan would make it end.

The perp rushed into an alley.

Dead end, asshole.

The killer didn't know the city as well as Duncan did.

His hold tightened on his weapon, and he leapt right into the entrance of that narrow alleyway. "Freeze!" Duncan roared. "FBI!"

The perp—a man with long, shaggy, blond hair—was facing the brick wall that ended the alley. At Duncan's shout, the man did freeze, for all of about twenty seconds. Then he started laughing as he spun to face Duncan and Elias.

"You humans are so out of your league," the blond snarled. His hands were up, and, as Duncan watched, the guy's nails began to transform—

Into long, black claws.

The blond laughed again. "Just the two of you? This should be so easy." His teeth were lengthening. Turning into sharp fangs. As Duncan watched, the man's face elongated. His bones snapped.

"Hell," Elias muttered from behind Duncan. "You were right. He's a wolf."

Duncan smiled, but didn't take his eyes off the killer before him. "I told you, vamps would never waste that much blood." Since Elias had just lost the bet, the guy owed him a hundred bucks. Duncan knew his werewolves.

The blond seemed to realize that they weren't exactly quaking in fear before him.

"What?" Duncan asked, lifting a brow. "Is this the part where we're supposed to act shocked because you can grow fur and howl at the moon?"

"You fuckin'—"

"Sorry," Duncan muttered, "but you're hardly the first Para that we've taken down." Actually, Duncan and Elias were part of an elite unit that *only* hunted the paranormals in Seattle.

The paranormals usually hid in plain sight, mostly managing to pass for humans.

Until they started to *eat* said humans. When the vampires and werewolves went bad and humans wound up as their prey of choice, well, that was when Duncan came in.

Someone had to keep the humans safe.

Duncan's words seemed to enrage the werewolf before him. The guy's lips peeled back—yeah, those teeth and claws were the weapons that had ended the lives of those four co-eds—and the fellow's body stretched as the power of the shift flooded through him.

Duncan kept his own body loose and ready. His gun was in his hand, but he wasn't firing unless the werewolf attacked him. His orders were to take the werewolf in, not to kill him.

The werewolf's elongated teeth snapped together.

Like I haven't seen all this shit before.

Unlike most humans, Duncan knew the score about the supernaturals. He'd known the truth since he'd been a kid.

"Humans aren't going to stop me!" The killer's cry was guttural. "You can't!" Fur burst along his skin. He fell to the ground, his knees and palms hitting the cement. His eyes glowed. "You don't have the power!" That last was more growl than human speech as the guy completed his shift…

And became a full on wolf.

The wolf launched at Duncan. *Not coming in alive.* Duncan's fingers tightened around the trigger. He fired. Once. Twice.

The bullets stopped the werewolf cold.

"Silver, dumb ass," Duncan said with a sad shake of his head as smoke drifted from the wolf's body. "It'll stop your kind every time." The fur slowly melted from the beast's body. The bones reshaped. In death, the monster became a man again. Well, not completely a man. A werewolf still kept his fangs and claws at death.

"Nice shots," Elias said, still from behind him.

Duncan grunted. He kept his weapon up as he eased closer to the body. Lowering the gun at this point would be a rookie mistake. Paras weren't like humans. Even if they *looked* dead, half the time, they weren't. They'd keep coming and coming and coming, just like the monsters in scary movies. Only this wasn't a movie.

Reality was scarier than the late-night horror shows.

"You hit him in the head," Elias said as he slid closer. "Don't worry, man, he's gone. He's—"

A growl sounded from the mouth of the alley. Duncan spun around.

Too late.

It wasn't just a lone werewolf they were hunting. He'd thought they were dealing with an isolated killer, a werewolf gone mad with bloodlust. That profile had been what the intel had showed him.

The intel was wrong.

Logan was gazing at a pack. Four other fully shifted werewolves were at the front of that alley.

They were leaping for Elias. And Elias had put up his weapon already. *Rookie mistake.*

Duncan rushed forward and shoved his partner to the side, barely dodging the claws of a werewolf. Duncan aimed his gun and started firing. Again and again.

One wolf down. Another—

He felt teeth tear into his shoulder.

Into his neck.

He could smell the wild, woodsy scent of the beasts. His own blood. He could *feel* his blood, trailing down his neck, soaking his shirt.

His gun wasn't firing. He'd used all the bullets.

More wolves were closing in…

Just as they'd closed in when he'd been four. When they'd killed his family.

When he'd lost everything but his life.

He hadn't been able to see the wolves then, but he'd heard their snarls and his mother's desperate cries. He could still hear those cries in his nightmares.

She hadn't survived the attack.

He had.

Only this time, Duncan knew he wouldn't be so lucky.

Elias was screaming. The beasts were howling.

And Duncan—Duncan was pretty sure that he was dying.

A NOTE FROM THE AUTHOR

Thank you so much for reading Jane and Aidan's journey. I've had such an incredible time writing the Blood & Moonlight books, and I really hope that you have enjoyed them. Jane and Aidan took us on lots of twists and turns, and I am very happy that those two got their happy ending.

If you'd like to stay updated on my new releases or book deals, please join my newsletter www.cynthiaeden.com/newsletter/. You can also check out my Facebook page www.facebook.com/cynthiaedenfanpage — I love to post giveaways and teasers there.

Best,
Cynthia Eden
www.cynthiaeden.com

ABOUT THE AUTHOR

Award-winning author Cynthia Eden writes dark tales of paranormal romance and romantic suspense. She is a *New York Times, USA Today, Digital Book World,* and *IndieReader* best-seller. Cynthia is also a three-time finalist for the RITA® award. Since she began writing full-time in 2005, Cynthia has written over fifty novels and novellas.

Cynthia is a southern girl who loves horror movies, chocolate, and happy endings. More information about Cynthia and her books may be found at: http://www.cynthiaeden.com or on her Facebook page at: http://www.facebook.com/cynthiaedenfanpage. Cynthia is also on Twitter at http://www.twitter.com/cynthiaeden.

PARANORMAL ROMANCE

Blood and Moonlight Series
- Bite The Dust (Blood and Moonlight, Book 1)
- Better Off Undead (Blood and Moonlight, Book 2)
- Bitter Blood (Blood and Moonlight, Book 3) - Available 04/12/2016

Purgatory Series
- The Wolf Within (Purgatory, Book 1)
- Marked By The Vampire (Purgatory, Book 2)
- Charming The Beast (Purgatory, Book 3)
- Deal with the Devil (Purgatory, Book 4)
- The Beasts Inside (Purgatory, Books 1-4)

Bound (Vampires/Werewolves) Series
- Bound By Blood (Bound Book 1)
- Bound In Darkness (Bound Book 2)
- Bound In Sin (Bound Book 3)
- Bound By The Night (Bound Book 4)
- Forever Bound (Bound Books 1-4)

- Bound in Death (Bound Book 5)

Night Watch Series
- Eternal Hunter (Night Watch Book 1)
- I'll Be Slaying You (Night Watch Book 2)
- Eternal Flame (Night Watch Book 3)

Phoenix Fire Series
- Burn For Me (Phoenix Fire, Book 1)
- Once Bitten, Twice Burned (Phoenix Fire, Book 2)
- Playing With Fire (Phoenix Fire, Book 3)

The Fallen Series
- Angel of Darkness (The Fallen Book 1)
- Angel Betrayed (The Fallen Book 2)
- Angel In Chains (The Fallen Book 3)
- Avenging Angel (The Fallen Book 4)

Midnight Trilogy
- Hotter After Midnight (Book One in the Midnight Trilogy)
- Midnight Sins (Book Two in the Midnight Trilogy)
- Midnight's Master (Book Three in the Midnight Trilogy)

Paranormal Anthologies
- A Vampire's Christmas Carol

Loved By Gods Series
- Bleed For Me

ImaJinn
- The Vampire's Kiss
- The Wizard's Spell

Other Paranormal
- Immortal Danger
- Never Cry Wolf
- A Bit of Bite
- Dark Nights, Dangerous Men

ROMANTIC SUSPENSE

LOST Series
- Broken (LOST, Book 1)
- Twisted (LOST, Book 2)
- Shattered (LOST, Book 3)
- Torn (LOST, Book 4) - Available 05/31/2016

Dark Obsession Series
- Watch Me (Dark Obsession, Book 1)
- Want Me (Dark Obsession, Book 2)
- Need Me (Dark Obsession, Book 3)
- Beware Of Me (Dark Obsession, Book 4)
- Only For Me (Dark Obsession, Books 1 to 4)

Mine Series
- Mine To Take (Mine, Book 1)
- Mine To Keep (Mine, Book 2)
- Mine To Hold (Mine, Book 3)
- Mine To Crave (Mine, Book 4)
- Mine To Have (Mine, Book 5)
- Mine To Protect (Mine, Book 6)

Montlake - For Me Series
- Die For Me (For Me, Book 1)
- Fear For Me (For Me, Book 2)
- Scream For Me (For Me, Book 3)

Harlequin Intrigue - The Battling McGuire Boys
- Confessions (Battling McGuire Boys...Book 1)
- Secrets (Battling McGuire Boys...Book 2)
- Suspicions (Battling McGuire Boys...Book 3)
- Reckonings (Battling McGuire Boys...Book 4)
- Deceptions (Battling McGuire Boys...Book 5) - Available 04/01/2016
- Allegiances (Battling McGuire Boys...Book 6) - Available 05/01/2016

Harlequin Intrigue - Shadow Agents Series
- Alpha One (Shadow Agents, Book 1)
- Guardian Ranger (Shadow Agents, Book 2)
- Sharpshooter (Shadow Agents, Book 3)
- Glitter And Gunfire (Shadow Agents, Book 4)
- Undercover Captor (Shadow Agents, Book 5)
- The Girl Next Door (Shadow Agents, Book 6)

- Evidence of Passion (Shadow Agents, Book 7)
- Way of the Shadows (Shadow Agents, Book 8)

Deadly Series
- Deadly Fear (Book One of the Deadly Series)
- Deadly Heat (Book Two of the Deadly Series)
- Deadly Lies (Book Three of the Deadly Series)

Contemporary Anthologies
- Wicked Firsts
- . Sinful Seconds
- First Taste of Darkness
- Sinful Secrets

Other Romantic Suspense
- Until Death
- Femme Fatale

YOUNG ADULT PARANORMAL

Other Young Adult Paranormal
- The Better To Bite (A Young Adult Paranormal Romance)

ANTHOLOGIES

Contemporary Anthologies
- "All I Want for Christmas" in The Naughty List
- Sinful Seconds
- All He Wants For Christmas

Paranormal Anthologies
- "New Year's Bites" in A Red Hot New Year
- "Wicked Ways" in When He Was Bad
- "Spellbound" in Everlasting Bad Boys
- "In the Dark" in Belong to the Night
- Howl For It

35249041R00204

Made in the USA
Middletown, DE
25 September 2016